One Month . . .

. . . was quiet time to spend with his past, sifting through memories of a magical childhood that had ended suddenly—and much too soon. . . .

. . . was quality time to spend with his son, exploring the wonders of the sea, the dunes and that special bond that linked father and son. . . .

. . . was not enough time to bask in the presence of Gracie Talbot, hearing her infectious laughter, feeling her comforting warmth. In her own way, Gracie put the past into perspective and made the present count, making Cameron believe that the best was yet to be.

For the month of August, Cameron McClellan was to be the master of Gull Cottage.

It would be a month he would never forget.

ABOUT THE AUTHOR

For Anne McAllister, ideas for stories are everywhere. She has found inspiration in a variety of sources—a childhood memory, a phone book, even a fortune cookie. In all her stories she writes about relationships—how they grow and how they challenge the people who share them. Anne makes her home in the Midwest with her husband and their four children.

Books by Anne McAllister

HARLEQUIN AMERICAN ROMANCE

HARLEQUIN ROMANCE

HARLEQUIN PRESENTS

Don't miss any of our special offers. Write to us at the following address for information on our newest releases.

Harlequin Reader Service
901 Fuhrmann Blvd., P.O. Box 1397, Buffalo, NY 14240
Canadian address: P.O. Box 603,
Fort Erie, Ont. L2A 5X3

SAVING GRACE

ANNE McALLISTER

Harlequin Books

TORONTO • NEW YORK • LONDON
AMSTERDAM • PARIS • SYDNEY • HAMBURG
STOCKHOLM • ATHENS • TOKYO • MILAN

For Barbara and Rosemary,
happy campers both.
I wouldn't have missed it for the world!
Thanks.

Published September 1989

First printing July 1989

ISBN 0-373-16309-6

Chapter One

New York City, July 1

"Trust me."

The words echoed around the peanut butter barrel with the authority of God speaking to Samuel. But the last time Gracie'd looked it wasn't God she'd been talking to.

Bent at the waist, she groped deep in the barrel for the last scoopful of chunky at the bottom, tamped it down into the jar, then straightened up and stared, just to be sure it was really Tony who'd uttered the words.

It was. He was sitting on a stack of hundredweight soybean bags, swinging his legs gleefully, looking as ungodly as he ever did—a twenty-three-year-old devil in Brooks Brothers casuals.

"Trust me," he said again. "When have I ever steered you wrong?"

She rolled her eyes. "This from the man who told me not to try out for *Cats*, that it would never last?"

Tony gave a sheepish shrug. "Besides that. I mean it, Gracie." He shifted his weight, shoved his straight brown hair out of his eyes and gave her his earnest young man expression. "You're a fool not to take me up on it. How many times have you been offered exclusive use of a cottage smack on the ocean at East Hampton for the entire month of August, for heaven's sake?"

"Well, never," Gracie admitted, screwing the cap on the peanut butter and handing it to the customer to take to the checkout. "But I'm still not sure."

"How can you not be? It's the chance of a lifetime," Tony persisted, following her as she wound her way through the crowded aisles to sort the just-delivered cheese shipment. "Two weeks on stage at the John Drew in a part like that. Lauren Bacall would kill for it."

Gracie rolled her eyes. "Lauren Bacall can have it. She can afford to live out there. She does live out there, as a matter of fact."

"Don't be smart." Tony shook his finger at her. "You can afford it, too, if you take me up on the offer. I suppose you want to scoop peanut butter and teach school at Mortimer Snerd for the rest of your life."

"Well, I—"

"You don't know how lucky you are. It could be your big break. Someone sees you as Cecily...remembers you the next time they're casting and...*voilà*, you're the next Ingrid Bergman."

"Or Lauren Bacall," Gracie said drily. "Or in my case—" she squinted at her choppy blond hair and round expressive face reflected in the dairy case "—Miss Piggy or, if I'm very lucky, Goldie Hawn."

"Whatever," Tony agreed blithely. "I say you should go for it. And my dad would agree."

"Now that I doubt."

Bluff and bossy, drama critic Laurence McClellan was considered by many—especially by himself—to be the "Oracle of Broadway," the "maker and breaker" of two generations of stage stars. If you were noticed by Laurence McClellan, your future, one way or another, was assured.

He had, to Gracie's great relief, never noticed her.

"Sure he would." Tony was positive. "If it's there, use it—that's his motto. So if he leaves the place empty, he'll be pleased that someone's staying in it."

"And you're sure it's empty?"

"He's in the south of France, has been since May. I got a post card from him last week. Gave it to someone to mail from Boston. Sounds like he's having a ball. So busy he didn't even remember to put the stamp on it." Tony gave a rueful shake of his head. "Cost me fifteen cents postage due."

Gracie was still skeptical. "If I had a cottage in the Hamptons and I wasn't going to use it for the summer, I'd rent it."

"Rent it? How plebeian can you get?" Tony swung himself up onto the cheese and yogurt case and shook his head at her. "You don't know my dad."

That was true. The closest she'd ever got to the esteemed Laurence McClellan was giving his son artificial resuscitation on a daytime soap opera two years earlier, a circumstance that the whimsical, teasing Tony declared meant he owed her his life—at least his "professional" life.

That, Gracie soon discovered, meant that Tony would show up at her apartment at odd hours to share his meager acting triumphs and more often to bemoan the lack of a "big break" in his career.

It also meant that he considered it his right to meddle in hers. But he'd never before shown the initiative he was showing right now.

"Dad would never rent," Tony went on. "Too tacky. Besides, he doesn't need the dough. He's got almost as much money as Mac."

Tony's half brother, Mac, was a corporate troubleshooter who got written up in business weeklies and sounded, in his own way, as intimidating as Tony's father. Gracie had never met him, either, and she didn't want to. Determined, goal-oriented hotshots were definitely not her type.

Tony grabbed her as she moved to go past him, clasped both her arms in his hands and held her prisoner between his knees. "Aren't you the one who always told me that your father told you to be all you could be?"

Gracie sighed. "You make him sound like an Army recruiter, not a minister."

Tony gave her his stern father look. "Well, didn't he?"

"Yes, but—"

"So, what have you got to lose?"

"I'll have to take Alice." A last ditch effort.

"So take her. It's a big house."

"I thought you said a cottage."

"Relative term. You'll see when you get there."

"*How* will I get there? With Alice?"

Alice, being a bullmastiff, was not a passenger welcomed with open arms by the Long Island Railroad.

"Never mind that. You'll go if I can figure out a way?"

"Well, I don't—" It seemed like such foolishness somehow. A break, if it was going to come, ought to appear before one had reached the ripe old age of twenty-six. And anyway, she wasn't sure. That was the story of Gracie's life—she was never sure, never wholeheartedly committed, always wondering if something better, different, more challenging might come along.

She looked out across the counters of Jack Sprat's Health and Wellness Store, across the rows of soybean bags, alfalfa sprouts, unpasteurized goat's milk and farmer's cheese that otherwise would be her summer.

She looked beyond them, in her mind's eye, to Admiral Byrd Public High School—called Mortimer Snerd by those who knew it well—six blocks away on New York's Upper West Side, where she had spent the better part of the last year as a long-term substitute drama teacher. A mecca of chalk dust, concealed weapons and concertina wire, Admiral Byrd was, if she ignored this opportunity, undoubtedly where her future lay.

Was that what she wanted? Did she even know what she wanted?

"You will. You have to." Tony gave her a confident nod, his mind made up. "Otherwise you won't know."

There was a pause. Then Gracie echoed, "Won't know?"

"Whether you could have had it all."

Long Island, August 1

"HOW MUCH FARTHER is it?"

Cameron, glancing up from the steady stream of traffic that was the Highway 27 extension of the Long Island Expressway, looked over at his son. "Where have I heard that before?" he teased.

Kip grinned. "Sacramento? Reno? Yellowstone? The Black Hills?"

"Sioux City, Davenport, Sandusky and points east," his father added. "But I actually think you started in Berkeley two weeks ago, about half an hour after we left home. You certainly know your lines."

"Line," Kip corrected.

Cameron shook his head. "No, you've got two. You forgot 'I'm hungry.' You do that one well, too."

"Speaking of which..." Kip bounced on the seat and rubbed his flat belly.

Cameron groaned. "You ate six blueberry pancakes three hours ago."

"That long?"

"My son, the bottomless pit."

"I bet you ate that much when you were ten," Kip challenged him.

When he was ten...when he was ten... Funny Kip should mention that.

When he was ten, Cameron had been on his way to East Hampton, too. On a train with his mother, his face pressed against the glass, anticipation increasing with every mile. Every year he'd relished it all—the trip out to his grandparents' house with his mother, the bonfires in the evening, the walks on the sand, the dips in the chilly Atlantic surf, the digging for clams, but especially the weekend visits from his city-bound father that culminated in August when he finally took two full weeks off.

It was odd how often Cameron had thought of it lately. Odd how much of what was happening this summer was dictated by the summer he'd had when he was ten. Perhaps he was being a fool, coming back this way, renting the house, stirring up memories. Everyone knew you couldn't go home again. But it was too uncanny—the ad offering Gull Cottage for rent, his housekeeper Sophia's grandchild being born and her needing to go to her daughter's to help out, Kip being ten.

"Well?"

Cameron frowned, jerked back to the moment at hand. "Well, what?"

"Are we gonna stop for lunch or what?"

Clearly, whether his father had been ravenous at ten was not the issue. Kip was hungry.

"Tell you what. We should hit East Hampton in about half an hour—forty five minutes if the traffic gets any worse. We'll catch a McDonald's or something there before we head for the house, okay?"

It was a stalling tactic on his part as much as a sop to Kip's incessant hunger, because—though he'd told himself he wanted this—the closer they got, the more trepidation Cameron was beginning to feel about coming here at all. What was he getting into?

Kip was satisfied with Cameron's offer. He gave a little bounce and settled back again to stare out the window at the wooded roadside, the developments, the acres of potato fields that they passed.

Cameron slanted a fond glance at his son, grateful for his even-tempered amenability. It wasn't exactly a family trait. The only one in his generation to have it was his half brother, and Cameron had once supposed Tony'd inherited it from his mother, Amaryllis.

But since then, Amaryllis had turned up anything but even-tempered, and Kip had. So Cameron thought perhaps, temperament-wise at least, his son was a throwback.

Maybe he'd got it from his maternal great-grandfather. Daniel Cameron had been a genial old man. Kip certainly didn't resemble the squash-faced old coot, though.

In looks the boy was a mirror image of himself at that age. Thick tousled dark hair with red highlights, a scattering of freckles across a straight nose and high cheekbones, deep blue eyes that someday girls would fight to drown in.

The way girls used to fight to drown in his, Cameron remembered dispassionately. And might still if he gave them the least encouragement.

He didn't.

These days he worked at active discouragement, which was one reason he was glad to be putting three thousand miles between Yvette de Jourlet and himself. She was a good friend, but he didn't need a wife like her, no matter what she thought.

He had his job and his son. He was satisfied. It was enough.

He reached over and tousled Kip's hair.

Finding a McDonald's in East Hampton was more difficult than he'd imagined. Food wasn't meant to be quick here, only quaint. He would happily have settled for one of the mom-and-pop cafés that had proliferated here during his youth, but they seemed to have vanished along with all signs of the slightly sleepy small town he remembered.

The buildings might be the same, and the gravestones, but everything else now looked to be on the cutting edge of the latest trend.

There was the Basketry, the Wickery, the Cookery and the Bookery, but not much sign of a grocery or bakery. Artsy boutiques had replaced simple dress shops, yuppie catering establishments had routed the corner grocery stores, and the newest food fads seemed to have taken over all the restaurants.

Two passes up and down the main streets reading the menus in the windows convinced Cameron of that.

"I guess you're going to have to choose between Madame Makarova's borscht and Papa Doc's linguine carbonara or Caribbean lime chicken," he told Kip.

"I don't like chicken. What's borscht?"

"Beet soup."

Kip made a face. "Whatever linguine carbonation is," he decided, "it's gotta be better than that."

The food itself wasn't bad. The dent it put in Cameron's wallet was. It was bad enough to have laid out eleven thou for a month in his father's house. He wasn't going to spend more on local cooking.

"Grocery store next," he decided on their way out of Papa Doc's, not willing to be stung again. "On the way home."

"Where is it?"

Cameron shrugged.

"You grew up here," Kip reminded him as they plunged back into the traffic in search of a grocery store.

"I spent summers here," Cameron corrected, "until I was ten."

But from what he could see, though the dirt beneath the asphalt might be the same, and some of the architecture was certainly historic, notably Hook Mill, there was very little else that he recognized from those summers years ago. The streets seemed narrower, the houses and shops smaller, as if they had shrunk rather than that Cameron had grown up.

He did, eventually, find the grocery store, and he and Kip trundled through. They wouldn't need a lot to start with, the realtor had promised his secretary. There had been tenants the first two months who had left plenty of goodies behind them.

"Don't bring a thing," Jeannie had told him. "Everything's furnished. You'll be all set."

But Cameron wasn't taking any chances. At last, groceries tucked in the back of the two-year-old Isuzu Trooper, they set off once more.

"How much farther is it?" Kip teased.

But this time Cameron didn't even smile.

They were entering more familiar territory now as they headed out toward the ocean. The road was narrow and tree lined. Here many of the houses hadn't changed a great deal, though he glimpsed more swimming pools now and at least one glassy add-on porch. Cameron drove with assurance, though his palms were damp and there was a dryness in his mouth.

"I can hear the ocean," Kip said, straining against his seat belt, craning his neck in vain to see over the dunes.

Cameron slowed the car and made the turn onto Frigate Alley. Then he stopped. "There."

Kip followed the direction of his father's nod toward the end of the road. There was a long, stunned silence broken only by the chirp of a cardinal and the muted crash of the waves.

Then, "Oh," Kip said. "Oh, wow."

Cameron knew exactly what he meant.

Even knowing what to expect never made the first sight of Gull Cottage less of a shock.

Atop the dunes it sat, like a slightly tattered dowager countess presiding with scandalized disapproval over an increasingly rowdy ball. Haughty, almost regal with its tall chimneys, steep roofs, and weathered shingles, it—unlike nearly everything he'd encountered so far today—hadn't changed a bit.

And despite its innate disapproval of today's East Hampton in general, it beckoned to him.

He smiled and breathed again. Everything was going to be all right. He hadn't been a fool after all.

He drove up the curving driveway, careful to keep to the center, as the edges, he noted with dismay, were crumbling a bit. Everything else, however, was just the same. The hedges were taller but still rambling, the lion's head door knocker still there and still in need of polishing.

"Oh, wow," Kip kept saying. "Oh, wow."

Cameron fished the key out of his pocket.

"Is it like you remember it, Dad?"

Cameron nodded, seeing in his mind's eye the slate foyer, the mission oak and wicker furniture that had crowded the living room, the heavy damask draperies of his grand-parents' old home.

Cameron turned the key in the lock and gave the door a shove. Then he stood in the foyer and stared.

The house, as far as the eye could see, was absolutely bare.

The floor stretched before him like an ocean. For the first time in his life he could see without impediment across the foyer, through the living room, right out the French doors to the sand and sea and beyond. What seemed an acre of parquet floor gleamed in the early afternoon sun.

"Oh, wow," Kip exclaimed with less awe now than en-thusiasm. He promptly kicked off his shoes and took off running to slide a good fifteen feet sock-footed across the floor.

"Oh, wow," Cameron agreed and groped for the built-in ledge along the foyer wall and sank down. So much for fur-nished, he thought.

"Neat, huh, Dad?" Kip slid past in the other direction.

"Mmm." Cameron's mind was working furiously. What was going on?

It wasn't so much that he wouldn't have rented the house if it had been advertised unfurnished, it was that the realtor very obviously thought it was.

"The owner uses the house all the time. He's only going to be gone for the summer," his secretary had reported back when she'd called about the ad. "Hasn't ever rented it be-fore, it means so much to him. In the family for a long time, you know. And he's quite sentimental. A very influential man, the realtor said. She said I'd recognize the name."

She would, too. But Cameron had played dumb, not wanting to admit he knew who the owner was. If he had, it would've just occasioned a lot of unnecessary questions like why he felt it necessary to rent a house from his own father.

He had no intention of explaining that it was the house he was interested in, not the "sentimental" old man.

"Just rent it," he'd told her. "And get the best price you can."

He didn't mind renting it, but he was damned if he was going to let the old devil gouge him out of a cent more than necessary. "And," he'd added, "take it in the name of the company. Don't mention my name."

Jeannie had done so, taking the house for the entire month of August. Cameron hadn't got involved. But he knew that he'd rented it furnished, for cripes sake.

Had the previous tenants decided to take it with them? A towel vanishing seemed in the realm of possibility. But a whole houseful of furniture?

"Wish I'd brought my skates," Kip grinned, skimming past once more.

Cameron rolled his eyes. He left Kip sliding from one end to the other of what amounted to a forty-foot roller rink while he went to explore the rest of the downstairs. Perhaps he'd find a chair here, a table there. He didn't.

The only things left were the photographs on the walls. And they, not surprisingly, were almost all of Laurence.

"What the hell are you trying to pull, you old shyster?" He scowled at his father's beaming countenance.

But Laurence, eight-by-ten, glossy and wholly unconcerned, didn't offer a clue.

Cameron scowled at him and moved on, curious now to see what else the ad had lied about.

A minute later he decided that if its sin of commission was bad, its sin of omission was worse—for there, in the solarium, he encountered unexpectedly the bane of his youthful existence.

"Awk! Beam me up, Scotty!"

"Ohmigod." Cameron's knuckles closed around the doorjamb for support. It couldn't be.

"Read the instructions! Read the instructions!"

But it was.

Boris.

After all these years.

Cameron closed his eyes and opened them again, then shook his head.

Boris shook his in perfect imitation. "Aren't you the pretty fellow?" he squawked.

Cameron glowered. "Stuff it, you mangy old bird."

There was no doubt in his mind at all that he knew this bird. And for a mynah who had to be twenty if he was a day, Boris was looking surprisingly chipper.

Cameron approached the cage warily. Boris edged along his perch. Cameron took a step; so did Boris. At last beady black eyes met blazing blue ones.

"What in the devil are you doing here?" Cameron demanded as if the bird could answer him.

Of course Boris didn't. He simply stared, his black eyes sharp but his beak silent, until Cameron felt the foolishness of his question, colored and started to move away.

"Give us a kiss, sugah," the bird drawled and followed it with an accurate smooching sound.

Cameron made an indeterminate grunt of rage, spun around and snatched the Post-it notes off the edge of Boris's cage.

"Who you talkin' to, Dad?" Kip bounded in and stopped dead, staring at the bird. "Him? We got a bird? Oh wow. Oh wow."

"It," Cameron said crossly. "*It*. And *it's* talking to me."

Kip's eyes grew to the size of baseballs. "He talks? What's his name? Can we keep him?"

"I don't think it's a matter of keeping him. It's a matter of being stuck with him."

Kip beamed. "Hi there, birdy. What's his name?"

Cameron sighed. "Boris."

"To be or not to be," Boris intoned sepulchrally, "that is the question."

Cameron rubbed a hand over his eyes. "I've got to talk to that real estate agent, and I've got to talk to her now." He turned on his heel and, leaving Kip to deal however he would with Boris, he strode toward the kitchen in search of the phone.

Like everything else, it wasn't there.

The cord dangled uselessly from the wall. Cameron just stared at it, rage building. Then he kicked the cupboard, hurt his toe, and shoved his hands into the pockets of his jeans to stand scowling out the glass toward the sand.

So much for his feeling of welcome.

He had half a mind to stuff Kip back into the car, turn around and head straight back to San Francisco where they'd come from. What in heaven's name was he going to do in a house with no furniture but a bird cage and, worse than that, a bird?

That bird in particular.

There'd been no love lost between Cameron and Boris since Cameron had come to his father's house the Easter after he'd turned sixteen to find that Boris had taken over his room.

"He's such a pet," his father had told Cameron. "Audrey gave him to me."

And knowing that his father doted on Audrey—had, in fact, "made" Audrey's career—Cameron knew he wasn't going to be able to budge the bird.

What he hadn't counted on was the bird budging him.

One night in the same room had sent him to sleep on the couch. The bird mumbled in its sleep hour after hour. And when it didn't mumble it quoted Shakespeare or Milton Berle or, even worse, Cameron's father.

Putting up with the old man's bossy pontificating all day was bad enough. Cameron was damned if he was going to listen to him all night, too.

But when he'd complained to his father about Boris's incessant nocturnal mutterings, Laurence had just laughed, scratching Boris on the chin while the bird had sung out, "For he's a jolly good fellow."

Cameron had been the first to deny it then. He didn't think things had changed much now.

"Hey, Dad." Kip interrupted his reverie. "Me and Boris are hungry. Can we bring in the groceries now?"

Cameron turned and his eyes widened. Boris was perched on Kip's left hand.

"It's out? You let it out?" Cameron croaked.

Kip shrugged. "Sure. Why not? He told me to. 'Lift the latch,' he said. 'Lift the latch.'"

Cameron took a step toward his son, took a look at Boris's unblinking stare, hesitated, remembered other times, other stares, other sharp, painful pecks. He stopped where he was. "Listen to me, Kip. The very last thing you are ever to do is anything that bird says. Do you understand?"

Kip swallowed audibly, not used to his father taking that tone of voice. "Well, yeah, sure, but—"

"It is not rational."

"He is hungry, though. He told me so," Kip argued. He cocked his head and looked at the bird, "Aren't you, Boris?"

"Yo, ho, ho, and a bottle of rum."

"See," Kip said proudly. "He's thirsty, too."

Cameron groaned. Then very quietly, speaking through his teeth, he said, "Put it back."

One look told Kip his father meant what he said.

While Kip put Boris back in his cage, Cameron brought in the groceries. Kip put them away, and Cameron, deliberately forgetting that Boris had told him to, read the instructions some previous sucker had stuck on his cage.

Whoever the earlier tenants were, they had obviously done their best by Boris. His cage was on the shady side of the room out of drafts. The bird himself was sleek and shiny, and if the floor was a mess all around his cage, that wasn't their fault. Cameron remembered Boris as a messy roommate. That obviously hadn't changed.

Cameron fixed Kip a peanut butter and jelly sandwich, then said, "I'm going to run back to town to call the real estate agent. Do you want to come?"

Kip, mouth full, shook his head. "Uh-uh. I'll stay here. With Boris."

"You won't let it out of the cage," Cameron reminded him.

"Aw, Dad."

Cameron lifted his eyebrows.

Kip sighed. "Not even for a little while?"

"Not even for a second."

"But—"

"Kip."

Kip sighed. "All right. Can I go exploring?"

"Only in the house," Cameron said. "And if it's as bare as the rest of the place, you won't want to bother." The entire first floor had yielded only Boris. The second floor he had given up on after checking out two completely barren bedrooms.

"I'll listen to the radio then," Kip said. "The Giants are in town playing the Mets."

"You'll be all right till I get back then?"

"Sure. And, Dad," Kip said as Cameron started toward the door.

"What?"

"You were right. I'm glad we came. This place is gonna be great."

THE REAL ESTATE AGENT in charge of Gull Cottage wasn't available that afternoon. Cameron's secretary wasn't so lucky.

"You've arrived then?" Jeannie sounded delighted to hear from him.

"I've arrived. Now I have some questions."

"Questions?" Jeannie knew him well and the tones of his voice even better. The delight in her voice was fading fast.

"Like I thought we were supposed to have furniture, and why the hell do we have this bird?"

"You don't have furniture?" Cameron could hear Jeannie fluttering through papers. "But I'm sure the agent said it was furnished. 'To provide for your every need,' I think the words were. Shall I look into it?"

"Please do."

"I'll just hang up and get right on it."

"Not yet."

"Not yet?"

"What about the bird?" It was his soft and deadly tone, the one he used when he told the corporate bigwigs that there was no hope, that if they wanted to save the company, some of them were going to be the first to go.

"Ah, yes." Jeannie laughed, obviously missing the deadliness in his voice. "The bird. I couldn't believe it when I first heard about that bird. It's got to be the most incredibly beloved and expensive bird in the world."

"What do you mean?"

"The agent said she had orders to reduce the rent four thousand dollars a month if you'd take care of it."

"Four thou—" Cameron's voice cracked.

"Mmm-hmm. That's what they meant in the ad when they said 'conditions negotiable.' Isn't that a stitch? Four thousand dollars to scatter a little birdseed."

"Erg."

"Anyway, I was sure you wouldn't mind. You said to get it as cheap as I could. And four thousand dollars..."

"I'd pay a million," Cameron muttered, "not to have to ever see that bird again."

"I beg your pardon?"

"Never mind." Cameron sighed. "I don't suppose when you call the agent, you'd like to see if she'll make other arrangements for it."

"Is it bothering you? Doesn't Kip like it?"

Cameron pressed his head against the glass of the phone booth. Heaven help him, yes, Kip liked it. Kip loved the damned thing.

That was half his problem. What was he going to say to the boy if he got the bird evicted? How could he explain a history like his and Boris's?

Who would ever believe him?

"Forget it," he muttered. "Just ask about the furniture. I'll call you back tomorrow. Right now I've got to go see about getting a phone."

The phone was easy.

"No problem," the lady at the phone company assured him when he called. "You supply the phone. We'll connect you tomorrow."

So Cameron bought phones. Like everything else in East Hampton, less was more. A plain white telephone or even a plain black one commanded a high price.

"So elegant," the lady at the Touch Someone Boutique assured him. "You won't be sorry."

"Mmm," Cameron said. If he wasn't, it was going to be the first thing he hadn't regretted all day.

He glanced at his watch, decided that Kip could last another hour or so on his own and set off for Bridgehampton where, he was told, he might find enough camping gear to get them through until such time as the furniture showed up.

If it ever did, of course.

He wondered idly, as he picked out sleeping bags and air mattresses, what had become of all his grandparents' stuff. He wouldn't have expected Laurence to give anything to him, even though it had been Cameron's mother's parents' house. That wasn't the way Laurence operated—not with his elder son at least.

But Cameron thought he might've let his son know if he was going to sell things off, just in case Cameron might've wanted to buy a piece or two for the sentiment attached.

He paid for the camping gear, stowed it in the Trooper and headed back toward East Hampton. Toward Kip. And, God help him, toward Boris.

The very thought made his head start to ache.

"Hi." Kip met him at the door when he returned. "Guess what I just found!"

"What?" Cameron said before the door behind opened farther. Once it did, the question was superfluous. Behind Kip stood the biggest, blackest dog in the world.

"What the—Where did that thing come from?"

Kip shrugged happily. "I dunno. I was in the solarium with Boris and all of a sudden, there he was."

"She," Cameron corrected, coming into the room carefully, never taking his eyes off the dog.

The dog repaid him in kind. But she didn't give him the shivers the way Boris did. In fact she was beginning to wag her tail.

Kip hopped from one foot to the other, enchanted with his new menagerie. "Isn't he—I mean, *she* great?"

"Mmm." Was this another of the "conditions negotiable?" Cameron wondered.

The dog looked well fed and well cared for. It also looked normal. Not the sort of animal one might abandon, as one might be tempted to abandon, say, Boris.

What was going on?

"Help me with the gear," he commanded Kip. "Then I want to take a look around."

Kip was delighted with the sleeping bag. "This is great, Dad. It'll be just like camping out." He lugged it into the solarium and began to unpack it.

"Not there, Kip."

"Why not? Boris is here."

"Exactly."

"But Boris will want the company."

"Boris doesn't need company."

"But—"

Cameron gave him a narrow look. "Upstairs."

Kip sighed. "But just for now?" he pleaded. "If I take it up later? If I promise?"

Cameron wavered, then shrugged. "Boris isn't exactly neat." His eyes scanned the room pointedly. "But if you want to risk it, it's all right with me."

Kip beamed happily. "Great."

He unrolled the sleeping bag and began to blow up the air mattress, supervised by Boris who kept up a running commentary. The dog, Cameron noted, took one look at Boris and headed the other way.

"You want to come with me?" he asked the dog.

She wagged her tail and nudged him with her nose. Cameron patted the huge head and set off up the stairs.

Whoever had blitzed the furniture downstairs had done the job upstairs as well. Besides the first two rooms, which he'd already checked, the pink-flowered bedroom that had been his mother's as a little girl was totally bare. So was her adjoining bathroom and the next two more sedately papered rooms he entered. The next bathroom, however, held a surprise.

Screwed into the wall next to the mirror was a slot machine in working order.

Three guesses, Cameron thought grimly, who'd put that there. His father's predilection for plays, ponies and pretty girls was legendary. Obviously he wasn't averse to other forms of gambling either.

Cameron jerked down the arm of the machine and got no response. A small electronic sign flickered. "Quarter required."

Just like the old man—out to fleece his guests. Cameron shook his head. First no furnishings, then Boris and a dog, now a slot machine.

What next?

The dog had wandered out and was headed down the hallway.

Cameron followed, then stopped dead in the doorway to the master bedroom. Here, at last, he found a piece of furniture—the most bizarre, incredible bed he'd ever seen.

But even more bizarre and incredible than the bed itself was the fact that in it there was a woman.

Chapter Two

The phrase "furnished to provide for your every need" echoed in his head.

Cameron stared hard at the woman, then shut his eyes and opened them again, as if she might just possibly go away.

She didn't.

Not surprisingly, neither did the bed.

It was high enough to require a ladder and broad enough to get lost in, and it looked as if in one of its former lives it had floated down the Nile. Even in the shadowy room Cameron could make out carved wooden gilt-encrusted serpents winding their way up its stylized legs and wrapping themselves around each other on the headboard. The spread was an equally elaborate gold-shot tapestry replete with pyramids, hieroglyphs and more reptiles.

The only thing it lacked was Cleopatra. Whoever the woman was, she definitely wasn't that. She had blond shaggy hair, lovely cheekbones and a wide, well-shaped mouth. In repose she looked vulnerable, tempting and entirely incongruous. Far more like Goldilocks than an Egyptian queen.

Amazed, bemused, completely befuddled, Cameron started to laugh.

The dog grinned and thumped her tail. "Rrroof." Then she launched herself at the bed, scrambling up it as best she could to land on the woman's back.

"Arrgh! Alllllice!" The woman woke and gave the dog a mighty shove as she rolled over.

That was when she saw Cameron.

Her eyes widened; she opened her mouth, then shut it again.

Cameron waited, not saying a word, curious, wondering how she would explain herself. She'd undoubtedly be furious to find out that she'd wasted a trip, that Laurence wasn't even here.

For there wasn't a doubt in Cameron's mind that Laurence was whom she'd come for.

He'd seen women throw themselves in his father's path as far back as he could remember. Anxious young actresses, looking for a good review and eager to show their "skill," had always been thick on the ground.

While he was growing up they probably could have carpeted the whole house with them.

This one, with her wide, astonished eyes, was a lot more attractive than the ones he remembered. Or maybe he was just old enough to appreciate them now.

Whichever... the woman had an extraordinarily expressive face. He read confusion in it, then fear, then determination not to show that fear.

"She can project her emotions," Laurence would have said.

Oh, yes.

Too bad they were wasted on him. Hardening his heart, Cameron gave the young woman a sardonic smile and stood his ground.

To his astonishment, she returned his smile with one of her own, and there was nothing sardonic about it at all.

"Hello." Her voice was soft and sleepy, slightly sultry.

Cameron felt as if something warm and wonderful had just tripped down the length of his spine. He stiffened.

"Hello." His own voice was deliberately gruff. There was no reason for her wasting her charm on him. Heaven knew he didn't want it.

The dog licked her face and she shoved it away again, swatting it lightly and laughing. "Quit it, Alice. Just quit."

"Her name is Alice?"

The woman nodded. "Mmm-hmm. And mine is Gracie. Gracie Talbot. What's yours?" She scrambled up so that she was kneeling on the bed, regarding him with wide inno-cent-looking brown eyes.

He paused, then said reluctantly, "Cameron."

Gracie Talbot offered him her hand. "I'm pleased to meet you, Mr. Cameron."

He should have corrected her, but for the moment he de-cided to let it ride. His eyes narrowed in surprise, though, at what she said. "You are?"

"Of course. I presume Tony sent you, too."

"You know *Tony*?" Was she Tony's girl then, not the old man's? Somehow that irritated him more.

"Oh, yes. I once saved his life. Figuratively anyway." Gracie laughed. "We were on a soap together. He was Beauregarde Calhoun, restless young stud, and I—" she gave a conspiratorial giggle here "—was Ethelmary Holt, nearsighted LPN." She crossed her eyes and grinned up at him. The effect was outrageous.

Cameron almost grinned. He didn't because his suspi-cions were confirmed; she was an actress. Enough said.

"What are you doing here? If you're an actress, I mean. Tony's not here. And my—er, Laurence McClellan isn't, either."

"And thank God for that!" Gracie appeared horrified at the mere suggestion.

Cameron stared at her, startled as much by the sentiment of the exclamation as by its vehemence. Not that he dis-agreed, of course. "You've, uh, met him?"

"No. And I don't want to, either."

She sounded sincere. Probably she was a *good* actress. He just wished she weren't so attractive. Cameron scowled. "I thought all actresses wanted to be noticed. Particularly by Laurence McClellan." All the ones he'd had the misfortune to meet certainly had.

"On stage maybe," Gracie agreed. "Not in his bedroom."

The thought made her roll her eyes, and she giggled again. It was an infectious giggle, a sound that seemed to invite him to join her.

Cameron ground his teeth. He stuck his hands in his pockets and rocked back on his heels. "You say Tony sent you here?"

"Yes. I got a part at the John Drew Theater. Chance of a lifetime. Big break, you know."

Oh, yes, he did know. Very well. But he didn't respond.

It didn't matter to Gracie Talbot. She went on, explaining, "I came down on the midnight train. It was the only way Tony could think they'd be nice enough to let me on with Alice. She's death to commuters. Then we started rehearsal at the crack of dawn this morning. It was exhausting. That's why I was zonked out now. I don't usually get into afternoon naps." She cocked her head and considered him. "What about you? I didn't see you there."

"I'm not an actor," Cameron said flatly.

Gracie leaned back. "Oh, that's too bad. Then, what are you doing here?"

"Renting the house."

"Renting..." Gracie looked at him askance. There was a long silence broken only by the far-off sound of Boris exclaiming and the steady thrum of the ocean. "Oh, dear."

Cameron's mouth quirked. "You're not, I take it."

"Er, no." Gracie gave an unhappy little shrug, flopped back on her bottom, cross her ankles, pulled her knees up and wrapped her arms around them. "Oh, dear, oh, dear."

Cameron's fists clenched in his pockets. She was very good. Damnably good. She had the "oh, poor me" look down pat with that woebegone expression on her face, that choppy dark blond hair slightly mussed from sleep. And she could do it at the drop of a hat.

Improvisation, it was called. He knew it well.

He'd had a good teacher.

"I guess you'll have to find somewhere else to live," he said, hardening his heart.

Gracie sighed, looked at him hopefully, apparently didn't find the commiseration she was looking for, and sighed again. "I guess." She reached over and rubbed Alice's head. The dog grinned at her. Gracie made a face at the dog. "Manhattan here I come," she murmured.

Cameron was about to second that, but suddenly there came the sound of footsteps in the hallway, and Kip skidded to a stop in the doorway.

"Gosh," he said, regarding Gracie wide-eyed, "a bird, a dog, and now you. And a bed, too," he added almost as an afterthought. He came into the room walking around it, surveying it from all angles.

Gracie laughed and swung her feet over the edge so they dangled. "Isn't it great? Want to come up?"

"No, he—"

"Sure." Kip hurtled past Cameron and was up the ladder almost before the invitation had been uttered. Cameron's attempt to decline had never even been heard.

Gracie held out her hand to him. "I'm Gracie."

"I'm Kip. D'you live here, too?"

"Well, I'd thought I might . . ." Gracie began. "But it seems you're renting it and I'm not. I was a sort of 'guest.'" She gave Cameron an apologetic look; he scowled.

"There's lots of room," Kip said, beginning to bounce a little. "This is a huge house!"

"I know, but . . ." Gracie paused.

"We wouldn't mind, would we, Dad?"

"Kip, Miss Talbot thought she had the place to herself."

"I share a one-bedroom apartment with three other girls in Manhattan," Gracie confided.

"See?" Kip said. "It's no big deal."

"Kip!"

The boy turned wide, guileless eyes on him. "Well, you always say to be generous, to share. Or maybe you wouldn't want to share with us, huh, Gracie?" He turned the same innocent eyes on her.

"No, Kip, of course I'd like to share with you, but—"

"So, it's settled then. Good. Can you cook? Is the dog yours?"

"Yes, I can cook. And yes, this is Alice." But while she was answering, Gracie shot a worried look at Cameron, as if she were trying to see how he would take Kip's resolution of her problem.

He wasn't taking it well, but he was in a quandary about exactly how to fix it. Damn kids, anyway. They were forever getting you over a barrel by throwing your own words of wisdom in your face. Expecting you to live up to the standards you set for them. Cameron chewed the inside of his cheek, stymied.

It wasn't only the philanthropist in Kip that annoyed him, it was the method the boy had used to get his way. There was more than a little of the bulldozing grandfather in the grandson. It wasn't a thought Cameron found comforting.

"Look, Dad, she likes me!" Kip said through Alice's long slurping licks of his face.

"Mmm. Maybe she's hungry, too."

Kip giggled and looked at Gracie. "Do you think she might be, Gracie? Can I feed her?"

"If you want," Gracie said magnanimously. "Did you see that turkey roaster on the counter in the kitchen?"

Kip shook his head.

"That's her dish," Gracie told him. "The dog chow is in the pantry. You start filling the roaster. I'll comb my hair and be down in a minute."

Kip was off the bed in a second. "C'mon, Alice."

Alice bounded off the bed with a grace that belied her size and loped out of the room after him.

"I'll leave," Gracie said the moment they had. She was getting down off the bed and groping around on the floor for her shoes with bare toes.

"Sure," Cameron said sourly.

She turned to face him. "You don't want me here."

"No." He wasn't going to lie about it.

"Well, then..."

"How'm I supposed to explain that to Kip?" He glared at her, annoyed at the innocence on her face. She had no right to it.

"You just say, 'Gracie left.'"

"And when he asks why?"

"You could tell him the truth."

"That I don't want you here."

"Mmm-hmm." She had located the shoes and was stuffing her feet into them, her eyes on Cameron.

"That'll just get me another question."

The big brown eyes got wider. "Ah, yes. I can see as how it might. He'll want to know why."

"Yes. He will."

"And you don't want to tell him."

"No. I don't."

Gracie went to the duffel bag on the floor and began rooting around in it. "Then lie to him," she said over her shoulder.

He scowled. "I don't lie to my kid."

Gracie found the hairbrush she had obviously been looking for and began tugging it through her hair. As she did so, she sat back on her heels and regarded Cameron with a smile. "You know what?"

"What?" He hated that smile. It made him want to smile back.

"I like you."

He stared at her, taken aback. "You like me? I'm evicting you."

"For good reason."

He looked at her suspiciously. "How do you know?"

"A man who encourages his son to be generous, to share, and who won't lie to him wouldn't evict me without a good reason."

Cameron raked his hand through his hair. "Oh, hell."

Gracie gave him a sweet smile and went on brushing.

He glowered at her, damning her, damning Kip, damning his father who had nothing—and everything—to do with any of this.

"All right. You can stay," he muttered ungraciously. "Just for tonight." And turning on his heel he strode out the door.

GRACIE WATCHED HIM GO with a mixture of relief and astonishment. And after he left she reached down and very carefully pinched herself just to be sure she hadn't been dreaming. It hurt.

But she still wasn't sure.

The only things she knew for certain were that 1) come morning, she was going to be out on her ear, 2) there were things in Laurence McClellan's life that Tony didn't know anything about, and 3) this Cameron person made her heart do the most amazing things in her chest.

The first she was going to have to give very serious consideration to. The second she already had. She'd even tried to call Tony yesterday before she remembered he was out of town.

But the third . . .

Gracie was used to being able to take men or leave them. In twenty-six years she'd found them charming, boyish, tough or boring; but always she'd found them dispensable. She'd never had an immediate reaction to one the way she'd reacted to this man.

Even glaring at her, he was worth a second glance with that thick dark hair, those vivid blue eyes, and that strong-boned face.

Gracie was very big on strong bones. They indicated character. They meant fortitude and stamina and stubbornness. All of which it seemed Mr. Cameron had plenty, if first impressions were any indication.

Yes, she liked his bones. And she liked the way his soft faded jeans hugged his thighs and the way his open-necked blue sport shirt gave a glimpse of a tanned, hair-roughened chest.

But more than his bones, his thighs and his chest, she liked the way he treated his son. Even when he was being outmaneuvered, she had to give him credit. He treated the boy with love, affection and respect.

He'd been gruff with her, of course, but that wasn't too surprising. After all, he'd hardly expected to find her in his bed like Goldilocks.

Yes, despite his attitude, she thought she'd like Mr. Cameron. She'd certainly like to know him better.

Was there, she wondered, a Mrs. Cameron?

There had been no mention of one. Kip hadn't said, "Mom won't mind," and his father hadn't said, "My wife won't want you here."

So maybe there wasn't. Though what good it would do her if she were going to be bounced out the following morning, she didn't know. Still, she was curious to find out. She straightened the spread, finished brushing her hair and went downstairs, eager to get off on a better footing.

She found Cameron and his son in the kitchen. They were alone except for Alice. No Mrs. Cameron in sight.

Of course that didn't mean there wasn't one somewhere. Perhaps instead of being a Happy Homemaker, Mrs. Cameron was a Happy Executive. These were liberated times, after all. In days past the mothers and kiddies used to summer in East Hampton and the fathers made weekend appearances. Perhaps the opposite was true of the Camerons.

She ventured a glance at Cameron senior. He was looking at her, too, but the moment their eyes met, his shied away. Gracie looked at him curiously.

"Is this enough?" Kip tipped the roaster up so she could see the amount of dog chow he'd added so far.

Gracie looked reluctantly away from Kip's father to gauge the amount of food Kip had given Alice. Given even Alice's voracious appetite, it could've lasted until Labor Day.

Gracie grinned. "I think she may get a little too fat on that much." She turned to share a smile with Kip's father, but he didn't smile back. Shrugging, Gracie helped Kip dump several pounds of chow back in the bag, then put the roaster on the floor.

The moment it was down Alice fell to eagerly, and Kip sank down onto the floor to watch, a rapt expression on his face.

Gracie smiled at them both, then ventured another glance at Cameron. He was leaning against the refrigerator, his dark hair drifting untidily across his forehead. Gracie's fingers itched to brush it back.

She jammed her hands into the pockets of her shorts, aghast at the impulse. Appreciation of the male of the species was one thing; the urge to paw it was something else.

"Well, the weather's certainly nice," she said briskly, rubbing her hands together.

"Mmm," said Cameron. He stared straight ahead.

Kip looked up from Alice's meal, shot his father a quick glance, then gave Gracie a heartwarming grin. "Yeah, it is."

"Have you been swimming yet?"

No comment from Cameron.

"Not yet," Kip said. "I can hardly wait. I can't believe this place is so close to the ocean."

"It's a great house," Gracie agreed. "You'll like it here." She turned to Cameron. "Have you been here before?"

He inclined his head. Gracie guessed that meant he had.

Kip, who missed the infinitesimal nod, looked at him, then at Gracie, then shrugged. "He has. I haven't."

"Have you taken it for the month, then?"

A vague lift of the shoulders.

"All of August," Kip said finally, in the face of Cameron's silence.

Gracie looked at Cameron narrowly. Good bones weren't everything, she decided. Nor was his attitude toward his son. It certainly didn't seem to extend to the rest of the human race. At least it didn't extend to her.

She didn't usually inspire such rudeness. She looked carefully at him. He looked just as carefully out the window. She felt a growing irritation. All this because she happened inadvertently to have ended up in his bed. After all, it wasn't her fault. Not really.

For heaven's sake, you'd have thought he was in it at the time! He could at least be pleasant. An initial shock was one thing. Prolonged surliness was something else. Unless he thought he had something specific against *her*. Which was ridiculous. They'd only just met. And no one disliked Gracie on first encounters. No one.

But Whoever-He-Was Cameron was certainly giving a good imitation of it.

Gracie tried to think of something to say, but for once her ability with small talk deserted her. Her mouth felt dry. She licked her lips.

A muscle ticked in Cameron's jaw, and Gracie heard a sound that could only be the gritting of teeth.

Oh, heavens. What on earth was his problem? But whatever it was, she didn't think he'd enjoy being asked. Anyway, Gracie knew an exit cue when she heard one.

"I think," she said brightly, "I'll just go take a walk on the beach."

THANK GOD, Cameron thought. At least he did until Kip looked up at him accusingly.

"You scared her away."

"I did not."

"Yes, you did."

Cameron looked offended. "I didn't say a word."

"You didn't have to. It's the way you looked."

"How did I look?"

"Like Sophia looked last winter when I brought home that dead mouse."

Cameron laughed.

"It isn't funny." Kip was indignant. "I think Gracie's a very nice lady."

"She's an actress."

Kip thought about that. "My mother was an actress," he said finally.

Precisely, Cameron almost said. He bit his tongue to stop himself, then he shoved away from the refrigerator and paced the room, raking his hand through his hair.

Out the window he could see Gracie's tiny figure disappearing down the beach, deserting him, leaving him to deal with a mess that—as far as he was concerned—she'd made.

Just like Dana.

His expression, he was sure, was exactly like the one Kip had accused him of moments before. Well, he had a right to. And Gracie Talbot had no right to come barging in here. No right at all.

What could Tony have been thinking of?

What was Gracie Talbot to Tony, anyway? She didn't seem Tony's type.

Unless his brother was branching out. Or maturing. Tony's taste had previously run to blond bimbos with big boobs and no brains. The only one of those criteria that Gracie filled was the color of her hair.

But Tony'd never had much staying power, either. Maybe he'd run through all the big-busted bimbos in New York and was having to make do with flat-chested intellectuals now.

Not fair, his conscience chided him.

Life wasn't fair, Cameron retorted. If it were he had a list as long as his arm of things that never should have happened to him.

And Gracie Talbot was definitely one of them. She was attractive—too damned attractive—but she was an actress. He wasn't going to be a fool again.

Deliberately he loosened his fingers and drew a deep breath. "Come on," he said to Kip. "Let's go for a swim."

GRACIE WALKED for miles. Not to Montauk, but close. At least it felt as if she'd gone that far by the time she dragged herself back in the dark.

She climbed the dune slowly, relieved that there were no lights on. She hoped that it meant both Camerons were asleep.

It might not, she knew. It could mean simply that whoever had taken the furniture had stripped the house of lightbulbs, too.

She hoped not.

She had spent the last four hours in constant contemplation of her circumstances, probing them for the window that her father assured her would open when God—or in this case, Mr. Cameron—closed the door.

So far she hadn't found it.

And if she didn't by tomorrow, she knew she'd have to resign her part. She didn't want to do that.

It wasn't that she was so desperately keen on having the role, though it promised to be fun, and she had learned a lot from the director, Herschel Dimante, in just one day. It was mostly that she felt that Tony was right. She should see if this was the break that would seal her fate.

Heaven knew something had to. She was twenty-six years old and she had no more idea of what she wanted to do with her life than she had when she was six or sixteen.

For years now she had been drifting this way and that, uncommitted, waiting for the clarion call of her vocation. And for years she'd waited in vain.

She might not have been so conscious of it if her father's "Be all you can be" hadn't echoed in her ears after so many sermons.

And she might not have cared as much if her sister Carrie hadn't decided at age six to become a kindergarten teacher, if her sister Suzanne at thirteen hadn't made up her

mind to be a lawyer, and if, apparently at birth, her young-
est sister Elsbeth hadn't fallen in love with the baby in the
next isolette and made up her mind to marry Danny Hobbs
twenty years later.

But given those auspicious examples of goal-oriented
commitment, Gracie felt like a dud. Surely sometime,
somewhere, her guardian angel would settle down on her
shoulder and proceed to make her life's plan clear to her.

In the meantime, she felt obliged to try everything, giving him all the help she could.

So she wouldn't quit unless she was forced to, but if
Cameron really did evict her tomorrow, she couldn't see any
choice.

Granted, rooms were available here and there even during the busy summer season, but none she could afford.
And everyone else in the cast already had as many roommates as they could stand.

Gracie sighed and stopped to stare up at Gull Cottage.

Cottage. What a laugh. Mansion, more like.

She could live there with Kip and his unfriendly father, his
mother and a half dozen brothers and sisters, and she'd bet
if she were careful, they'd never even see her.

But she couldn't see herself proposing such a solution to
Mr. Cameron. Not unless he had a terrific change of heart.

Sighing, she climbed the steps that led up the dune from
the beach and let herself in the gate so she could go in the
kitchen door.

All seemed quiet within. Not even Alice seemed to be
stirring.

Normally Alice would have been at her heels when she
left. Tonight she hadn't even paid any attention when
Gracie'd walked out. Of course she had been eating, but
food was rarely a consideration when walks were in the off-
ing. The temptation was Kip. Alice, Gracie had long suspected, had always wanted a boy of her own.

She smiled as she opened the back door and slipped silently into the kitchen. She liked Kip, too. She even liked, as

she had earlier admitted, his father, despite his odd behavior.

She wondered why he didn't like her.

"About time."

The sudden voice in the darkness of the hall startled her. Her heart skipped a beat. "Oh!"

The faint sliver of moonlight was enough for her to see Cameron standing bare-chested in the hallway, his thumbs hooked in the belt loops of his jeans. "I thought you might've found another more welcome bed for the evening."

There was no mistaking the mocking tone of his voice or the meaning that underlay his words. Gracie stiffened, shocked at the insinuation.

She looked at him, her eyes wide. For a long moment he looked back as if challenging her to deny the veiled accusation. Electricity surged between them, grounded by astonishment on Gracie's part and a completely baffling anger on Cameron's.

"I beg your pardon?" she said icily.

He looked almost defiant for a moment, then his gaze flickered away, before coming back to meet hers again. "Sorry. That was uncalled for."

"Yes," Gracie said. "It was."

He looked as if he might say something else. Gracie waited, curious. An explanation wouldn't be out of line, she didn't think. But finally Cameron shrugged awkwardly, then made a faint grimace as he brushed past her. "Forget it," he muttered. "I'll lock up."

Gracie stared after him wonderingly.

Who was this man?

Where had he come from?

Why was he angry?

What was he doing here?

Renting, yes. She knew the answer to that, at least. One out of four.

But why?

He seemed to know Tony. But Tony hadn't known the house was for rent. So, what was his connection to the family?

He didn't look much like the sort of man who would be friends with Laurence McClellan. He looked far too hard-bitten and businesslike to put up with a pompous, conceited old walrus like Laurence. Not the sort to suffer fools gladly was Mr. Cameron.

Gracie wanted some answers. She waited by the stairs for him. He didn't look pleased to find her there.

"You said you were renting this place?" She concentrated on his face, her eyes carefully avoiding his hair-roughened chest, though looking at his lips wasn't much better.

"Yes."

"From who?"

"Laurence McClellan, of course."

"But Tony didn't know it was for rent."

"I'm not surprised. Tony's only his son, after all." There was a wealth of bitterness in his voice, which surprised her.

"So, how'd you hear about it?" she asked.

"I saw an ad in the paper."

Gracie sagged, relieved, though she couldn't have said why. "Oh. You don't know him, then."

Cameron's lips pressed together for a moment. "I know him."

"You do? How?"

"He's my father."

Chapter Three

Gracie simply stared at him, dumbfounded. "I don't—" she faltered, shaking her head.

"Believe it?" Cameron finished mockingly. He shrugged. "Neither do I most of the time. And I try hard not to think about it at all." He stepped around her. "Good-night, Ms. Talbot."

"Er, good-night, Mr. Cameron. I mean...Mr. McClellan. Oh, Lord," Gracie muttered as she watched him go into the bedroom and quietly shut the door.

She felt chagrined, embarrassed and suddenly angry. How was she supposed to know who he was, for heaven's sake?

She'd certainly never heard Tony mention a brother named Cameron. The only one she'd ever heard of was the hard-nosed businessman that Tony continually referred to with awe and reverence as Mac.

Was this Mac, then?

He was hard-nosed, she'd give him that. And the granite jaw would go well in boardrooms, Gracie decided. So would the fathomless eyes. She had a hard time reconciling what she'd heard about Mac with the bemused father of the well loved Kip. But she didn't see who else it could be.

As far as she had determined, Tony only had Mac and a twin sister, Emmy, whom she had met and who was even more of a dandelion-head than he was.

Ergo, Cameron McClellan was Mac.

"Eureka," Gracie muttered, but she wasn't pleased at the discovery.

"People are contradictions," Herschel, her director, had boomed at them just this morning. "They have many facets, many faces."

"No kidding," she said to herself.

"It is your job to know them all." Herschel had fixed them with his beady little eyes. "Great actors know that— they study people, they learn all their faces, all their facets. And then they bring that knowledge to the stage. Remember that. Do it always. Learn people. Know them. Understand what makes them tick." He'd paused and smiled at them. "That way, my children, you can tell the clocks from the bombs."

Gracie sank down on the top step of the landing and tried to decide what it was that made Cameron McClellan tick. Resting her chin in her hand, she tried to put together what she knew about the Mac Tony had spoken of with the man she'd just met.

It wasn't easy.

Tony's half brother was brilliant, with an economics degree from Harvard and an MBA from Yale. But he was more than book smart—he was savvy as well. Street smart, Tony said. And as far as goal orientation went, he made Gracie's sisters look like underachievers.

He had swiftly climbed to the top of the corporate ladder in a multinational road equipment firm before leaving it to start out on his own as a troubleshooter. He had been equally successful taking on failing companies and making them sound again.

These days when he walked into boardrooms, Tony said CEOs fell on their knees in worshipful awe. He was an oracle, a minor—perhaps even major—prophet. He was knowledgeable, insightful and powerful.

"Doesn't sound much like you," Gracie had remarked to Tony.

"Not a bit," he'd agreed blithely, not at all offended. "Chalk and cheese, we are. But it's Mac who's the misfit. My dad is horrified, hates business. So mundane and uncreative. He swears they found Mac under a cabbage leaf. Personally," he confided, "I've always thought it was probably a bank ledger."

Gracie wasn't sure where she thought Cameron McClellan had sprung from. But there wasn't much question in her mind about whether he was a clock or a bomb.

The question was: would she manage to get out of the way before he went off?

WHEN HE GOT UP in the morning, she was gone.

Cameron felt an incredible sense of relief, then asked himself why he should. Getting control of the routine of Gull Cottage wasn't any different than taking charge of a floundering company. It was just a matter of seeing what needed to be done and doing it. Like getting rid of Gracie Talbot. He smiled and poured himself a cup of coffee.

That was when he spotted Alice asleep on the deck.

Cameron's jaw tightened and his fingers clenched around his coffee mug.

Footsteps came thudding down the stairs. "Where's Gracie?" Kip demanded. "She's not in her bed."

Cameron turned just in time to field the tennis ball Kip tossed at him.

"And a very pleasant good morning to you, too," he retorted sharply.

Kip looked momentarily abashed. "Oh, yeah. Morning. So, where is she?"

"I don't know."

Kip looked around worriedly. "She didn't leave, did she?"

Cameron gave the dog a grim look. "She didn't leave." She'd probably just gone to rehearsal. But she would leave later. He'd see to that.

Kip breathed a sigh of relief. "Oh, good."

"Kip, I don't think you should get too attached to her."

The boy looked at him wide-eyed. "Why not? You told me to make friends here. You told me to be nice to people."

"Of course you should be nice to people and make friends. But—Oh, hell." Cameron thumped his coffee mug on the table in frustration.

Kip was rooting in the refrigerator. "You're afraid she'll want to be your girlfriend," he said matter-of-factly over his shoulder.

Cameron scowled. "That's ridiculous."

Kip put the milk on the counter, then got out a serving size packet of cereal, opened it meticulously and proceeded to pour milk on it. "No, it isn't. You came clear out here to get away from Yvette, and you don't want another Yvette here. I don't think Gracie would be one," he told his father seriously.

"Kip!"

"It's true."

Cameron rubbed a hand around the back of his neck, easing an already open collar that suddenly seemed to be strangling him. He'd thought his relationship with Yvette de Jourlet had been clearly platonic to Kip. It certainly wasn't one he wanted to become serious, even though Yvette did. She was quite obviously ready to become the next Mrs. Cameron McClellan.

Cameron himself couldn't see it. Nothing in him wanted to marry her, though he couldn't put his finger on why. She was pretty enough, pleasant enough, smart enough, successful enough.

Still . . . he dragged his feet.

It wasn't that he never wanted to remarry, it was just that he was going to be damned cautious this time. No credence was going to be given to hormones, physical attraction, hearts that went pit-a-pat, or any other unreliable indicators. He'd done that once. In fact from that standpoint, Yvette was well nigh perfect. But still he couldn't find it in him to propose.

"This has nothing to do with Yvette," he muttered.

Kip shrugged. "But now we've lost her," he said, his mind still on Gracie Talbot. He looked glumly into his cereal bowl.

"The dog is out by the pool," Cameron said gruffly.

Kip's face lit up. He bounded to his feet to peer out the window, all now right with the world. "Great. Hey, can I eat my cereal out there with Alice?"

"May I," Cameron corrected automatically.

"Sure. C'mon." Kip was out the door before Cameron could protest.

And what was he going to protest anyway?

It seemed to Cameron that in fact he'd been protesting entirely too much. He needed to leave well enough alone.

Irritably he snagged another packet of cereal out of the package, then went to join Kip on the deck.

After they ate, Kip threw the ball for Alice. Then, when Alice tired of that and came to lay her chin on Cameron's knee and look adoringly up into his eyes, Kip wanted to go talk to Boris.

"Be my guest," Cameron said.

"Shall I feed him?" Kip asked.

"Read the instructions."

Kip dashed off and Cameron sat, absently patting Alice's head. Then, when he realized what he was doing, he stood up abruptly and carried the dishes back into the kitchen. Alice followed and sat right beside him while he rinsed them.

"Go away," Cameron commanded. Alice thumped her tail.

Ignoring her, he went upstairs and rolled up the sleeping bags. Alice dogged his footsteps, making him trip over her every time he turned around.

"Alice." He scowled at her. She grinned back at him. She had the same cheerful innocence her mistress had. Determinedly Cameron turned away. He went back out and sat on the deck to read the paper until the man from the phone company came; Alice sat beside him with her chin on his feet.

Cameron did his best to pretend she wasn't there.

When the phone company man came, it got easier.

"Cost a pretty penny, hooking up all this," the man told him as he worked. "Surprised it wasn't done before when everything split up. Must've only had old lines out here."

"Must've," Cameron agreed. What it meant to him was that his father hadn't been using Gull Cottage recently.

"Just buy the place?"

"I'm renting."

"Hope they don't stick you with the bill, then." The man looked up from the wires he was twisting and gave Cameron a gap-toothed grin.

"They won't." Cameron intended to see to that.

It took the rest of the morning to do the whole house and the outside wiring. When the man came clattering down the stairs, Cameron, with Alice alongside, was there to meet him. "Well, you're all set." The man started out, then paused and gave Cameron a sly smile. "That's some bed."

"What?"

"The bed. All them snakes. Wow."

"Oh, er, yeah."

The man winked. "Must be a hell of an inspiration."

Cameron, remembering how Gracie Talbot had looked lying in it, gave him a tight grin and followed him out.

The man got into his truck, glanced back at the house and paused again. "You been up on that roof?"

"No. Why?"

"Pray it don't rain."

Cameron shut her eyes and groaned. Something else to talk to the realtor about.

THE REAL ESTATE AGENCY proved singularly unhelpful.

"Mrs. Geller?" a woman's voice said when he reached the office on the phone. "I'm sorry, sir. Mrs. Geller is . . . well . . . not working here any longer."

"Not working there?"

"She, er...had a...breakdown. Stress, you know."

Cameron rolled his eyes. He was getting a very good idea. "Well, if Mrs. Geller isn't there, you'll have to help me. What about the furniture, then? Before she stressed out, your Mrs. Geller told my secretary this place was rented furnished."

"I, er, believe that the, er, furnishings, um, disappearing had something to do with the, er...stress, sir."

Cameron could believe that. "So what're you going to do about it?"

"Well, the owner is out of the country, I'm afraid, and until he returns, I can't say..."

"You don't have to say," Cameron told her briskly. "But when you talk to him, tell him I get furniture or I get a refund of a third of the rent."

"But, sir—"

"I understand the roof leaks, too."

The woman bristled. "Where on earth have you heard such a thing?"

"Just a rumor so far. But if it does, I'll expect an adjustment there, too."

"Well, I—"

"Now, about that bird..."

"Bird?" She said the word as if it were a bomb about to go off.

"We don't want it."

"But—"

"No buts. It's got to go." He'd spent the night thinking about Boris, and he'd made his decision. Kip might be upset, but it was nothing to what Cameron would be if he had to spend a month babysitting that bird.

"On the contrary, sir," the realtor said, apparently feeling she had to draw the line somewhere. "When your firm agreed to take the house, such matters were discussed—the conditions negotiated. I'm sorry, sir, but it's quite clear in your lease; *You took the bird.*"

He certainly had, Cameron thought bitterly. "That was before I'd *met* the bird."

"Well, I don't know about that." Her tones were clipped. "But a contract is a contract."

"As in furnishings..." Cameron let the word hang in the air.

She sighed, caught. There was a heavy silence on the line. Cameron wasn't about to be the one who broke it.

Finally she said, "I can't do anything about retrieving the furnishings, sir. And I can't do anything about the roof without the owner's permission. And I'm afraid I can't remove the bird. Not at this late date. He's very sensitive, you see. Needs stability in his life."

Cameron snorted.

"But if you'll agree to keep the bird," she went on, undaunted, "I'm sure that the owner will be only too happy to pick up the cost of any furnishings you might require. And I will get in touch with him about the roof, so if it does rain, we can then authorize repair of the roof, too. I know he'll be only too happy to comply."

"You think so?" Cameron didn't. Not for a minute. The house wasn't bare and leaky because his father had suddenly got religion and had given away all his worldly goods, including the roof shingles.

"Certainly I'm sure," the woman assured him. "So, do we have a deal?"

Cameron thought about a month with Boris. He shuddered. But then he thought again about trying to convince Kip that Boris had an invitation elsewhere. He thought about telling Gracie Talbot he didn't lie to his son. He thought about the roof and the furnishings and about backing his father into a corner, about just once ruffling that almighty and unshakable Laurence McClellan aplomb. A month with Boris might be a fair trade.

"All right," he said.

"Oh, sir, you won't regret it," the realtor gushed.

Cameron wasn't so sure.

HE CALLED JEANNIE, gave her his new phone number and told her the way things were.

"So you've settled it then?" She sounded relieved.

"More or less."

"I knew you would. You always do."

"Yeah." But Cameron, for the first time, found himself wondering about that.

"Good. Roger called."

"Ackley?" Cameron's interest perked up.

"Yes. He was apologetic about calling. He knows you've taken the month off, but he said it was urgent. He did say, though, that he'd understand if you didn't call back."

There wasn't any question that he would, though.

Roger Ackley had been Cameron's best friend since college. They'd roomed together, studied together, doubledated together. Cameron had been Roger's best man, and Roger had been his. Cameron had been godfather to Roger's oldest child; Roger was godfather to Kip.

But even more than the high points they had shared, Roger had been there for Cameron when his marriage fell apart. He and his wife, Julie, had bolstered Cameron through some very rough years. They and their three little girls had been the bastion of normality and sanity that Cameron had clung to while he tried to be a successful businessman and, at the same time, both mother and father to Kip.

If Roger said "urgent," there was no way that Cameron was going to neglect his call.

But unfortunately Roger wasn't there.

"I know he wants to talk to you," his secretary told Cameron. "But I can't disturb him now. He's in a meeting. I'll tell him you called, shall I?"

"Please." Cameron gave her the number.

He should have bought a portable phone, he thought after three hours had passed during which he didn't venture beyond phone-ringing range and Roger didn't call.

Kip was getting bored with sliding from one end of the living room to the other, even with Alice for company. He wanted Cameron to go swimming with him at the beach or, failing that, at least in the pool. But they couldn't hear the phone out there.

Then, at quarter past two, Gracie came in.

All day Cameron had been hoping his reaction to her would have moderated a bit. After all, there was nothing so special about a choppy haired blonde. They were a dime a dozen, particularly along the seashore. Besides, yesterday had been trying in the extreme. His hormones could have gone into overdrive purely as a result of that.

One look told him they hadn't. One look at Gracie Talbot and he was searching out all available escape routes.

"Hey, super, you're here!" Kip said to her, then turned to his father. "I bet Gracie'd listen for the phone while we swim."

"Miss Talbot was just leaving," Cameron said implacably.

Gracie cleared her throat. "I was wondering if we could maybe...talk about that?"

"Talk about what?"

"My, er...leaving."

"What about it?"

"I talked to my director today. Herschel Dimante. Maybe you know him?" She sounded young and hopeful.

Cameron eyed her narrowly, shaking his head.

"Oh." Gracie gave a helpless little shrug. "Well, he's quite well known in some circles. I mean, very highly thought of. Your father probably—"

"No doubt," Cameron said flatly. "I don't."

"Er, right. Well, I talked to him about getting a replacement for me. He wasn't exactly keen—which I'm glad of, of course," Gracie admitted ingenuously. "But he didn't know of a place for me to live, either. One of the women, Tracy, thinks I might be able to live with her. But she had to check with her boyfriend to see if he minds me being on the couch.

So I was wondering . . . would it be all right if I stayed just one more day?''

She was looking at him like a pet-shop puppy looked at a kid through the window. It was an act, Cameron told himself. Wistful, hopeful, gentle. But only an act. He gritted his teeth.

Gracie continued to smile hopefully.

Alice wagged her tail.

Kip shifted from one foot to the other. ''She could answer the phone, Dad,'' he put in finally after the silence went on and on.

Cameron looked at his son, looked at Gracie, then looked out the French doors across the sand that swept down to the sea. Oh hell, he thought. Oh hell.

Why did life always have to do this to you? Why, when you were all set to hit a fastball down the middle, did God suddenly throw a curve?

He didn't want Gracie Talbot here another day. She was a danger to his emotional health. She tempted him. He scarcely knew her; still he was attracted to her.

And that wasn't what he'd come to East Hampton for at all. He'd come for Kip, for memories of his childhood. He had not come to be confronted by a woman who brought back other memories, who made him feel the way another woman had once made him feel.

''Think of the worst possible scenario,'' he often told the CEOs he worked with. ''Imagine it in great detail. Think what you would do if it came to pass.''

That's what he did now, facing the prospect of Gracie Talbot.

And when they'd done it, ''Can you handle it?'' he always asked them.

''Yes,'' they always said, for their fears were always worse in vague terms than when they dealt with them step by step.

Could he handle his worst fear?

As long as he could see through her act, yes. As long as he kept at the forefront of his mind just exactly who she was and what that meant, he could handle it. He was thirty-six years old now. He'd been around the track. No green lad, he. Not any longer.

So as long as he never got taken in again, what difference did it make?

Hell, he thought recklessly, it might even be a good thing, test his immunity and all that.

He drew a deep breath and gave Gracie a level look. "One more day."

Gracie's face looked like the sun came out. She looked as if she were going to leap on him and hug him. Cameron's back went stiff against the wall.

But all she said was, "I'd be delighted to answer the phone."

It was Kip she hugged.

GRACIE STOOD at the windows and watched Kip and Cameron cavorting on the beach. First they'd swum, then they'd tossed a Frisbee, and now they were digging trenches and tunnels and building castles, their faces by turns smiling and serious, laughing and thoughtful. Her eyes followed them, entranced.

How could a man who laughed and played with his child be so sullen and stiff with her? she wondered. What was it about Cameron McClellan that made him behave that way? What was it about *her*?

The question continued to nag her, intrigue her, tantalize her.

No, to be honest, it wasn't the question; it was the man. He was such a paradox, she found him fascinating. Warm and laughing one minute, cold and gruff the next. She'd seen love and gentleness and decency in him. Always with Kip; when pressed, with her. Yet always, too, there was also a shell around him, a reserve that challenged her to crack it.

She sensed anger in him, resentment, hurt. All of it for some reason directed at her. She didn't understand the reason for any of those things.

But she wanted to.

She wasn't even sure why. Always one for puzzles, Gracie thought that might be it. Perhaps it was a whim, mere perversity that made her want to find out what made him tick.

She suspected, though, that it might be something else.

There was so much she didn't know. She still didn't even know if there was a Mrs. McClellan. She began to suspect there wasn't, but it wasn't the sort of question you asked a man as prickly as Cameron. Being here on sufferance meant keeping as low a profile as possible. Still, the questions wouldn't go away.

Alice whined and pushed at the door with her nose, then nudged Gracie's hand.

"You want to go out?"

Another whine and a harder nudge.

Gracie pressed her nose against the glass, watching as Kip took a scooper full of water and dashed it at his father. Cameron retaliated, then chased the boy into the surf. "Me, too," she murmured.

She wished the phone would ring. Then she could go out and tell him, swim with him, get to know him a little better.

"For all the good it will do you," she reminded herself. For she feared that, however much she was intrigued by the puzzle that Cameron McClellan presented, she wasn't going to get a chance to solve it. Not when she had less than twenty-four hours as a part of his life.

CAMERON SWAM with Kip, then threw the Frisbee, then built a sandcastle complete with moat and drizzled sand towers. It was exactly the sort of afternoon he'd envisioned since he'd come up with the notion of "going home again."

It was also the first time anything remotely resembling what he'd planned had actually happened since he'd set foot in Gull Cottage the day before.

His only discomfort was knowing that he owed it to Gracie Talbot.

He cast the occasional glance back at the house, wondering what she was doing while she waited for the phone to ring, then told himself he didn't care.

Kip stared back at the house, too, then said, "The ocean's great. Why'd they ever build a pool?"

"Prestige," Cameron answered promptly. "It was the thing to do."

He even remembered when. He'd been in his freshman year in college and had come to spend the summer holidays with his father, Amaryllis and the twins. Since Cameron's grandparents had died the year before, the house had somehow come into his father's hands. Just how—since it had belonged to his mother's parents—he'd never determined.

But for whatever reason, Laurence McClellan owned it, and for a change he had been spending the summer there. So Cameron had steeled himself against his memories and had come to visit. He had taken a taxi from the train station and had walked up Frigate Alley because he wanted some time to prepare himself.

But nothing had prepared him to find his grandmother's precious herb garden under several tons of sand and a monstrous hole where his grandfather's brick patio had once been.

He'd stopped dead and stared, and had been standing there slack-jawed when his father had seen him from the house and had bustled out.

"What's going on?" Cameron had asked.

Laurence had looked momentarily discomfitted, then said firmly, "Amaryllis wanted a pool. They're in this year."

Laurence was notoriously indulgent to his actress wife and to the clever, creative twins she had borne him. Cameron resented his father's blithe indulgence of his second wife and family because Laurence so grudgingly had anything at all to do with him. But he couldn't resent Amaryllis or the twins because they bore him no ill will at all.

On the contrary, they were invariably glad to see him whenever he turned up. Amaryllis always wanted to hear what he thought of the new part she was trying out for, and Tony and Emmy were always demanding he watch them perform some new skit that one or the other of them had written.

It was only his father who never seemed able to give him the time of day.

"Sound investment. You see if it's not." Laurence thrust his jaw out. "Besides, that herb garden was a mess. Covered with dead branches and leaves half the time."

"Compost," Cameron said quietly.

"A trash heap," Laurence said, nodding. "Much better this way. Everyone agrees."

Cameron hadn't. But he hadn't said so then or later.

For him the magic had already gone from Gull Cottage. What he'd found there at ten had, by eighteen, vanished into thin air. He made plans to leave almost as soon as he'd come.

"I'm cold," Kip said suddenly, teeth chattering.

Cameron glanced at his son, hauled back to the present.

"Come on," he said to Kip. "You're turning blue. Time to go in."

They clambered back up the dunes to the house and found Gracie in the kitchen making supper.

"Meat loaf," she announced when they came through the door. "Suit you?"

"You didn't have to—" Cameron began, but Kip cut him off.

"Great! My favorite. Mashed potatoes, too?"

Gracie smiled. "Sure. If you want."

"I want."

"Go get a shower then, and you can peel them for me," Gracie told him.

Kip's face fell. "Peel them?"

"Do you make mashed potatoes with the skins left on?" she asked, a twinkle in her eye.

"Well, I've never exactly made 'em, but..." He gave a little shrug. "I'll be right back."

He dashed up the back steps.

Cameron lingered in the kitchen, discomfitted. He couldn't help admiring the way Gracie had so neatly got Kip to help with the preparations; on the other hand, it seemed like one more inch she'd got her foot in the door.

He cleared his throat and shifted from one sandy foot to the other. "You didn't have to make us dinner."

"I know." Gracie went right on shaping the meat loaf.

"It doesn't mean I'm going to relent," he went on, determinedly.

She looked at him. "Really?"

He felt the hot rush of blood to his cheeks. He gritted his teeth.

Gracie bent and put the meat loaf pan into the oven. Glancing up over her shoulder, she fixed him with her gaze. "Perhaps you'd prefer to eat separately? Me in the kitchen and you two in the dining room?"

Cameron opened his mouth, then closed it. Spelled out it made him sound like an idiot. Damn her.

Cornered and knowing it, he did his best to salvage what he could, attempting to take another page out of the book that he used to counsel his clients.

Whenever you have to compromise, he always told them, do it gracefully.

"Let me get cleaned up," he said gruffly, "and I'll make a salad."

"Sounds good." Gracie blessed him with a cheerful grin.

The sheer power of it made Cameron look away. No corporate executives ever took compromises quite like that.

Shaken, he realized that compromise with Gracie Talbot could be a very difficult thing.

Chapter Four

The meat loaf was delicious, the salad tasty, and the potatoes lumpy. But surprisingly no one cared or even seemed to notice.

They'd worked together in the kitchen, Kip peeling the potatoes and Cameron tossing the salad while Gracie regaled them with stories of how she used to try to get out of similar kitchen chores while growing up.

"Did you really hide in the attic so you didn't have to set the table?" Kip demanded when they were eating at last.

"I really did," Gracie assured him. "I was the bane of my mother's existence. She began to wonder if she'd ever make a lady of me."

"Did she?" Cameron asked dryly before he could help himself.

Gracie tossed her hair. "I don't know. What do you think?" she asked impishly, batting her eyelashes.

Cameron felt his cheeks warm and his loins tighten. He cleared his throat, took a gulp of water from his glass and looked away.

Gracie shrugged and shook her head. "No comment?" She smiled. "My mother would probably agree with you."

Cameron didn't know about that. She certainly had all the right parts. And she knew all the buttons to push. He wished the meal would end. Quick.

"I'll do the dishes," he volunteered the moment it did.

But Gracie would hear none of it. "I ate, I'll help," she said. "That's the way it always was at my house."

"You don't have to," he said.

"I want to."

What was he supposed to say to that? *You can't?*

So the three of them pitched in—Cameron washing, Gracie drying, and Kip putting the dishes away.

The stories then moved from Gracie's childhood to life in the fifth-floor walk-up she shared with a series of revolving roommates.

"They all come and go," she said. "All but one." She reached out and fondled the mastiff's head. And then, while Kip dumped dog chow in Alice's roaster, Gracie told them of how one snowy afternoon three winters ago, she was standing outside Bloomingdale's, bell ringing for the Salvation Army, when a huge black dog had come up and sat down beside her, and how, at five that evening, the huge black dog had simply followed her home.

"And that was Alice?" Kip's eyes were like saucers.

"That was Alice."

Kip set the roaster on the floor and watched as Alice proceeded to gobble. Then he looked up, considering. "But how did you know she was called Alice?"

"She told me," Gracie said guilelessly.

And Cameron, who had been listening to all of her stories without saying a word, watched her big brown eyes and gently upturned smile and actually found himself believing her.

He shook himself. Ridiculous. All she was was an actress. But a consummate actress, for all that. She had Kip—and very nearly him—eating out of her hand.

He made a pointed effort to concentrate on scrubbing the meat loaf pan. But steel himself as he might, he wasn't entirely immune. Gracie Talbot, effervescing, was hard to resist. He stole glances at her, watching the way she seemed to light up when she was remembering something joyful, the

way serenity seemed to emanate from her when she re-
counted something moving or thought provoking.

She seemed to be sharing herself and her memories un-
stintingly, confiding in them, trusting them with herself.

Despite all his misgivings, it made him want to share, too.
Eventually he could maintain a stony silence no longer.

When Kip asked him if he'd ever had a dog, he told them
about Blackie.

Blackie was the first pet Cameron had ever had—and the
last.

He had come to Cameron the summer he was ten rather
like Alice had come to Gracie. Scarcely more than a puppy
when he had followed Cameron back to Gull Cottage, he
was a scruffy black mongrel—nothing to look at, certainly
a far cry from the pampered poodles and pedigreed yorkies
that were de riguer in East Hampton at the time, but Cameron loved him.

When no one claimed him, he settled in. Cameron
romped on the beach with Blackie, scrambled through the
woods with Blackie, even—to his mother's dismay—
scratched fleas with Blackie.

All summer they were inseparable. But when summer
ended, so did Cameron's life with Blackie.

"New York City was, according to my father, no place for
animals. Or rather, there were enough animals there already—of the two-legged variety, you know," he said in a
surprisingly adept imitation of Laurence McClellan's
pompous tone.

Kip giggled and Gracie smiled.

Cameron smiled, too, albeit ruefully. "There was no way
my father was going to take Blackie along."

"So what happened?" Kip asked, clambering up onto the
counter to put the plates away.

"So we went back to New York in September and Blackie
didn't."

"Where'd he go?"

"He was supposed to stay with my grandparents right here."

"Did he?"

"I don't know."

Kip frowned. "Was he here the next summer?"

Cameron shrugged. "I don't know. I wasn't."

Kip just looked at him. "But didn't you ever see him again?"

"No. My grandfather had a stroke that fall." Cameron pulled the plug in the sink and watched the water swirl noisily down the drain. "My parents got a divorce."

His hands lay limply against the lip of the sink. He looked at them, then at Kip and saw in him the innocent he'd been at that age. He remembered how he had felt. On the one hand it seemed an aeon ago, on the other, no more than an hour.

"It was years before I ever got back. But when I did, suffice to say, there was no more Blackie. I suppose they...gave him away, found him a good home." He hoped they had, anyway. He'd never let himself think about what else might have happened. "Anyway," he said briskly, "it's a long time ago now. That's all water under the bridge."

He wiped his hands on the sides of his jeans, embarrassed at how much he might have revealed in front of Gracie. "I'm going to go try to call Roger."

There was a phone in the kitchen, but he didn't use it, choosing instead to take refuge upstairs.

Roger was at the hospital, according to Julie. "Dad had a heart attack last week, wouldn't you know? He retires to take it easy, is off less than a month and winds up in the hospital."

"How is he?" Cameron had always liked Roger's father, a gnomelike, cheerful man quite unlike his own, who had spent his life building bicycles and making a living at it.

"Holding his own. But he has crises now and then. Roger's been there a lot. I'll tell him you called."

Cameron hung up and sat on the edge of his sleeping bag. He should go back downstairs with Kip, but that meant going back down with Gracie, too, and he felt a definite reluctance to do that.

He was scared of her. On the face of it, that sounded foolish. She was a pint-sized woman. He was a strapping, muscular man. But that had nothing to do with his fear. She piqued his curiosity, nettled and tantalized him the way he hadn't been nettled or tantalized in years.

Not since Dana, in fact.

Remember that, he cautioned himself.

Like other men remembered the Alamo, Cameron McClellan made himself remember Dana Bryce.

The antagonist of his very own personal cautionary tale, his wife had very definitely left her mark.

An actress, he reminded himself. A woman just like Gracie Talbot.

If Gracie Talbot were anything other than an actress, he admitted to himself, things would be different. He might even consider her surprise residency here an asset. He certainly wasn't averse to women, except ones like Yvette who were determined to infiltrate his life further than he wanted.

Gracie Talbot had an elfin quality that could enchant him if he'd let it. There was an openness about her, an innocence. She reminded him of the Brownies who used to come to the door selling cookies. With that "happy camper" look on her face, who could refuse her?

But how much of that, he wondered, was really Gracie Talbot and how much was an act?

And what did it matter, anyway?

One more day, he'd promised her. He glanced at his watch. He lifted his eyes heavenward. In less than eighteen hours, please God, she would be out of his life.

In the meantime, he'd do his best to ignore her. He scrambled over and rooted through the duffel at the head of his sleeping bag for the mini-chess set he and Kip had brought. If it occurred to him that perhaps it wasn't the most polite maneuver to propose a two-person game in a three-person household, he shoved the thought ruthlessly out of his mind.

Kip looked a bit askance at his father's suggestion about starting a chess game, but Gracie didn't seem to mind.

"I'll watch."

It wasn't what Cameron had in mind. But short of saying no she couldn't, what could he do about it?

Muttering under his breath, Cameron led the way into the living room. He built a fire in the fireplace, more for the nostalgic value than because it was necessary. They began to play. First Kip moved, then Cameron.

Gracie watched, her bright eyes shining. She shoved the hair away from her face and leaned closer. Cameron could smell the soft scent of wildflowers now. It raised the hairs on the back of his neck.

He tried to ignore it, tried to concentrate on chess strategy. He felt as if he were a prairie dog with a hawk circling overhead. Conscious. Aware. Nervous.

The fire spat and crackled. Kip moved. Cameron moved again. The game went on.

Gracie crossed her legs, rested an elbow on one knee and lay her chin in her hand. Cameron could hear her breathe.

Kip moved his castle.

Cameron licked his lips, then moved his castle.

Gracie shifted her weight and made a soft approving sound in her throat. Out of the corner of his eye Cameron could see her bare toes painted pink, flexing slowly. He swallowed.

Kip moved again.

So did Cameron.

"I thought bishops couldn't move straight forward," Kip said.

"What? No, of course they can't!" Cameron raked his fingers through his hair. He cleared his throat, grinned lamely and changed his move. "Just wanted to see if you were on your toes."

"I am," Kip assured him.

"Right."

"He's very good," Gracie interpolated.

"Very," Cameron agreed. His voice was hoarse.

He glanced at his watch, wondering rather desperately if Roger might be back yet. Kip took his knight.

Cameron scowled at him.

"Nice," Gracie approved.

Kip grinned and shrugged.

A log shifted in the fireplace and Gracie got up to adjust it. From where he sat on the floor Cameron could appreciate her slim form silhouetted against the fire. She bent over the fireplace and Cameron watched the flames lick up behind her, outlining the curve of her bottom, the length of her legs. He shifted uncomfortably.

"Your move," Kip said.

Cameron glanced cursorily down at the board and moved his castle, his eyes already drawn back to Gracie.

"Checkmate," said Kip.

"What!" Cameron's gaze jerked around to stare at his son.

Kip gestured toward the board.

Cameron stared at it, studied the positions of the remaining pieces, moved his castle, his bishop, his king in his head. He had nowhere to go. He was boxed in. His eyes lifted and he looked at Kip accusingly. "You little—"

"Genius?" Kip offered.

Cameron shook his head slowly. "Genius," he concurred, grinning, as he reached out and ruffled the boy's hair.

"You gotta pay attention, Dad. That's what you always tell me. Can't defend yourself if you don't." Kip got up and stretched mightily.

Let that be a lesson to you, Cameron told himself. He allowed himself a long hard look at Gracie Talbot, still standing with her back to the fire, looking elemental, tantalizing, untamed. She could do the same thing to him if he weren't careful.

"How about some popcorn?" she suggested. "I'll make it."

"Great," Kip said, bounding up to help her.

Cameron knew how Adam felt when offered the apple. "No, thank you. I've got to call Roger." He headed for the stairs without looking back.

STILL NO ROGER.

"I'll have him call you first thing in the morning," Julie said. "I hope you haven't been hanging around waiting, Cam."

"No. No, that's all right."

Cameron hung the phone up slowly and lay back on his sleeping bag to stare at the ceiling. Through the curtainless window a soft breeze blew in off the sea, and the sound of the waves reached his ears. He could hear Kip's giggle coming from downstairs, then Gracie's soft, almost sultry laughter, and Alice's woof.

It sounded homey, seductive, enticing. He lay there, stiff and silent, resisting.

The sounds reminded him of when he'd been a child. Night after night he'd lain upstairs and strained his ears to hear life going on down below. In those days the sounds of his mother's laughter, of his father's deep tones and his grandmother's gentle ones, of his grandfather's periodic throat clearing and Blackie's staccato yaps had spelled security to him. They'd given him satisfaction, warmth, love.

They'd fueled his dreams. They'd taught him to plan, to hope, to desire. Those memories had given him ideals that he'd coveted and aspired to. He'd wanted a home like that, a wife like that, a life like that. It was exactly what he'd sought when he'd married Dana.

And now?

Now he felt lost, bereft, almost as if he were grieving. He was lying here aching for something beyond him, something gone or lost or simply—now and always—out of reach.

He sighed. *Stop it,* he told himself. *Just stop.*

Usually he could. Usually it was easy enough to put ideals behind him and get on with the reality at hand. But it wasn't easy tonight. But whether he owed this perversity of mind and emotion to Gull Cottage or to Gracie Talbot or to a combination of the two, he really didn't know.

Suddenly Kip poked his head in the door. "We thought you were on the phone."

Cameron sat up, shaking his head, trying to reorient himself. "No. Roger wasn't there."

"Oh. Well, Gracie told me to get ready for bed and she'd read me a book we found in one of the cupboards downstairs."

"*Gracie* told you ...?" Cameron found himself bristling.

"You don't mind, do you?" Gracie peered in the room at him. "I don't mean to usurp your role. But we thought you'd be on the phone longer. And it is getting late."

"I know how late it is," Cameron snapped irritably. "Kip doesn't go to bed with the chickens in the summer."

"I didn't mean to imply—"

"Forget it." He was overreacting again. He raked a hand through his hair. "Go ahead. Read to him. I don't care."

Gracie gave him a tentative smile. "You can listen, if you like."

"No, thanks."

He turned his back on her, got to his feet and went to stand at the window, staring out into the blackness. For a long moment he didn't think she was going to move. Then, almost soundlessly he heard her slip away.

A few minutes later he heard her reading. He didn't move, just stood there, letting the sound of the waves and the words wash over him. Her voice was husky, but soft, soothing and gentle, the way his own mother's had been.

He wished life were as simple as it had been when he was a child like Kip, being read to by his mother. He wished he felt the sense of possibility, of promise that he'd felt then.

"Do you really?" he asked himself doubtfully. Wasn't it better to know that life wasn't always rosy, that hopes didn't always materialize, that dreams sometimes didn't come true?

"Yes," he said firmly. "Yes."

But even so, he was drawn out into the hallway by her voice, and he found himself leaning against the wall, listening as she read.

It was a book he remembered, a book he'd read himself as a child. A book about a summer in which a boy longs for someone to play with and finds when the clock strikes thirteen, that the present meshes with the past and that the house in which he is living and the people who used to live in it exist for him both then and now.

The boy's longing was one that Cameron, as an only child, had known. It was in fact not unlike the feeling that had brought him back here this summer. Nor was it unlike the feeling that was blowing about inside his soul tonight.

He closed his eyes and leaned his head back against the wall, his throat curiously tight.

He was still standing there when Gracie reached the end of the chapter and Kip said, "But what happens next?"

"You'll find out."

"Can't we read another chapter?" Kip begged.

"Not tonight."

"But—"

"It's late," Gracie told him firmly, "and I told you *one* chapter." A pause. "Didn't I?"

"Yeah," Kip mumbled. "But you can read me another one tomorrow, can't you?"

There was another pause, longer this time. Then Gracie said, "I don't think I'm going to be here tomorrow night, Kip. But you can read it yourself, or perhaps your father will."

Kip sighed. "Yeah, I guess." The floor creaked as he shifted in his sleeping bag. "G'night, Gracie."

Cameron heard Gracie getting to her feet and moved quickly away from the wall.

"Good night, Kip."

She came out the door and spotted Cameron looking as if he were just coming down the hall. "Oh, there you are. Thanks for letting me read to him. I enjoyed it."

The eager warmth of her smile hurt more than Cameron would have thought possible. He swallowed against the lump in his throat, not trusting himself to say a word. It wasn't until he'd edged past her into Kip's room that he dared to say, "You're welcome."

WHEN SHE WAS in high school, Gracie had latched on to acting as a way to find out who she was and what she wanted out of life. Never clear in purpose the way her sisters were, she hit upon theater as a means of checking things out. After all, one's life's circumstances generally prevented one from trying out too many life-styles in fact. But in fantasy the roles were limitless. She could try out life as a bar girl, an ingenue, a revolutionary, a career woman, a dancer. Whatever the casting director permitted her to be.

And someday, Gracie was convinced, such efforts would pay off. Either she would find her niche as an actress per se, or she would find the role that fit her like a glove—the one she was made for, or the one that was made for her.

How would she know? she asked herself. Would a voice come down from on high and inform her? Would a choir of angels burst into hallelujahs when she finally got her act together?

Something eventful surely ought to happen, she thought.

But tonight as she sat propped against the bow of the barge bed, with her arms clasped around her drawn up knees, she thought it was possibly more subtle than that.

She wasn't sure, of course. No one with her track record for indecision and dithering could be. But somehow, tonight, she'd felt as if she'd just slipped her hand into a surprisingly comfortable glove. She liked being with Kip and his prickly, well defended father.

Despite the fact that the prickly, well defended father certainly seemed averse to her.

Did that mean she wanted to be a wife and mother?

Sometimes she'd thought so—in a vague, abstract, Gracie-Talbot sort of way. But whenever she'd had offers along those lines—and she had—they'd never intrigued her in the least.

What was it about this time that was different?

The boy, of course. Who could not like Kip?

But the man?

Gracie sighed. There was a lot not to like about Cameron McClellan, not the least of which was the way he acted toward her. But, if she were honest, a part of his attraction *was* the way he acted around her. She wasn't a masochist; she didn't like it. But she did want to understand it, wanted to understand *him*. She didn't think it was a natural aversion. She thought something had provoked it. And she wanted to know what.

It was like Herschel said, an effort to try to figure people out, know what made them tick.

And then what? she asked herself.

Well, that remained to be seen.

But for someone who was going to be booted out on her rear end tomorrow, she felt astonishingly settled and calm, rooted almost. It was as if her congenital restlessness was fading, as if she were preparing to dig in, stay in East Hampton one way or another—not just to play Cecily at the John Drew Theater—but mainly to find out whether this sense of rightness she was beginning to feel was just one more false alarm or, finally, the real thing come at last.

SHE WAS IN HIS BED.

Kissing him. Running her hands over him. Teasing.

Tempting. He held himself rigid, resisting. Gritting his teeth. Clenching his fists. Aching. Needing. *Wanting*.

The phone rang almost in his ear.

Cameron jerked and fell off the air mattress, cracking his elbow on the hardwood floor. "Damn."

It rang again. He groped for it, not knowing whether he was relieved or angry to find he was alone, that Gracie Talbot and her tantalizing hands were nothing more than an erotic dream. He only knew that he was frustrated as hell.

"Rotten time to bother you," Roger Ackley said cheerfully when Cameron finally answered. "Vacationers should get to sleep in."

Cameron rolled over onto his back and shook himself from head to toe, trying desperately to banish the dream of silky skin warm and fragrant against his. "What's up?"

"Me. All night."

Me, too, Cameron thought distractedly. Then, "How's your dad?"

"Holding his own right now. It's the company I'm worried about.

"What do you mean?"

"Aw, you know my dad. He made a good product, but he didn't manage well. He was always more interested in bicycles than in ledgers and profit and loss. We're going to lose the company if I don't get it sorted out."

"I'll take a look," Cameron offered.

"I hate to do this to you. I know you were counting on this month just with Kip."

"You're only in Massachusetts," Cameron said. "It's not as if I had to go back out to San Francisco."

"I know, but—"

"I can bring the paperwork home. Don't worry. It's what friends are for."

Roger sighed. "I really do appreciate it. I know if the heart attack doesn't kill him, losing the company will."

"No sweat. I'll be there."

"You and Kip can stay with us. I know it isn't the same as your 'roots' bit, but we're here and there's some history in Boston he can absorb."

"We'll see. I'll talk to him and call you back."

Cameron got up and dressed, then went to find Kip on the deck with Alice. He looked perfectly content tossing the ball to the dog. But, Cameron told himself, the dog wouldn't be here after today. Then Kip would probably be pleased to go to Boston and spend time with Roger and his family.

Kip, when asked, said, "Yuck."

He tossed the ball into the pool and Alice leaped after it. "You don't mean it, do you, Dad?"

"Boston's a great place. Paul Revere, the Boston Tea Party—" he cast around for another example "—the Celtics."

"Girls," Kip gagged, making a horrible face. "All those yucky girls."

"Roger's girls?"

More gagging.

"There's nothing wrong with Sarah, Anne, and Caroline," Cameron said defensively.

Kip stopped gagging long enough to look at him to see if he was joking.

He wasn't, but unfortunately he could remember being ten well enough to know how Kip felt. Oh, hell.

"I have to go, Kip," he said helplessly. "I owe it to Roger. I told him I'd be there as soon as possible. We probably won't have to be gone long. A few days. A week altogether at most."

"An hour is too long," Kip said. He took the ball from Alice and, disgruntled, flung it to the far end of the pool.

The dog threw herself into the pool after it, drenching both of them.

Kip beamed at the soaking, then scowled as he remembered a further grievance. "An' that Sarah keeps trying to kiss me."

Cameron wiped the water off his face. "In a few years you might want her to."

The boy gave him a baleful look. "I'll wait."

Cameron scowled and cast around for another enticement, trying to think of something to counteract the obviously negative influence of Roger's daughters.

"I could stay here," Kip said offhandedly.

"No way. Not alone. You're far too young."

"Not alone. With Gracie."

Alice plunged into the pool once more. Cameron stared at Kip, hoping that it was his turn to joke. One look told him there wasn't a chance. He could almost see the wheels turning in the boy's head.

"She wouldn't mind," Kip said quickly. "I'm sure she wouldn't."

"No. You don't even know her."

"Sure I know her. She swam in the pool with me last night, *and* fixed us meat loaf, *and* we made popcorn, *and* she read me *Tom's Midnight Garden.* Anyway, I know I like her. And I *looooove* Alice." Kip flung his arms around the soaking wet dog as she floundered out of the pool and dropped the ball at his feet.

Cameron scowled at them both. "It's ridiculous. We couldn't impose on her."

"We could ask," Kip said logically. "You're always telling me you never know unless you ask."

"Not about this."

"The principle's the same," Kip argued. "You say that a lot, too."

Cameron thought once again that there were definitely times he should have kept his big mouth shut.

"Why would it be so terrible? Can't we just ask her? She needs a place to stay. It would solve everybody's problems."

Not mine, Cameron thought.

"I won't do anything awful. And I think she likes me," Kip added hesitantly. He looked up at his father. "Don't you think she likes me?"

The boy's expression made Cameron's heart turn over. It was the same worried, defenseless look he'd seen on Kip in the months right after Dana had left them. Was he that unlovable? Kip seemed to ask. Was that why she'd left?

"Of course she likes you," Cameron said gruffly.

Kip brightened. "Well, then... *I'll* ask her. She'd prob'ly take it better from me than you, anyway."

Surprisingly that nettled, though Cameron knew Kip was probably right. After his surly performance the first time they met and the way he'd acted around her yesterday, he would be the last person Gracie Talbot would be expecting to ask her for a favor.

Still, he didn't want to do it. He didn't want to give Gracie Talbot even a toehold in his life.

He might not have either, if he hadn't gone back into the house just then.

He heard a scuttling on the perch, a rattling of the cage.

"My life is one demd horrid grind," Boris quoted in stentorian tones, then he shrieked and kicked seed at Cameron.

That was when the awful realization hit.

He might be able to take Kip to Boston, but he certainly couldn't take Boris.

Never. No way. Not in a million years.

Chapter Five

Gracie saw Cameron standing on the porch the moment she turned her bicycle onto Frigate Alley. She glanced around hastily, half-expecting to see her bags scattered across the front lawn.

She was surprised not to.

He was standing in what Herschel would describe as a "gunslinger stance," his feet spread slightly apart, his chin up, his thumbs hooked into the belt loops of his jeans. Not the posture of a man with welcoming arms.

"We speak with our bodies," Herschel had said today at rehearsal.

Gracie kept pedaling and steeled herself to face a body telling her to get lost.

Cameron met her at the steps. "I've got a proposition for you."

It was so astonishingly unexpected that she put her feet down suddenly and the back tire ran right over her foot. "P—" she licked her lips "—prop—proposition?"

Gracie suddenly felt as if the ride from town had taken all the breath right out of her.

"Not that kind of proposition," he said scathingly enough to make her feel a fool for having even a second's worth of romantic fantasy. "I need a baby-sitter."

Gracie stared. "Baby-sitter?"

"I have to go up to Boston to do some work for a friend on his business. I intended to take Kip, but he doesn't much want to come." There was a pause, and Cameron eased his collar away from his neck. "He's not crazy about my friend's daughters."

Gracie couldn't help smiling.

Cameron scowled and went stolidly on. "He seems to think that if he's not too horrible, you might agree to stay with him here."

"I—"

"I wouldn't ask you myself, but—"

"No," Gracie said, irritated. "I don't suppose you would."

Cameron looked slightly uncomfortable, but plunged on. "I won't be gone long. But I may have to go back and forth now and then, and I can't leave Kip alone. So if you haven't found another place...I suppose we could work out a trade."

So saying he stared at her, jaw thrust out, fists clenched, as if he dared her to argue.

Gracie wasn't about to; she felt as if a roast duck had just flown over and fallen into her mouth. But she was afraid to trust this miracle just yet. "So why are you asking, then?"

There was a pause. "I called Tony." He grimaced. "He thinks you're the greatest thing since sliced bread. If Sarah Bernhardt had married Dr. Spock, the end result would have been you, he said."

Gracie blushed. "Tony exaggerates."

"We can but hope."

"I'd be happy to stay with Kip," she said hastily. She propped her bike against the front porch. "It would be a pleasure."

"Boris, too," Cameron reminded her darkly, obviously determined to put the bleakest complexion possible on the situation.

"Of course."

He looked at her suspiciously. "You don't mind Boris?"

"He's a sweet old bird."

Cameron gave a disbelieving snort.

"He just wants attention. He's lonely."

"And if you believe that, I've got a bridge in Brooklyn I'd like to sell you."

Gracie made a tsking sound. "You don't like Boris."

"Too right."

"Then don't even worry about him. Leave everything to me." She gave him a cheerful smile.

He scowled back.

Seeing that further conversation was going to get them nowhere, and unwilling to make things worse, Gracie brushed past him and went into the house. "Hi, Kip," she said to the boy using Alice as a pillow in the family room. "I hear we're going to be housemates after all."

Kip's face betrayed both shock and delight. His eyes skipped from Gracie to his father. "You asked her? And she didn't turn you down?"

"Thanks very much," Cameron said dryly.

But his discomfort caused Gracie some enjoyment. It was a pleasure to see a man with Cameron's command of his life find himself even momentarily at a loss. She thought she even detected a bit of a flush across his cheekbones as well.

She savored it for a moment, then assured Kip, "He asked me very nicely, and I was delighted. It isn't often Alice and I have the opportunity to spend time with such a handsome young man."

Now it was Kip's turn to blush. He made a face at her, then ducked his head and burrowed against Alice's dark fur. Gracie smiled and was gratified to notice that briefly Cameron smiled, too.

"Which bedroom would you like me to take?" she asked him.

He looked momentarily startled, then cleared his throat. "I, uh, I guess you might as well keep the one you have."

"But it's the only one with the bed, and since you're paying rent and I'm here on sufferance..."

"Keep the bed."

"Well, if you decide you want it—"

"I won't." Cameron's words were sharp and short. "The sleeping bag is fine with me. And I have the realtor's blessing to buy some furniture."

"Well, all right," Gracie agreed dubiously.

"Can I come with you tomorrow, then?" Kip asked Gracie.

"Sure."

"No," Cameron said at the same moment.

Both Kip and Gracie stared at him.

"No?" Gracie said.

"No."

"I do have to rehearse," she reminded him quietly after a moment. "It's what I'm doing here."

Cameron scowled. "I forgot. I didn't think. I don't want..." He hesitated, clearly in a quandary, though what the problem was, Gracie didn't know. "Forget it," he said abruptly. "I'll make other arrangements."

"Dad!" Kip protested.

Gracie put her arm across Kip's shoulders. "Mr. McClellan, for all its innuendo, *The Importance of Being Earnest* is not what I would call a risqué play. If it was, I wouldn't let Kip anywhere near it."

Cameron still glowered. "It's not that."

Gracie stared at him, bewildered. "Then what is it?"

Cameron sighed. He opened his mouth, then closed it again, then shook his head. He raked a hand through his hair, he paced the length of the room. He sighed again and muttered. Gracie watched him worriedly.

"He's prob'ly afraid I'll bother everybody," Kip said finally when his father seemed still at a loss for words. The boy's expression was resigned and glum. "Make a nuisance of myself."

Gracie looked at Cameron closely, unsure if that was the reason or not.

"I don't think you would," she said to Kip. "But I suppose I could try to find a local baby-sitter for the times I have to be gone."

Cameron traced the line of wood in the floor with his toe. "Oh, hell, never mind. I—It doesn't matter," he said finally. He sighed again. "Just do whatever's most convenient for you."

"I can go?" Kip asked.

His father fixed him with a stern frown. "If you take a book to read."

"I wanta watch," Kip replied.

"Take a book."

"You might want a book, Kip," Gracie said hastily, aware that Cameron was a hair's breadth from changing his mind again. "It can get pretty boring watching the same scene over and over again."

"Yes," Cameron said, "it can." He glanced at his watch and turned away abruptly. "Excuse me. I've got to see about getting to Boston."

HE DECIDED TO LEAVE as soon as possible. The quicker he got Roger's problems taken care of, the better. Better for Roger, better for his father.

Better for himself, a small inner voice mocked. He shoved it away, but even as he did so, he knew he didn't want to spend another night on the floor, wide awake and aware of Gracie Talbot across the hall in her Nile barge bed.

A niggling little voice in the back of his mind told him that he was a fool to leave the boy here. It meant exposing the boy to the theater, to rehearsal, to the same idiotic temptations that had enticed his mother. That worried the hell out of him, but he certainly wasn't going to tell Gracie about it. He never talked about it at all.

Besides that, it meant trusting Gracie Talbot. They didn't know her well enough for that.

But another voice reminded him again that Tony did, and that Tony had vouched for her explicitly.

"Leave Kip with her? Of course. She'd love it. She'd love Kip."

"Are you sure about her . . . I mean—"

"You couldn't find a better person. One of her roommates has nieces and nephews who are always underfoot. The roommate ignores them, but Gracie spends hours with them whenever they come over."

It wasn't her expertise with children that Cameron had found immediately noticeable. "She doesn't live with you, then?" He hated himself for having to ask.

Tony gave a short bark of laughter. "Don't I wish! Believe me, I've asked."

"She said no?"

"You'd better believe it. Pure as driven snow, that's our Gracie."

In spite of himself, Cameron felt a sense of relief.

"You interested?" Tony asked.

"No!" The explosive force of it was obvious.

"I see," Tony said.

Cameron hoped not. "I guess she can manage then," he went on.

"You won't regret it," Tony assured him, then something else occurred to him. "Hey, Mac, you never did say what you were doing there, anyway. I thought you put thumbs down on all Dad's olive branches. I sure didn't think you'd take him up on an offer to spend time out at the cottage."

"Yeah, well . . . you never know."

All Laurence's "olive branches" had ever consisted of were offers to allow Cameron back into the worshipful circle that venerated his father. And Tony was right, Cameron wanted nothing to do with those.

But he didn't really want to tell his brother that he was renting the place, either. Tony obviously had no idea that Laurence was renting out Gull Cottage at all, or he wouldn't have sent Gracie out to spend the month here.

So it was all a deep dark secret. Cameron doubted it would remain a mystery forever. But he was relieved for once to know that Laurence hadn't taken Tony into his confidence any more than he had Cameron.

Why should he, after all? They were only his family.

Cameron sighed. Why did he care so much? He had Kip. He didn't need anyone else.

He put it all out of his mind and arranged to charter a small private plane to take him to Logan. Then he packed a bag, changed his clothes, and went back downstairs.

Kip and Gracie were on the beach. Kip was tossing a stick out into the waves, and Alice was thundering after it, bringing it back, and shaking water all over him. Kip was clearly delighted.

Gracie sat on a beach towel a few yards away, reading a book and glancing up periodically to check on things or to reply with a grin to Kip's continuing commentary.

Cameron stood on the deck and watched them, feeling briefly rueful and envious. It was the sort of setting in which he had often imagined himself—man, wife, boy and dog. *Dream on,* he chided himself.

"Hey, Dad, c'mon down!" Kip shouted.

Cameron wavered, tempted. Then he glanced at his watch, dropped the duffel bag and kicked off his shoes. He could spare fifteen minutes, and it would be good for Kip if he went down. It had nothing whatever to do with wanting one last glimpse of Gracie Talbot.

He padded down the steps and across the sand.

She squinted up at him, smiling. "Are you leaving now?"

Her smiles had the damnedest effect on him. They seemed to make his mind blur and his heart rev. He cleared his throat and said gruffly, "Yeah. I left a phone number by the telephone. Also a list of instructions."

"You and Boris." The smile turned into a cheeky grin.

Cameron scowled at her.

"We'll be fine," Gracie assured him. "Won't we, Kip?"

Kip nodded, hopping from one foot to the other, obviously eager to get back to playing with Alice. "When'll you be back?"

"Don't know yet. I'll call you tonight."

"'Kay. See you." Kip bounced forward so that his father could drop a kiss on his forehead without getting covered with sand, then he gave a little wave and ran off, whistling for Alice.

Cameron watched them go and felt a twinge of envy, wishing for a moment he was staying.

Then he looked at Gracie Talbot, felt his heart beat faster and changed his mind. He began to back away.

"I'll, uh, see you."

"Okay." She opened her book again.

"Or I'll call you."

She didn't look up. "Fine."

"Don't hesitate to call me."

"I won't."

There was a long pause. What're you waiting for? Cameron asked himself. His teeth clenched. He swallowed and stuck his hands in his pockets.

His shadow still fell across her legs. Finally she shut her book and smiled, her eyes twinkling as she squinted up at him. "Want a kiss good-bye?"

He took off up the beach like a shot.

A MAN LIKE THAT could give a woman a complex.

Could give? Hah. If she didn't know better she'd think she had some sort of hex mark on her forehead, or obvious signs of infectious disease, or, at the very least, terminal bad breath.

She watched Cameron go with mixed emotions, almost sorry she'd plagued him with the offer of a kiss, but sorrier still that he hadn't let her give him one. She wondered what it would be like. Could she turn a crochety toad into the prince of her dreams if she did?

Did she want Cameron McClellan to be the prince of her dreams?

Good question.

ABSENCE MADE the heart grow fonder. It was insane, Cameron told himself, because he hardly knew the woman. Still, there it was; all the time he was in Boston he couldn't keep his mind off Gracie Talbot.

As a rule all he had to do was set foot in the offices of whatever company he was working with and all thought of the rest of the world fled. His single-mindedness was legendary.

His mind scattered like buckshot now.

Now when he found himself staring off into space he wasn't envisioning long-range projections for Ackley Bicycle Company. Rather he was daydreaming about the golden gleam of choppy blond hair. And when Roger droned on about what he was doing to salvage the business, Cameron found himself remembering the sound of slightly husky feminine laughter instead. Worst of all, when he concentrated on the rows of figures on Ackley Bicycle ledger sheets, the numbers all seemed to register as 34-25-34.

He was, Cameron decided, losing his mind.

"I can't concentrate," he complained to Roger the second afternoon as he stuffed his hands in his pockets and stared blindly out the window of Roger's Brookline home. He had spent twenty-four hours trying to, and he was beginning to think it was a lost cause.

"You're worried about Kip," Roger prophesied. "You should have brought him along."

"Yeah," Cameron said. Then he would have got Gracie Talbot out of his house and, with luck, out of his head.

And Boris, too? he asked himself. Would you have brought him? To banish Gracie Talbot it might have been well worth it.

"Why don't you give Kip a call? Set your mind at ease."

Cameron hesitated. He had called last night because he'd promised Kip he would, and it hadn't set his mind at ease at all.

Kip had barely found time to talk to him. Things were terrific, he'd said. He and Gracie were having a wonderful time. Stupendous. Simply super. And he'd met some neighboring boys, so he had to go now because they were playing Frisbee on the beach with Alice. Then, without giving Cameron a chance to say a word, he'd handed the phone to Gracie.

And that was the main reason his mind was like buckshot. Her soft sultry voice was still plaguing Cameron today.

"All's well," she had told him. "We swam, went into town for groceries on the bikes, had spaghetti for supper, and coming back he met some kids who live down the alley. They seem quite nice. Jeff and Danny Bates are their names. They're staying with their grandparents. Perhaps you know them?"

"Mmm." Cameron couldn't have said right then whether he did or not. He couldn't think at all; he was mesmerized by the sound of her voice.

It had only happened to him like this once before—with Dana. He gritted his teeth.

"Anyway, not to worry," Gracie went on. "Everything is fine." There was a pause during which he couldn't think of a thing to say. Then Gracie asked, "Is there anything else you want to know?"

"Er...no. Not really. I was just...checking."

"Okay, bye." And she was gone.

But her voice had haunted him all night and day. If he'd thought getting away from her was the answer, he was wrong. Things seemed to be getting worse rather than better.

"I think," he told Roger, "that I'll call Yvette."

Roger's eyebrows went up. A hint of a smile tugged at the corner of his mouth. "Like that, is it?"

Cameron shrugged irritably. Let Roger think what he would.

"You could do worse," Roger said.

Undoubtedly he could. And his thoughts about Gracie Talbot went a long way toward proving it.

Roger gathered up the projections they had been going over. "I'll just make myself scarce for a while then," he said, heading for the door. "Don't hurry. You're doing me a big enough favor as it is."

Cameron gave him an absent smile, already beginning to dial. Roger shouldn't be counting his chickens, he thought. Heaven only knew if his faith would be justified. At the moment he wondered if he had enough good sense left to keep Ackley Bicycles together until they hatched.

Maybe—he hoped—Yvette could restore it for him. Maybe he was just particularly susceptible at the moment. Maybe he would react the same way when he heard Yvette's voice on the phone.

He leaned back in the chair and rested his stocking-clad feet on the desk of Roger's study, drumming his fingers on the arm of the swivel chair while he listened to the phone ring.

"De Jourlet Interiors," a briskly efficient voice said.

"I'd like to speak to Ms. de Jourlet, please."

"I'm sorry, sir. Ms. de Jourlet is busy with a client right now."

"Tell her Cameron McClellan called, then, and—"

"One moment, Mr. McClellan." The line went dead.

Seconds later it was picked up again and an enthusiastic voice said, "Cameron, *mon chéri*, how are you?"

He felt nothing.

"Cameron?"

"What?"

"I said, how are you, *chéri*?"

Worried, he wanted to say. Frantic. Desperate. And getting more so by the minute. He said, "Missing you," and found that he wished it were true.

But Yvette's voice sent no shivers down his spine, gave no jolts to his heart. It was the same as it always was.

Yvette apparently didn't think so. "Ahh, yes." She let out a slight sigh. "Just as I am missing you, *chéri*. I am so glad you called. I did not think you would. You said—"

Cameron knew what he'd said. He'd said this time was for him and Kip. No work, no women. And he'd meant it.

He'd had to compromise the work restriction for Roger. But he could handle that.

It was the woman restriction that he was worried about. Thanks to Gracie Talbot, he needed help, but it wasn't the sort of thing you could just come right out and say.

"Well, you know how it is," he said, purposely vague.

"I hope I do." Yvette laughed lightly. "So when are you coming home?"

"Don't know yet."

"Sooner than you'd planned?"

"Perhaps."

She gave a small satisfied sound. "You *are* missing me."

Cameron eased his shirt collar away from his neck, knowing she was getting the wrong impression. "We're . . . good friends, Yvette," he hedged.

"I should hope, *chéri*," she said seductively.

He ignored the innuendo, going on doggedly, "And I just had some free time so I thought I'd give you a call, see how things were going." He tried to sound matter-of-fact, brisk.

"Things are going very well. Better and better—now," she added.

He didn't need an advanced degree in mind reading to understand what she meant. Calling Yvette had been a very stupid idea.

He swung his feet down off the desk and stood up, clearing his throat. "Well, good," he said heartily. "I'm glad to hear it. Good to talk to you. I'd better get going now, though."

"Can't keep Kip waiting," agreed Yvette.

"Er, right."

"Don't keep me waiting too long, either, *chéri*."

"No." Cameron swallowed hard.

"I am so glad you called, Cameron darling," she told him. "It sets my mind at ease."

"I don't know, Yvette. I—"

"I know you said you were going to concentrate purely on Kip this month," she went on. "But I thought— Well, you know what I thought. East Hampton must have its fair share of beautiful women, and you are a handsome man. An eligible man. Still—" she finished optimistically "—if you're already calling me up, well, things are not as bad as I feared."

"Uh, no, of course not," Cameron said faintly.

But as he set the receiver gently back into its cradle, he disagreed. He thought things were a damned sight worse.

GRACIE HAD NEVER HAD a ten-year-old boy of her own. Not for days at a time at any rate. She found she liked it very much.

"It's because you're ten, too, at heart," Tony told her when he called the second afternoon to see how she was doing.

"There is that possibility," Gracie agreed, the receiver tucked between her chin and her shoulder as she slapped peanut butter onto slices of bread for the snack she and Kip were going to take to the beach.

"Seriously, kiddo, do you know what you're doing?"

Gracie had never heard Tony sound quite that serious before. It surprised her. "What's to know?" she asked. "I'm only baby-sitting."

"Yeah, but...Mac?"

"I'm not babysitting Mac."

Tony laughed. "No, I know that. But his kid. I mean, you could've knocked me over with a feather when I heard he was out there. Not the sort of move he'd make."

"No?" Gracie was cautiously curious. She didn't want Tony to know how interested she really was. Since Cameron had been gone, her interest hadn't abated. In fact it had grown more intense. Even though he was businesslike and even abrupt with her, she sensed a struggle in him. And everything she'd learned about Kip and the things he said about his father suggested that Cameron McClellan was a man worth knowing. Gracie's hormones seconded that.

"He and the old man don't get along," Tony was saying. "Surprised the hell out of me when he called and asked me about you."

"Yes, well, he surprised me, too," Gracie admitted. "I didn't expect anyone here."

"I'll bet." Tony laughed. "Still, you're my guest. What can he say?"

A lot, Gracie thought. *Especially since he's paying rent and I'm not.* But since Cameron apparently hadn't told him, she wouldn't, either.

"He can be a demanding son-of-a-gun," Tony went on. "Stubborn, hard-nosed. Thinks he's the Almighty sometimes. Don't let him push you around."

"No."

"Maybe I'll just catch the train out to see you some weekend," Tony went on. "If I don't get a part."

"You'll get a part," Gracie assured him. She didn't want to say, don't come, but it was what she meant.

"Maybe. D'you like yours?"

"Yes. It's fun."

"Glad I talked you into it?"

"Yes."

"See," he said triumphantly. "There. Told you so. You only needed a meaty part and you'll take off like a rocket. I've got faith in you, Gracie. You'll knock 'em dead and somebody'll notice. My dad, even. And you'll get your big break. Casting directors will beat a path to your door. You'll have the rest of your life laid out for you. It's happened before. Right there in East Hampton."

"Oh, Tony." Gracie found his optimism endearing but unbelievable.

"Hey," he sounded offended, "you don't believe me, you just ask Cameron." He paused. "On second thought, don't."

"No fear." She certainly wasn't asking Cameron. It didn't take a genius to figure out that there was something about theater that Cameron didn't like. Most likely, if he didn't get along with his father, that was it.

"Come to think of it," Tony said suddenly, "maybe that's why he hasn't been back."

"What?"

"Cameron..." Tony said vaguely. "He hasn't been out to the cottage in years. Not since the summer Kip was a baby. I've been thinking it was because of Dad, but—" there was a pause "—I can see where he might have other reasons." His voice drifted off as if he'd just had a revelation that needed further consideration.

Gracie waited, hoping he'd say more. But for once the normally garrulous Tony did not.

"Anyway, I'm glad you're hitting it off," he said briskly. "In fact, all things considered, I'm surprised you *are* hitting it off. He doesn't have much time for actresses."

So that was it. "Actresses?" Gracie probed gently.

But Tony said, "Sorry, gotta run. Take good care of my nephew."

"I will."

"And my brother." Tony paused. "I'd say be good to him, but I don't think there's a chance in hell he'd let you do that."

ENDURE, Cameron counseled himself. It was only a month. Less now. August 6 and counting. You can do it.

He knew he sounded like an aerobics tape gone haywire. But there was nothing else for it. He was flying home to Gracie Talbot in less than two hours and he was simply going to have to cope.

There was a storm warning posted for eastern Suffolk county from midday on, and he'd tried to get his work wrapped up at Roger's in time to beat them. No such luck.

He mislaid a folder, then he got caught in a traffic jam, then there was a bottleneck returning the rental car. It was close to two before he made it to the charter terminal, and almost three before the pilot got clearance to take off.

Heavy pewter clouds hung on the horizon to the south, threatening but as yet doing nothing. Not in Boston at least.

"Raining all across Suffolk County," the pilot said.

"Much?"

"We'll have to see." And they headed down the runway into the wind and swooped up and out, banking over Boston Harbor and heading into the clouds.

It wasn't long until Cameron got his answer. Less than fifteen minutes out of Boston the rain sluiced down the window and lowered the horizon so that sky and ocean blended into a uniform gunmetal gray. The water continued to bucket down throughout the rest of the flight, and Cameron forgot everything but sending up prayers to keep them in the air.

He sent up one of thanksgiving for the pilot's competence when the plane set down at last at the local airport.

Cameron tried to call home but the phones weren't working. He could have waited it out, but they were expecting him and, having come this far and already soaked to the skin, he ran to his car and set off into the storm.

No lights lit the windows of Gull Cottage when he turned into the bottom of Frigate Alley. No welcoming committee stood in the door.

The rain thundered down, drumming on the car roof, fogging the windows, making Cameron squint as he headed up the drive. The wind picked up, rattling the leaves of the trees and buffeting the car.

He pulled up just outside the door to the solarium, shut off the lights and the engine, grabbed his bag and drew a deep breath.

Courage, he told himself. Fortitude. Endurance.

But it wasn't the storm he was worried about braving. It was Gracie Talbot.

He made a run for it, shoving the French doors open and letting the wind slam it shut behind him.

"Awk! Look what the cat dragged in."

Cameron jerked to a halt. Dropping his bag, he glowered at Boris. Out of the dimness Boris glowered right back at him.

"Where is everybody?" Cameron muttered.

Boris gave a little hop. "Where have all the flowers gone?" he said, cocking his head.

Cameron gave him a dirty look, kicked off his shoes and squelched across the bare floor in his socks. "Kip?"

There was no answer. He hit the light switch and got nothing.

"Kip?" he called again.

The only sign of habitation was the fire in the fireplace in the family room.

"Kip? Gracie?" he added after a moment. "Anybody home?"

"Up here!" came a muffled voice. Not Kip's.

Cameron's heart did an odd little flip-flop in his chest. His very own Pavlovian response to Gracie Talbot's voice. He grimaced and his jaw clenched.

Shape up, he told himself. *You're not a sex-starved adolescent. You have control.*

He did, too, as long as he climbed the stairs. He was a tower of indifference, of disinterest. And then he walked into Kip's bedroom.

Gracie was bent over, setting out a variety of pots and dishes under a multitude of persistent leaks. Her hair was wet, her T-shirt damp and clinging. She lifted her head at the sound of his footsteps and gave him the most incredible grin. "Welcome home."

All Cameron's pep talks went right down the drain. The sight and sound of Gracie rooted him to the spot.

"Hey, Dad, you're just in time!" Kip splashed through the puddles and flung his arms around Cameron.

Cameron swallowed hard. For a moment he didn't even register his son or his surroundings or the significance of the pots and the pans. He had eyes only for her.

Then Gracie straightened up and brush a lock of damp hair away from her face. "The roof leaks," she said matter-of-factly.

"Yes," Cameron managed.

"These ceilings are a wreck."

"Yes." So was he. He cleared his throat and wiped his hands on damp slacks and tried to scrape his mind into some semblance of good sense.

The roof, he told himself. Concentrate on the roof. "How many . . . other rooms are getting it?"

"Everything that isn't covered by the attic." Gracie bent down to catch another stream with a coffee pot. "And we're almost out of containers." She straightened up again. Beneath the wet T-shirt he could see the lace of her bra.

He looked away, rubbed his hand against the back of his neck, tugged at his shirt collar. Containers, he told himself. Peanut butter jars. Paint cans. He had to consciously remind himself what they were. "Er, there must be some in the garage," he said at last.

"Good idea." Gracie handed the pressure cooker and dented pie pan to Kip. "I'll go look."

"No, I will," Cameron said hastily. "I'm already wet."

Gracie looked him up and down, which made his body temperature go up so much he was surprised the dampness didn't turn to steam. She seemed suddenly to be breathing hard, too.

"No, I will," she said abruptly, and, brushing past him, she was out of the room and down the stairs before he could object.

SPACE. She needed the space.

All day long Gracie had been preparing herself for Cameron's return. Ever since Kip had announced that his father would be coming home today, she'd been psyching herself up, telling herself that her earlier reactions were nothing more than aberrations. He was just another man, she'd told herself. No different than Herschel. Or Tony.

He was only Tony's brother. Kip's father. No big deal.

He didn't even like her.

But the moment she saw him again everything she told herself went for naught. Her heart started beating faster, her mouth got dry, her palms damp. She felt tongue-tied and awkward and wholly unprepared. She tried to sound chipper and matter-of-fact.

For the first time in her life she questioned her ability to act.

The garage was a good twenty yards from the house, and the rain was still coming down in sheets. Good, Gracie thought as she plunged out into it. She could use some cooling off.

Dodging past Cameron's car, she took off running. She was soaked to the skin before she'd gone five yards, and her jeans and shirt were plastered to her body by the time she'd wrenched open the door to the garage. Breathing hard, she sagged against the door and let her eyes become accustomed to the dimness.

She'd only been in the garage a handful of times since she'd arrived. Only to get the bicycle Tony had assured her was there, to ride it to rehearsal and, afterward, to put it back.

But a quick glimpse had told her that, though the house might have been stripped of its contents, nobody had touched the garage.

Nothing in it was worth the effort. Old saw horses and rickety ladders were the order of the day. There were a few old tools hanging on the wall. Hammers, saws, screwdrivers, that sort of thing. Gracie surveyed them all without finding a thing that would suit her purpose.

She poked her way toward the back and found the ladder that led to the second-story loft. She craned her neck and wished she had a flashlight. All she could make out were what looked like shadowy shelves and stacks of paint cans.

The shelves wouldn't help. But if the paint cans were almost empty, they might. She could take a couple back at least.

Then she wouldn't have to go back empty-handed. That would be the worst thing she could do. If she did, it would be obvious she had only come out here to flee Cameron. And with her luck, he would come out here looking afterward and find a cache that she had missed. She might be a fool, but she didn't want to look like one.

Relieved and determined, Gracie began to climb.

The wood was rough and dry under her fingers. It was a good thing she had worn old clothes, she thought as it scraped her jeans. And a good thing she'd had the eyesight to spot the cans. And a good thing she wouldn't have to go back empty-handed.

She was three rungs from the top when all the good things she thought about couldn't save her. There was a splintering sound. Her feet scrabbled, her fingernails clutched thin air, and the rungs began to crack.

Chapter Six

Cameron thought it might make more sense to forget looking for containers and simply start building an ark. The telephone man certainly hadn't been wrong about the roof. What could his father have been thinking of, letting the place go like this?

It was probably a blessing that the furniture was gone, otherwise it would have been destroyed, too.

He surveyed the damage and did some arithmetic in his head, then thought he wouldn't like to be his father. The cost would be outrageous unless you could do it yourself. He laughed at the thought of Laurence McClellan reroofing the house.

He stripped off his wet clothes and changed into a pair of dry jeans and a sweatshirt while Gracie was in the garage. He also congratulated himself on getting through his first encounter with her.

It was undoubtedly the most difficult. First encounters always were. But he had survived it, and now it would just be a matter of maintaining outward indifference.

So, where in heaven's name was she so he could be indifferent to her?

He glanced at his watch. How long did it take to rustle up half a dozen containers?

He went to the window of Kip's bedroom and scowled out at the garage. The door was closed. There were, of course, no lights. Rain thundered down outside and spattered down from the ceiling, wetting his socks.

What was taking her so long? Couldn't she find anything? Cameron jammed his hands into his pockets and stared at the garage. He'd be willing to bet there were hundreds of containers of one sort or another. His grandfather had squirreled away almost everything. Unless of course they, too, had been stolen away.

Finally when he could stand it no longer, he stuffed his feet into his loafers and clattered down the stairs.

Kip was in the solarium talking to Boris.

"Did Gracie come back in?" Cameron asked him.

Kip shook his head. A bolt of lighting lit the room, then thunder shook it. "Haven't seen her. Want me to go look?"

"No."

"You gonna go?"

"No."

"But—"

"She's probably waiting for the rain to slow down."

"It isn't raining any harder now that it was when she left," Kip said.

Cameron shrugged.

Lightning flickered again, followed by a powerful clap of thunder.

"Sturm and drang!" cawed Boris. "Damn the torpedoes. Full speed ahead!"

Cameron glowered at him. "Stow it," he snarled at the bird. "Or I'll use your cage as a bucket, you old fleabag." Then he stomped back upstairs again.

His sleeping bag was soaked. All the available pans had still only taken care of half of the leaks. *For heaven's sake, Gracie, come on!* Grimacing, Cameron picked up the sleeping bag, dragged it into the bathroom, and tossed it in the tub. He should have stayed in Boston, he thought. At least he'd have had a dry place to sleep.

But he wouldn't have wanted to strand Kip in this. Or Gracie.

Gracie.

Damn the woman. Where *was* she?

Maybe she was lying in wait for him out there in the garage? Could she be sitting there in the dark hoping he'd come looking for her so they'd have a few moments alone?

Didn't he wish!

Cameron scowled. The water was running in rivulets across his bedroom floor. Suppose she couldn't find any buckets.... Suppose she had more than she could carry.... Suppose she really was waiting out there for him....

He headed back down the stairs. "I'm going out to the garage."

"I'll come," Kip volunteered.

"No."

"But—"

"You stay put." Rain pelted him as he raced for the garage and hauled open the door.

"Gracie?" He peered into the darkness of the garage, trying to see her.

"Over here." A shaky voice came from the gloom. "I'm toward the back."

He spotted her now, lying on the floor. "Gracie! What the—"

She lifted herself on her elbows and gave him a weak grin. "I found some great cans. But they were just a bit out of reach."

Cameron hunkered down beside her. "What in heaven's name did you do?"

"I tried to climb the ladder. It broke."

He could see that now. Could see the splintered wood, the shattered rungs. His eyes lifted toward the loft and his heart lurched, grateful she hadn't got higher. "You could have been killed!"

"I wasn't," she said tartly.

"You should have let me do it," he said angrily.

"You're heavier than I am," Gracie pointed out.

"I wouldn't have done anything so stupid."

Gracie glared at him. "Thank you very much."

He crouched down beside her, trembling, wanting to run his hands over, to touch her, to reassure herself that she was all right. He didn't dare. He didn't even dare offer her his hand. Because if he did, he didn't think he would want to stop there. "Can you get up?"

"No."

"*No?* Why not?" Oh, cripes, was he going to have to lift her?

"Because I twisted my leg and jammed my wrist," Gracie said patiently, as if he were slightly dim. "I don't think either of them are broken, but I can't get the leverage to get myself up. And I don't know if I can put any weight on my leg when I do."

He *was* going to have to lift her. Cameron swallowed. He licked his lips. He sucked in a deep breath. He wiped damp palms on even damper thighs. "I'll...carry you."

Gracie looked no more pleased than he felt, which was oddly annoying. He didn't want to have to touch her, but he didn't like the idea that she didn't want him to, either.

She didn't say anything, just looked at him. Cameron looked back. The rain pounded down, thrumming loudly on the garage roof, which perversely didn't leak at all.

"Right," Cameron said.

"Okay," Cameron said.

"Of course," Cameron said. "No problem at all."

But all the words in the world didn't give him the detachment he sought. He moved alongside her, then moved back. He edged forward, then back. He lifted his arms, dropped them, considered, cleared his throat, sighed, moved closer, knelt, bit down on his lower lip, drew a deep breath—paused—then slid his arms under her.

Lightning sizzled. Thunder cracked.

"Electrical storm," Gracie muttered, her breath touching his cheek.

"And how," Cameron muttered back.

He held her snugly against him, trying to keep a grip, trying not to hurt her leg, and trying to remain indifferent at the same time. Two out of three wasn't bad.

He shouldered his way out the door and moved quickly up the drive. By the time he got back to the house he was breathing hard, and it had nothing to do with exertion at all.

Kip flung open the door. "What happened?"

"I fell," Gracie said. "I'm all right."

"You're not," Cameron argued. "You can't even walk."

"Of course I can now," Gracie said. She struggled against his grip. "I just didn't, coming across there, because in the rain it would take too long."

Cameron looked down at her. "Are you sure?"

"Of course."

"Okay." Eagerly he set her down.

She crumpled at his feet.

"Cripes!" Unceremoniously he hauled her up again and glared at her. "Not smart."

"Damn," Gracie mumbled, looking oddly close to tears. "Oh, damn."

"Come on," Cameron said irritably. "We'll take you to the hospital."

"I don't need—"

"You're not in any position to say what you need, are you?" he demanded.

Gracie gulped.

"Don't look back, something may be gaining on you," Boris counseled from his perch. He gave a little hop and preened when they turned to look at him. "Sock it to me, baby."

Gracie grinned. "No," she said. "I guess at the moment I'm not."

Neither was Cameron, but he wasn't saying so. He just turned around, carried her back outside and slid her into the car. Then he motioned Kip into the back and headed for the hospital.

"We don't have to go now," Gracie protested. "I'm not going to get any worse. What about the paint cans, the leaks, the bedrooms?"

"Don't worry. I'll take care of them." Cameron started the engine. "You're first."

"But—"

But he wasn't up to any more tonight. He turned and gave her as genial a smile as he could muster. "Shut up, Grace."

THE DOCTOR SAID she had strained the tendons in her knee and had compressed something noncompressible in her wrist. At least that was what Gracie's layman's brain got out of the long-winded medical explanation she'd been given for the ice packs, knee immobilizer, crutches and painkillers she was given.

"Take her home," the doctor told Cameron. "Take her to bed and baby her a bit."

Gracie looked at Cameron and saw a flush high along his cheekbones. He looked at her and she knew he saw the same on hers.

"Right," Cameron said hoarsely. He jammed his hands into his pockets.

Then, with Kip trailing after them, they left.

The rain had slowed considerably. The lightning and thunder had receded to only a far-off flicker and rumble out at sea. Just as well, Gracie thought, because she was making very slow progress. Cameron wasn't carrying her now. He wasn't even touching her. You could have stretched a barge pole between them.

The moment the doctor had given her the crutches it had been "hands off." She could only use one, her jammed wrist preventing her from putting any weight on the other. But since he so obviously wanted nothing to do with her, at least she could keep upright and manage on her own.

And thank heavens for that. She'd had quite enough of him, too. For other reasons, though. Even her throbbing knee and painful wrist couldn't quite obliterate her awareness of him. And the remark from the doctor made it even worse.

So did Cameron's reaction to it.

Gracie found it disconcerting to be that aware of a man who not only seemed to abhor her touch, but shrank from it at every turn as well.

She hobbled over to the car and, with Kip's help, slid in. Cameron went around and got in beside her. He rested his hands on the steering wheel for a moment, as if he were drawing strength from it.

If the truth were known, he was. At least he was trying to. *Take her to bed.* The doctor's words rang in his ears. *Take her to bed. Take her to bed.*

Wouldn't he love to! Just once, he reckoned, and this ridiculous hunger would go away. It was a thought, anyway.

But he didn't see how he was going to manage it. Not tonight. Tonight he was going to have to stay as far away from her as possible.

Thank heavens for the crutches. At least he didn't have to touch her.

He turned the key in the ignition, and they headed home.

The lights were back on by the time they arrived. The rain had all but stopped.

"I'm going to get the containers anyway," Cameron said briskly. "You never know when it might start up again. Can you manage all right?"

Gracie just looked at him. "I'm fine," she said and gamely hobbled toward the door. "Kip can help me if I need it."

Cameron hesitated a moment, then nodded. "Of course."

Gracie made it as far as the solarium and gave up, sinking down onto the bare wooden floor.

"Oh, my aching back," said Boris, hopping nimbly along his perch.

Gracie gave him a baleful look.

"I'll get my sleeping bag for you to sit on," Kip volunteered.

Gracie smiled at him. "That would be nice."

He had her ensconced in the sleeping bag and was bringing her a cup of instant cocoa when Cameron got back, both arms filled with paint cans, a dirt smudge on his face and sawdust in his damp hair.

"You didn't fall, too?" Gracie asked him, regarding him over the rim of the cup.

Cameron shook his head. "But I had a hard time finding a ladder that would hold me. Made a couple of false starts." He gave an awkward, almost sheepish shrug.

"Want some cocoa, Dad?" Kip offered.

"In a few minutes. I'm going to take these upstairs and change my clothes."

As it happened, he couldn't. All the rest of his clothes, left in his duffel bag on the floor, were soaked. Grimly he set out the cans, glared at the freshly painted ceilings, understanding now why they had been, and went back downstairs.

Gracie was still in Kip's sleeping bag, propped against the wall where he had left her. She was still damp and disheveled from her escapade. She was also still as desirable as ever.

Cameron looked at her narrowly. Her teeth were chattering, but she didn't say a word.

"You're cold," he accused.

"A little."

"There's a fire in the living room, remember? Why don't you go in there?"

Gracie looked at the doorway, then at the crutches, then at her leg. "I think I'll just stay here," she said. "I'm all right."

She wasn't, and Cameron knew it.

"For heaven's sake," he muttered, and before he could think better of it, he stalked across the room, scooped her up, sleeping bag and all, in his arms and strode into the family room with her. Depositing her by the hearth, he jerked open the screen, added another log, stirred the embers, shut the screen again, and lifted her onto the hearth.

Then he stepped back and stuck his hands in his pockets again.

"Better?"

Gracie smiled at him. "Yes, thank you. Much." Except for the fact that he acted as though she had a contagious disease. She wriggled her toes. The fire popped and snapped. Alice meandered over and laid her head on Gracie's lap. At least someone was willing to get close to her.

"You didn't change your clothes," she said.

"Nothing dry." He grimaced, then realized she hadn't, either. He said so.

"I will," Gracie said, "when I go upstairs."

Both of their minds seemed to home right in on what they would entail. Fires seemed to crackle and snap within as well as without.

Cameron cleared his throat. "I think I'll just go see about that cocoa Kip promised me."

But just then Kip appeared. His escape foiled, Cameron took the cocoa and reluctantly came back to sit down on the floor in front of the fire. Gracie, of course, was directly in his line of vision. Just what he needed. But he could hardly face the other way.

He found he didn't want to. She looked like an orphan of the wars. Her hair was mussed, her face dirty. Her clothes were undoubtedly clammy from the rain. But he found his eyes tracing the line of her uptilted nose, her firm chin, her delicate jaw and marveling at her beauty. He also marveled that she didn't complain. Instead she sat carefully balanced, her bad leg cushioned by Kip's jacket, her weight resting on her rear end and her one good arm, while she and Kip proceeded to tell him about how the storm began and when they first noticed the leaky roof.

Outside the wind picked up and the rain began again. Kip went to the window to peer out, saying, "I was listenin' to the radio in the kitchen. It's so bad out there the announcer said pretty soon they'd have to name the storm."

"Well, we're all home and dry," Gracie said, smiling at him.

"At least home," Cameron corrected wryly, grinning.

His eyes caught Gracie's and held. And Gracie's breath caught, too, because this look was for her. And in it she found for the first time a hint of warmth, of laughter, of tenderness.

Oh, dear Lord, she thought desperately, because somehow that made everything else worse.

She finished her cocoa, declined a second cup, then yawned, stretched and carefully lowered her immobilized leg.

Cameron frowned. "What're you doing?"

"Going up to bed." She eased herself around and began to raise herself gingerly using her left arm for support.

He got to his feet quickly, then stood there, hesitant, unsure whether to help or not. But when he spotted the grimace of pain that flickered briefly across Gracie's face, he hesitated no longer.

"I'll carry you."

"It's all right." She let the sleeping bag fall around her feet, then attempted to step out of it, almost stumbling in the process.

Cameron sucked in his breath. Three strides took him across the floor. "Don't be an idiot, Talbot," he growled, and with as much gentleness as he could muster, he swung her up into his arms.

It was the third time he'd carried her tonight, and it didn't get any easier. He met her eyes, wide and wondering, for a split second, then lifted his own and looked straight ahead, mounting the stairway as quickly as he could.

He set her on the side of the asp bed and stepped back, folding his arms across his chest, nodding his head as if congratulating himself on a job well done.

"All set?" he said with hearty encouragement.

Gracie smiled, trying to figure him out. Sometimes she thought he was interested in her, found her attractive; seconds later she thought he could hardly wait to escape her clutches. What was it about this man? "Yes," she said carefully. "Thanks."

He turned and walked quickly out the door. "Call if you need anything," he tossed over his shoulder.

She needed help with the buttons on her shirt, but at last she managed them. She had the devil's own time fumbling her bra off, but she coped with that, too. She even got the oversized T-shirt she slept in out of her duffel bag without disaster.

In fact she would have managed fine if the floor hadn't been damp from Cameron's shoes. But it was, and the one-legged hop she needed to get back to where she could lean against the bed, did her in when she hit the slippery wood. The next thing she knew, her foot slid, she gave a little cry of dismay and went down on her bottom.

"Ow! Damn!"

Footsteps thundered up the stairs. First Cameron, then Kip.

Gracie groped to pull the T-shirt in front of her naked breasts, her face flaming, her wrist and leg throbbing with pain. She wasn't quick enough. They both got a very good view.

"Cripes," Cameron muttered. Then, "Go feed the bird, Kip."

"But—"

"Go feed the bird."

Kip looked at his father in amazement, then shrugged and vanished out the door.

Cameron and Gracie stared at each other. He hesitated, then sucked in his breath and came over to hunker down next to her. "Did you break anything this time?"

Gracie shook her head. "I don't think so."

"I'm surprised," he said dryly. "I said I'd help you."

"I didn't think you wanted..." she began.

But they both knew what she'd thought, and moreover that she'd been right.

"You should have called," was all he said. He took the T-shirt out of her hands, his eyes deliberately avoiding her bare breasts. "Raise your arms." His voice was gruff.

She did and felt Cameron slip the T-shirt over her head, settling the cool cotton against her damp, flushed skin.

"What else?"

"What?"

"What else do you need?"

Gracie snagged some clean underwear from the pile. "Just this," she mumbled.

"All right." He lifted her up once more and carried her back to the bed. Then, without giving her a chance to protest, he undid the snap of her jeans, unzipped them and peeled the jeans down her legs. Then he tossed her a quilt to cover herself.

"Can you handle it from here?" he asked. There was a strained note in his voice.

Gracie flushed. "Oh, yes."

"Good," he muttered and promptly fled.

Trembling, Gracie slid off her damp underclothes and put on the clean dry ones beneath the cover of the quilt. Then she lay back against the pillows and stared at the ceiling, her heart thundering, her leg and arm aching.

What a day. First the storm and then Cameron. Then her fall and Cameron. Then her wet clothes . . . and Cameron.

Cameron.

Stiff, unyielding, warm, caring. Tender in spite of himself. A regular armadillo, though, with his shell held tight around him. She smiled, remembering a bit of trivia picked up from one of her student's papers; armadillos had soft bellies.

Did Cameron?

She snuggled down into the bed, warm and dry and in bed and willing to contemplate that. It would while away the hours for her. Let the storm rage, she thought. Nothing else could befall her here.

THEY'D REPOSSESSED the whiskey, too. Or drunk it all. Which was a damned sight more likely, Cameron thought savagely as he paced the entire length of the downstairs, prowling through the cupboards, searching out every nook and cranny he could think of where his father's stash of whiskey might have gone unnoted and untouched.

No such luck.

And he shouldn't be surprised, either. If the damned place turned into a sieve every time it rained, there was no wonder nothing was left.

But Lord knew he needed something. He was at the end of his rope. If he'd thought the visions of Gracie Talbot that had danced in his head throughout three days and nights in Boston were hard to deal with, they were nothing compared to the reality of her in his arms.

How much was a man expected to stand?

"What's wrong, Dad?"

He whirled to see Kip standing in the doorway.

Cameron wiped a hand over his face. "Nothing."

"I...fed Boris."

"Yeah, uh...thanks."

"I've seen a lady's boobs before, Dad."

"Kip!" Cameron's voice was strangled. He glowered at his son.

Kip gave a small shrug. "Well, that's why you sent me out, wasn't it?"

Cameron sighed. "Sort of. I—" But what could he say? That was why he'd sent Kip out. That and because he hadn't been able to predict his own reaction under the circumstances.

Kip walked over to the fire and sat down in front of it, pulled up his knees and wrapped his arms around them, then looked up at his father. "Gracie has very nice boobs, doesn't she?"

Cameron choked. "I don't think—"

"I suppose other women's might be bigger. *Some* other women's," Kip qualified, as if he'd given the matter serious consideration. "But size isn't the most important thing, is it?"

"N-no. Of course not." Cameron sagged against the wall, feeling more in need of the whiskey than ever.

"Did my mother have big breasts?"

"Kip!"

"I just wondered." Kip looked at him levelly. "I don't remember."

Cameron shut his eyes and counted to ten. Then twenty. When he opened them Kip's gaze was still fixed on his face, obviously awaiting an answer. The fire sizzled and popped. The wind gusted and rain lashed once more against the windows.

"They were ... bigger than Gracie's," Cameron said at last.

"Ah-ha." Kip nodded. There was a considerable silence during which Cameron found himself feeling like the man with the noose around his neck awaiting the hangman's jerk.

"I thought so," Kip said at last. "I fed Alice again, too. After I fed Boris," he added after a moment. Another pause. "She didn't need it, either."

He lifted his eyes and met Cameron's gaze. A long look passed between them. A father-son chat in complete silence.

"Thank you," Cameron said gravely.

Kip gave him a small, almost gentle smile. "Don't mention it."

WHAT ELSE could possibly happen?

Cameron couldn't imagine. Even in the worst of all possible worlds, everything he could think of already had.

At least until he and Kip went upstairs to go to bed.

"What about my sleeping bag?" Kip asked him, hauling it into the bathroom where Cameron stood brushing his teeth.

"What about it?"

Kip held it up. "I let Gracie use it, and she was wearin' wet clothes."

"Use mine," Cameron said and then remembered that his was in the bathtub because it was even wetter.

He and Kip stared at each other, father stymied, son considering. Then Kip brightened.

"No problem."

"What do you mean?"

But Kip was already on his way out of the room. "I'll sleep with Gracie."

"Kip! You can't! There isn't room."

Kip paused in the doorway to her bedroom. "Sure there is. It's a big bed. Huge, in fact. Can't I, Gracie?"

Gracie, who'd just drifted off to sleep, came around in time to hear only the last part of the question. "Huh?"

"My sleeping bag's wet an' I need a place to sleep. Can I sleep with you?"

Gracie blinked. "Uh, sure."

Kip shot his father a triumphant look. "See, what'd I tell you?"

Cameron didn't reply. He was lucky he didn't swallow his toothpaste. Kip was going to sleep with Gracie Talbot? He closed his eyes. Dear Lord.

Kip scampered off to his bedroom, ferreted a pair of dry sweats out of his duffel bag which, fortunately, hadn't got soaked, then galloped back to Gracie's room, Alice at his heels.

Gracie had moved over to one edge and Kip climbed in. So did Alice, stretching herself along the foot of the bed.

"See? Lotsa room." Kip grinned at Cameron who had come to stand in the door, his thumbs hooked in his belt loops. He patted the space still available in the bed. "We got lotsa room, huh, Gracie?"

"Lots," Gracie parroted dutifully. Cameron felt her eyes on him.

"Where you gonna sleep, Dad?"

Cameron's thumb twisted in the belt loop.

"His sleepin' bag's soaked," Kip confided to Gracie.

"Is it?"

"Oh, yeah. Sopping."

"I'll manage," Cameron said tightly.

"He could fit, too, couldn't he?" Kip asked.

"I don't need to fit, Kip," Cameron said harshly.

"You could, you know," Gracie said, lifting herself on her one good arm.

He stiffened. "It isn't necessary."

"But, Dad—"

"Going to sleep on the soft brick hearth, maybe?" Gracie suggested. "Or next to Boris perhaps?" She gave him a teasing smile.

Cameron ground his teeth.

"You oughta at least stay in this room," Kip said reasonably. "In case Gracie has to get up. She might need you."

Cameron hadn't thought of that. His eyes met hers for a moment, wary and worried. Then he looked away.

"All right. I'll get an air mattress," he said gruffly and stalked out.

He dragged Kip's back, tossed it on the floor, snapped out the light and flung himself down on it.

"You comfortable?" Kip asked him.

"I'm fine," Cameron snapped. "Go to sleep."

"'Kay. 'Night," Kip mumbled.

Alice gave a whuffle and began to snore.

"'Night," Cameron said sourly.

Gracie didn't say a word.

Kip's air mattress had been the drier of the two, but five minutes on it proved that it really wasn't very dry. Half an hour and Cameron was going nuts. His shirt clung, clammy and cold against his back. His jeans, already damp, felt even damper. He twisted, then turned, sighed, then dragged the jacket he was using as a blanket up around him. His teeth began to chatter.

"Still comfortable?" he heard Gracie Talbot whisper.

He grunted and turned over.

She raised herself on her arm again so she could peer down at him in the darkness. "We don't want any unhappy campers, now."

"Stuff it," Cameron muttered, which would have been more effective if he hadn't sneezed right after.

"For heaven's sake," Gracie snapped. "You're going to freeze to death down there."

"I hardly think I'm in any danger," Cameron growled back. "Not many people die from frostbite on Long Island in August."

"Not many people die from sharing a bed with two people and a dog, either."

"I don't think I'll die." He sat up and glared at her.

"Then what do you think?" she asked, meeting his glare. "Ever since you met me, you've been acting as if you'll get something horrible from me."

"I haven't—"

"Or maybe that isn't it at all. Maybe you're afraid that if you do, I'm going to ravish you?"

Cameron felt his cheeks burn. His gaze went immediately to Kip who was, thank heavens, asleep.

"You needn't worry," Gracie said icily. "I'm not in the habit of forcing my attentions on unwilling gentlemen. And anyway," she added, "I'm sure between them, Kip and Alice could protect you."

Cameron had had enough. He said a very rude word, surged to his feet, stripped off the clammy shirt and shucked the damp jeans. If that was the way she wanted it, fine. He jerked back the comforter and crawled into the blessed warmth of the bed, then lay there rigid and shivering next to Kip. He felt goaded, harassed, at the end of his tether.

Gracie lay back down. "That's better."

Was it? Cameron asked himself as he lay there, letting the heat from the boy's warm body and Alice's heavy fur seep into him.

Was it really? Because if the truth were known, Gracie Talbot had hit him very close to home.

Only the real truth was that his fear wasn't that she would ravish him. It was that—in spite of himself, his better judgment, his experience and every bit of common sense he could muster—heaven help him, he wished she would!

Chapter Seven

The night was not as long and sleepless as Cameron thought it would be. He stayed awake for a long time, wavering between astonishment and dismay at the circumstances in which he found himself.

But eventually the rigors of the day overcame him, the welcome heat of the boy and the dog soothed him, and slowly his eyelids lowered, his breathing deepened, and he went to sleep.

When he awoke it was to sunshine, to the cawing of the gulls, to the easy rhythm of a now calm sea washing a storm-battered shore.

And when he awoke he was alone.

For the first few moments he didn't remember much. But when he did, his eyes jerked open and he lifted his head, staring about wildly. No one was there.

He lay back again, staring at the ceiling, getting his bearings. And when he'd got them, he sat up, tossed back the comforter and swung his legs over the side of the bed.

"Ah, you're up." Gracie appeared in the doorway, leaning on one crutch.

Bearings scattered, self-consciously aware that he wore only his underwear, Cameron yanked the comforter back over his hips, then felt like a fool when Gracie hid a smile. He scowled at her.

She smiled back openly, making him feel even worse. "I've hung most of the clothes out along the fence by the deck, and I think several of your T-shirts and shorts might be dry. Shall I have Kip bring you some?"

"Please." He grudged her a smile. "You didn't have to do that."

"I didn't mind. I'm better today. But I still don't balance too well."

"Do you still hurt?"

"Not quite as specifically." She grimaced. "Now I just ache all over."

"I'm sorry." He felt surprisingly sympathetic.

Gracie shrugged. "I'll live. But I do have a favor to ask of you."

Cameron looked at her warily. "What?"

"I have to be at rehearsal at eleven today. And I can't ride the bike. I was wondering if you'd mind driving me. I can call a cab, but . . ." She looked at him hopefully.

Rehearsal. The moment he started having positive thoughts about her, she reminded him. *And a good thing, too, fella,* he told himself.

"Of course," he said tightly. "It's the least I can do."

There was a long pause while Gracie just looked at him. Then, "So you'll do it," he heard her say under her breath as she hobbled toward the stairs.

IF THERE WERE any other way that she could afford to get to the theater, Gracie would have taken it. She was tired of being made to feel like some sort of third-class person. So what if Cameron McClellan didn't like actresses; she was still a human being.

She had thought he might have mellowed a bit after his night with her, Kip and Alice in the barge bed. A man with a sense of humor would have.

But when it came to her, Cameron seemed to have no sense of humor. It was positively perverse that she should find him so attractive. There was absolutely no reason for it. None. There were a million better men in the world.

Well, a hundred thousand at least.

"When'd Dad come in the bed?" Kip asked, bounding into the kitchen, trailed by Alice. They'd been down at the beach since before Gracie had been up. He'd waved at her, but this was the first time they'd spoken this morning.

Gracie smiled at him, telling herself she was amazed such a surly man could have such a nice kid. "Not long after you went to sleep."

Kip smiled. "I figured you could convince him."

Gracie grimaced, remembering the way it had been. "Well, something like that."

She fixed him breakfast. Then they carried it out onto the deck as had become their custom, and sat with their backs against the wall of the house while he ate it.

"D'you like New York?" Kip asked her between mouthfuls.

"Yes."

"D'you like here better?"

"It's . . . nice here," Gracie said. Then she tweaked his nose. "A bit overpowering at times. All these 'cottages' aren't quite what I'm used to, but I must admit I do like the company." She grinned at him.

"All of it?"

"What do you mean?"

"My dad."

Gracie's fingers tightened around her coffee mug. "Of course I like your father."

Kip looked relieved. "Good. Sometimes he hasn't been very polite."

Gracie's eyes widened at this frank observation.

Kip gave her a guileless shrug. "He hasn't."

"Well, perhaps he's just been a bit distracted," she said awkwardly.

"That's no excuse," Kip said. "That's what he always tells me whenever I'm rude."

"I see." Gracie bit down on the corners of her mouth to keep from smiling.

"Anyway, I'm glad you're not mad at him, and I hope you keep givin' him a chance." So saying, he tipped his bowl to his lips and drained the milk. "If Danny comes, will you tell 'im me 'n' Alice are down at the beach?"

Gracie nodded wordlessly, her mind preoccupied with wondering what sort of "chance" Kip McClellan had in mind.

Danny came, and she sent him down to play with Kip and Alice, then went in and set about cleaning up the dishes. That's what she was doing when Cameron came down the stairs. He was wearing a pair of faded blue corduroy shorts and a gold T-shirt with the Golden Gate Bridge stenciled on it in vivid red. But for all his informal attire, he was all business with her.

"Are you ready?" His voice was gruff.

"Almost." She still had her coffee mug to wash. Gracie hobbled toward the counter with it when she found it lifted from her hands.

"I'll clear up," Cameron said. "You go get in the car."

"I can—"

He looked at her leg brace pointedly. "Go get in the car."

The implication was that however long it took, he was damned if he was going to carry her again.

Well, good for him. That was fine with her! Gracie spun around and limped toward the solarium with as much dignity as she could muster.

Cameron appeared just as she was opening the door to the Trooper. He stopped in the doorway for a moment, regarding her painful efforts, then sighed and strode forward to help her up. His touch had the same electrifying effect on her this morning that it had last night and she jerked.

"Electrical storm?" Cameron mocked. But when Gracie's eyes flew to his face, his expression was grim, his lips tight.

He drove her into town and deposited her at the door of the John Drew Theater in total silence. He made no comment about the debris in the road or the scattered fallen limbs, residue from last night's storm. Gracie noticed them and almost commented. But one look at him and she decided not to. He might be driving along Main Street, but his mind looked to be a million miles away.

"This is it," she said unnecessarily when they approached the theater, for Cameron had already come to a double-parked stop. "Thank you very much."

"You're welcome." He didn't look her way.

She eased open the door and stuck her crutch out to catch herself, wobbling as she did so. Cameron ground his teeth audibly, shut off the engine, got out and came around to help her.

"Here." Strong arms gripped her just above the waist and lifted her onto the sidewalk. Warm breath caressed the side of her face. Then he set her onto the sidewalk and his hands fell away. "Can you manage now?"

Gracie, who needed more time to recover from his touch than from her injuries, nodded jerkily. "Yes. Yes, of course." She lifted her gaze to meet his and gave him a bright smile. "The show must go on, right?"

His jaw clenched. He gave her a curt nod, strode back to the driver's side and jumped into the Trooper. "Do you need a ride back?"

"I—er..."

"What time do you get done?"

"Oh, er, I'm not sure really. Herschel sometimes keeps us over the allotted time. Depends, you know."

"I know." His voice was hard.

"How about three?" she offered.

"Three." And without glancing at her again, he gunned the engine and sped off.

"WHO'S THAT?"

Gracie turned toward the stage door to see Tracy Mullens, her almost-roommate, standing there watching Cameron leave.

"My landlord."

Tracy rolled her eyes. "I could do with a landlord like that. Why on earth were you looking for another place to stay?"

"Because at the time I needed one. Now we've reached a compromise."

Tracy grinned at her. "I'll bet."

"It isn't what you think." Gracie edged her way past a plump woman in designer togs who was almost at the door, too.

Tracy sighed. "No, you're too pure, aren't you?"

Was she?

Gracie wondered. Well, the question would never come up. There was no chance of it. If there was one thing she was quite clear on, it was that Cameron McClellan wanted as little as possible to do with her.

"What happened to you?" Tracy asked now, holding the door open for her.

Gracie related the gist of the accident as they walked toward the stage where Herschel and the rest of the crew were assembling.

"Fell out of a loft? Good heavens!" Herschel exclaimed, rushing up, taking her by the arms and surveying her carefully. "You are all right?"

"I will be," Gracie promised.

"You are sure?"

"Yes. Truly."

He seemed still not quite convinced, but when she bobbed her head reassuringly several times, at last he smiled. "Good, good. We cannot lose you now. You are our little star."

Gracie blinked.

"It's true, my dear." He patted her shoulder. "Indeed you are. The others act. You sparkle. You make everyone

forget their cares to care only about you.'' His hand
squeezed her shoulder gently. ''You steal the show.''

Gracie's face flushed at this astonishing praise. She had
known she liked the part, had enjoyed the work, had felt
good after. But to be told she ''sparkled,'' that she ''stole
the show,'' was quite beyond anything she expected to hear.
Especially from a demanding director like Herschel.

''We shall go carefully today,'' he told her. ''Not to put
pressure, yes?''

Gracie swallowed. ''Sure. Whatever.''

He beamed. ''Whatever,'' he mimicked as if she were a
child who had just said a marvelous new word. ''You see
how gracious she is,'' he said to the rest of the cast.

They grinned at her. Gracie felt her face must be red as a
beet. She hadn't expected the compliments, and she surely
never expected Herschel to go out of his way to make things
easy for her today, but he did. In fact he worked around her
scenes frequently, so she could sit down in the audience and
rest her leg.

After the rehearsal was over he came and sat beside her.
''You must take care of yourself, my dear.''

Gracie gave an awkward little shrug. ''It was an accident. I do try.''

''Yes, well, try harder. I was not fooling earlier. You have
something special. A God-given talent. You can go far, my
dear, if you work, if you study.'' He looked at her braced
leg, then smiled at her. ''If you are careful.''

''Rest assured,'' Gracie promised. ''I won't climb any
more ladders.''

Herschel smiled. ''Not unless you have a hero there to
catch you at least.''

Gracie's mind flickered not to the men who played Jack
or Algy in Wilde's play, but straight to Cameron McClellan.
For all the good it does you, she chastised herself. Angrily
she pushed the thought away.

DÉJÀ VU, Cameron told himself as he drove back to Gull Cottage, was a dangerous thing. It could remind a man of things he'd rather forget, of dreams that never saw reality, of a future that wasn't his to touch.

Driving Gracie to the theater was one of those.

When he'd been young and newly married, he'd done the same for Dana. Had dropped her off at the door, and blissfully watched her disappear, thinking that he had it all. Young and confident, he'd leaned back in his MG, closed his eyes and envisioned a future of days like those: a house like Gull Cottage, a couple of kids, a dog, perhaps. Most of all, a wife who shared his dreams.

And he'd got . . . what?

Well, not that, certainly.

He had got one kid at least. One terrific kid. But the rest? He gritted his teeth, then sighed and turned onto Frigate Alley. It was better not to think about that.

It would have been better not to come to East Hampton at all, he told himself for the hundredth time. Better to have put nostalgia and memories where they belonged—in the past. Memories were treacherous things. They could seduce and destroy, tempt and torment.

And it wasn't only the memory of what he had thought he wanted with Dana that could do that to him. It was the realization that now he had a memory of a night in bed with Gracie Talbot to add to his list.

GRACIE FOUND CAMERON drumming his fingers on the steering wheel of the Trooper when she came out of the theater. She might've asked if he'd been waiting long, but his impatience told her that however long he'd been there it was too long. She tried to offer a smile, but he wasn't looking at her.

Obviously he was going to be just as genial this trip as he had been the last. Annoyed, she clambered silently into the seat next to him. Doing so was awkward, but she knew from experience that it would be more awkward still if he offered to help her.

Happily he didn't. He just waited, the essence of impatience with a patient veneer.

"Thank you," she said, "for coming to get me."

Cameron didn't say a word. And the moment she was in he shot away from the curb.

Irritated, Gracie waited, unwilling to speak again. It was his turn now. Surely he could be polite enough to do that. After all, it wasn't as if they were strangers. They'd spent the night in bed together. That thought made her cheeks burn, though the fact was innocent in the extreme. It was because she hadn't wished it were. She didn't want to think about that.

She waited patiently, thinking eventually he'd have to say something. He didn't.

When they'd gone six blocks in total silence, she'd had enough. "Where's Kip?"

For a moment she didn't even think he was going to answer that. But then he said, "Playing baseball. He's over at Bates's house."

"Ah, yes. Danny, wasn't it?" She knew it was, but hoped that would keep the conversation going.

"Mmm."

Gracie glowered, then went doggedly on. "He said his family had lived here for years. I thought you might know them."

"Mmm."

A course in conversational English wouldn't have hurt him a bit. She tried another tack. "The play is going really well. You'll have to come see it."

There was no response whatever to that.

They were caught in some sort of traffic jam, now, and the heat was building up again after yesterday's storm. Apparently there was going to be no respite at all, Gracie thought. Neither from the humidity nor from Cameron's moodiness.

"We're not going home?" she ventured when he took a road that led toward the highway rather than toward the shore.

"No."

Gracie just looked at him. "Is this twenty questions, then?"

He shot her a hard glare.

"Where are we going? Or can I ask only questions that can be answered with yes or no?"

"To get furniture," he bit out. "We need some. Beds in particular, in case you hadn't noticed. And roofing shingles if we're ever going to survive another storm. I was on the phone this morning talking to the realtor and with Roger so I didn't have time then. I'm taking time now."

No question about whether she wanted to come along, no query as to whether she had other plans. Nothing. He was driving and she was along for the ride. Arrogant jerk.

Cameron's fingers kneaded the steering wheel. He took the next corner sharply, swung into the lot of a furniture store and pulled into a parking space.

Then he blew air out of his cheeks and jerked the key from the ignition.

Gracie didn't move. "Cameron?"

"What?"

"Can I ask you a question?"

He sighed, staring straight ahead. "Ask," he muttered finally.

"What do you have against me?"

Cars swished past on the highway. Two spaces away a harried mother fastened a screaming toddler into a car seat. From overhead came the audible buzz of a plane headed for the city. Cameron's hands clenched and unclenched, strong and powerful against his thighs. Gracie swallowed, wondering if he was even going to answer her.

"Nothing," he said at last and moved to open the door.

"Wait just a damned minute," Gracie snapped. "You can't act the way you do with me and tell me that." She grabbed his arm to hold him, determined to get this out in the open once and for all.

Cameron jerked back as if he'd been stung. Knowing she'd gone too far, Gracie let go at once, eyeing him warily.

He turned to face her, hard blue eyes boring into her. "I don't have anything against you."

He gave each word equal weight. The trick, Gracie thought, was to determine which one deserved it. But she didn't have time for that right now.

"Sure," she said with enough sarcasm to make Herschel proud. "That's why you act as if you wish I were at the other end of the earth, as if I had an infectious disease or something. That's why you jerked away just now!"

"For cripe's sake!"

"I'm not stupid; I can tell when I'm not wanted."

Cameron gave a short, harsh, mocking laugh. "Can you?"

"Yes." The word came out as a hiss. "You're the man who told me he didn't lie to his kid."

"So?"

"So why don't you stop lying to me? Why don't you play fair, Cameron McClellan? Why don't you tell me just exactly what the problem is?"

His dark eyes glittered. One corner of his mouth lifted in a parody of a smile. "You want to know what the problem is, Gracie Talbot?"

She faced him defiantly. "Yes, I do."

"You really want to know?" He sounded as if he was taunting her.

"Just tell me."

"I'll do more than tell you. I'll show you!"

And before Gracie could say another word, he had reached for her, hauling her across the stick shift into his arms and touching his mouth to hers.

Gracie had had her share of kisses. Tentative kisses, sweet kisses, hungry kisses, even one or two passionate kisses. But she'd never ever been kissed like this. This was an angry kiss, a frustrated kiss, heated and demanding, desperate and eager, yet at the same time resisting precisely what it asked for.

Cameron's arms betrayed the same emotion. They were hard around her and yet they held her away as much as they drew her near. He fought himself as much or more than he fought her.

Gracie wasn't fighting at all. She was too astonished, too amazed. *Cameron McClellan was kissing her!*

But before she could react further, he thrust her away, dropped his arms and was wiping his mouth on the back of his hand. His breathing came in short, harsh gasps as they stared at each other.

"That's the problem, Gracie Talbot," he said roughly. "That, by God, is the problem."

Then he jerked open the door and was out, striding into the furniture store as if all the devils in hell were on his tail.

Gracie sat stunned in the Trooper, her fingers brushing her lips tentatively.

I can tell when I'm not wanted. Her pompous words came back to her, chiding her, taunting her. Her fingers traced her lips again.

"Oh, Gracie," she murmured to the dazed reflection in the window. "What a fool you are."

Chapter Eight

Cameron was a fool, and he knew it.

If there was one thing stupider than continuing to live day after day in the same house with Gracie Talbot, it was kissing her. Even in anger.

Especially in anger.

Because it had ceased to be anger almost at once. It had started because he was goaded. Tired, worried, tempted, aroused, needy, and a whole host of other things he should have kept under control. He hadn't. He had taken it out on her.

And within seconds he was taking it out on himself. Because he couldn't maintain the anger. He could only taste the gentleness, the astonishment, the innocence that was Gracie Talbot. He might have begun trying to shock the socks off her. He had ended by shocking himself.

He wandered aimlessly through the furniture store, seeing nothing, hearing nothing, brushing off the sales clerk as if she were no more bothersome than a gnat. He paced the aisles, his hands in his pockets, his head bent. He passed sofas, recliners, dining room tables, chairs, buffets, kitchen sets.

Way to go, McClellan, he congratulated himself with as much sarcasm as Gracie had mustered when she'd challenged his feelings about her. *Way to go.*

But the question was—which way was he going to go now.

He wasn't exactly sure when he became aware of someone following him. At first he thought it was the sales clerk,
back for another stab. But she didn't speak, didn't point out
the wonders of the inner spring mattress or the truly re-
fined patina of the cherry wood armoire. She only walked
behind him silent as a ghost and when, at last, he stopped
in front of a row of sofas, he realized who it was.

For a moment he didn't say anything. Then he said the
only thing he could say. "I'm sorry," he muttered, head
bent.

Gracie Talbot blessed him with a tentative smile.

Another woman would have run fifty miles in the other
direction. Another woman would have slapped his face.
Gracie Talbot should have done both. Instead she was
looking at him as if she were worried about him.

Cameron choked back a half sob, half laugh. No more
than he was worried about himself.

He walked on. She walked beside him. He stopped and
fingered the rough tweed of a recliner, looked at it, at her.
His eyes asked what she thought of it.

Briefly she nodded her head.

They did the same throughout the rest of the store. He
touched a sofa, a matching chair. Table and chairs. Dressers. Lamps. Beds.

And with a nod or a slight negative movement, Gracie
made her opinions known. Mostly they agreed. She approved his taste for understated, plain, timeless lines; for
oak and walnut; for the one irresistibly frivolous wicker
rocker.

All in silence. As if words were too harsh, as if were either
of them to speak, only misunderstanding could occur.

It was true. Cameron was grateful. In fact he was convinced.

They didn't have understanding. They had a truce, and
the terms of the truce were as yet undecided. It was simply
that both of them understood that, given the way things

were, they had to get better. It was the only way things could go.

Cameron thought afterward that the sales clerk could easily have thought they'd lost their minds. Neither spoke and yet they bought a houseful of furniture.

He charged it to Laurence.

Gracie stared at him wide-eyed.

Cameron shrugged. "It's his."

It wasn't until they got back in the car, and Cameron had stuck the key in the ignition, that Gracie spoke.

"I think we ought to talk." Another woman could have made that line as sarcastic as her earlier ones. This contained no sarcasm at all.

Cameron nodded. "Now?"

Gracie shrugged. "Whenever."

Cameron glanced at his watch. "I think maybe we'd better get back to the house first. I left Kip at Bates's but I don't want him to wear out his welcome."

"That's fine." Gracie folded her hands in her lap and stared out the window.

Cameron expected she might say more, might well insist on talking now. He wouldn't have blamed her. But she didn't. She was the most amazing woman he'd ever met.

They stopped at a lumberyard on the way home. The furniture had been a necessity, but no more than the shingles that Cameron ordered delivered.

"Be weeks before anybody can get around to reroofing," the man at the lumberyard told him. "Everybody's at work on the new developments."

"I'll do it myself." Physical labor wouldn't kill him, Cameron thought. In fact it might do some good. Hammering in all those nails might displace a bit of the frustration he felt about not being able to hammer himself into Gracie Talbot.

How crude is that, McClellan? he asked himself. And the answer was, *very.* But if Cameron wasn't lying to Kip or Gracie, he wasn't going to lie to himself, either.

BY THE TIME they picked up Kip at Bates's it was after five o'clock. The boy looked semi-amazed to see them together. But after a brief glance from one to the other during which he didn't seem to detect emotional gunfire, he hopped into the back and launched into a long account of the pond he and Danny had explored, and the pick-up baseball game that they'd participated in.

Then he sank back against the seat and rubbed his stomach. "I'm starved. What's for supper?"

Cameron glanced at Gracie. She glanced back. Neither spoke.

"Let's eat out," Cameron said after a moment.

"You can drop me off before you go," Gracie said quickly. She didn't want to impose on him or make him feel in the least as if he had to ask her.

Cameron turned his head and his eyes met hers. "I meant the three of us."

"But—"

"Please."

What was he thinking now? Why the change of heart? Did she really want to know? Or was it enough just to accept it for the moment? Finally she gave a jerky little nod. "Thank you, then. I'd like that."

Out of the corner of her eye she saw Kip's eyes widen and his mouth drop open. Then he reached forward and gave his father a pat on the back. Cameron's mouth seemed to develop a wry twist for just a moment, but he didn't say a word.

They went back into town and drove down the main business streets looking for possibilities.

"They've got funny food here," Kip confided to Gracie. "Beet soup an' carbonated chicken with spaghetti an' stuff like that. No McDonald's at all."

"I think we're in the mood for something a little more posh anyway," Cameron said.

"Fast food is fine with me," Gracie assured him.

"Not with me," he told her. "There," he pointed at a place they were passing. "How about Chinese? Kip likes that."

"Wonderful," Gracie agreed.

Called the Wokery, the restaurant Cameron ushered them into seemed more interested in trendsetting than place settings. Used to menus given over to things like Cashew Chicken and Sweet and Sour Pork, Gracie was amused to find that The Wokery went in for Cashew Capon and Sweet and Sour Quail. Her eyebrows lifted.

Cameron shrugged and grinned—a grin that threatened to dissolve Gracie right where she stood. "It's East Hampton," he said. "What can you expect?"

Gracie thought she ought to have given up on expectations long ago. She certainly had none right now. She didn't even know what Cameron's immediate intentions were.

When she'd said they had to talk and he'd agreed, she'd thought he would rush her back to Gull Cottage, sit her down, and proceed in bullheaded Cameron McClellan fashion to explain that he meant nothing by the kiss, that for a few moments his hormones had simply got out of control.

He hadn't. Instead he'd been treading softly, smiling gently, speaking low, soothing words.

It was, she decided, probably what made him such a terrific success in business. Cameron McClellan was a past master at keeping his adversaries off balance. Heaven knew he off-balanced her.

They ordered the dinner for three which netted them the capon, the quail and a veal dish with bamboo shoots and something listed—Gracie hoped, erroneously—as wood ears.

There was also sizzling rice and bowls of piping hot egg drop soup, which Kip said always reminded him of snot, a comment that elicited a glare from Cameron and gales of laughter from Gracie.

Whatever tension that had remained between them broke.

Dinner became almost fun. Kip showed Gracie how to use chopsticks, was tolerant of her eventually retreating to a fork, and Cameron actually praised her, saying, "You tried. That's what matters."

"I would keep trying," Gracie said, "except I might starve before I finish. I'll try again when I'm not famished."

Cameron gave her an approving nod, and Gracie felt her heart expand.

It was silly, she tried telling herself. Nothing had changed. And, of course, in one sense, that was true. But, intangibly perhaps, things were different. Just as the world seemed a calmer, better place even in the aftermath of the storm, so did Gracie's world after Cameron's kiss.

It had enflamed her, yes. But it had righted her world as well. It made sense of things at last. It wasn't an unknown she was dealing with any longer. Or at least in a swirling confusion of unknowns, she now had one less.

The implications of that kiss she wouldn't even let herself consider.

They would talk. Cameron had promised. And just as he was honest, he would be, she was certain, a man who kept his vows.

In the meantime, she would take life as it came. And if that meant Cashew Capon, wood ears, and a fortune cookie that assured her "blue skies just ahead," she was not going to complain.

CAMERON WAS GOOD at talking. Negotiating. Listening. All that communication business was part of his life. He could do it in his sleep, he sometimes thought. He was in a blue funk whenever he thought about talking to Gracie.

He thought of a thousand reasons not to. A thousand excuses that would legitimate his refusal to say a word. He wasn't accustomed to opening himself, to sharing his feelings, to explaining them to other people. Certainly not to a woman like Gracie.

A woman like Gracie... What did that mean?

Once he'd thought he knew. Right off, the moment he'd seen her lying asleep in that ridiculous barge of a bed, he'd been convinced he had her pegged: ditzy actress ready to do anything for the big break.

But the more he was around her, the less certain he was. She seemed so innocent, so guileless and yet so aware of the feelings of others. She certainly evoked an incredible variety of feelings in him.

He climbed up onto the roof after supper to check it out before he started shingling in the morning. And while he was there he tried to sort those feelings out. A little perspective, he told himself, wouldn't hurt a bit.

But the only perspective he got was one that allowed him to look down on her as she sat on the deck watching Kip and Alice paddling around in the pool. And the only conclusion he came to was how right they looked together that way.

So he was apprehensive later when he shut out the light in Kip's room and slowly made his way back downstairs.

Gracie wasn't in the family room or in the kitchen. And Cameron felt a moment's hopefulness that she had somehow forgotten his promise and had gone off to bed. Then he saw a silhouette move out on the deck and Gracie's soft voice said, "Out here."

She was sitting on the edge of the pool, her knee brace discarded once more, her feet dangling in the water. Like a mermaid, Cameron thought, and wished she were. It would be a lot easier if he knew she were simply the product of his fantasies and not a red-blooded, wholly real and tempting woman.

He opened the screen door and came out, crossed the deck slowly and stood looking out across the pool. Excuses clamored in his head. He tried to sort through them, to pick the most plausible, the one that would get him off the hook.

"Sit down," Gracie invited.

He hesitated. To sit down would be to commit himself to the discussion, to settle in for the long haul. Cameron stuck his hands in the back pockets of his shorts and rocked back and forth. He stared out past the pool toward the darkness of the sea, to the running lights of some boat heading for... where?

It didn't matter. He wished he were on it, wished he were anywhere but here.

He sighed, then ducked his head and saw Gracie looking up at him. Her gaze was rapt and slightly worried. The only person he could ever remember looking at him that way was his mother.

Was he equating Gracie with his mother now? Given the state he was in, who knew?

"Aw hell," he muttered and sat. He laced his fingers, then flexed them, then leaned forward and rested his forearms on this thighs and stared down into the shadowy depths of the pool. Beside him he could feel the warmth radiating from Gracie Talbot, and the patience—as if she would wait for him to get to the point, however long it took.

"I don't like actresses," he said at last.

She shifted slightly. He didn't turn his head to see her expression, but kept his eyes cast down. She didn't reply for ages, and he wondered if that would be that.

Finally she ventured, "Because of your father's job?"

"Because of my wife."

Most of the time he could talk about Dana with indifference. He could shrug off her defection, her carelessness, her determination. He didn't manage it here. And he could tell from the way Gracie's fingers tightened into a fist against her leg that she heard every ounce of bitterness and pain in his voice.

"She was an actress, I take it."

Cameron slanted her a glance. "You don't know?"

Gracie shook her head.

"You've heard of Dana Bryce?"

"Oh, yes." Then her eyes widened.

"My wife."

"Oh, my heavens. I mean. I'm terribly sorry. Her death was such a shock. Were you . . . I mean, I'm sorry about . . . I never . . ."

"My *ex*-wife," Cameron corrected. "Spare me the condolences." He'd got a lot of them even though he hadn't been her husband when she'd died in a horseback riding accident five years before. His fingers clenched, gripping the curved edge of the pool.

"When did you . . . ?" Gracie voice tapered off. "I mean, when did she . . . ?"

"Get divorced?" Cameron finished for her. "Kip wasn't even two."

There was a long silence between them. Cameron waited for the questions that would come if the platitudes didn't. Gracie didn't say a word. She just sat quietly, her fingers kneading the tops of her thighs. Then she lifted one hand as if she might have reached out to touch him. But her other hand reached up and knotted with it and they both fell to her lap.

Thank heavens, Cameron thought. He couldn't have survived her touch just then. He couldn't have taken Gracie Talbot's pity.

"She was in summer theater like you," Cameron said in a low voice. His mouth twisted. "At the John Drew. Also like you."

He spared her a quick glance. "It was a good part. Second lead. Demanding. Challenging. All the things," he concluded wryly, "that motherhood and marriage were not." He chewed on his lip, then a sigh escaped him. "Ah, hell, what can you expect?"

"More than you got," Gracie said softly. "I'm not . . ."

"Not interested?" Cameron grimaced. "I don't blame you. I shouldn't have even brought it up. But I'd promised to explain and—"

"I *am* interested," Gracie told him. "I just . . . I don't want to be nosy."

"You're not asking. I'm telling you. Trying to explain why I've been acting like such an ass."

"I don't think—"

"Don't excuse me. I know what I've been doing. And if I didn't, Kip's only too willing to tell me."

"Kip?"

"Thinks I've been rude as hell." Cameron raked a hand through his hair. "And he's right. But I've had to be. It was the only way I could keep my distance, and I damned well needed to do that." His eyes met hers ruefully.

"I'm . . . not Dana," Gracie said softly.

Far off in the direction of town, he could hear the sound of a horn honking. Closer, he heard the continuous rush of waves against the shore. Nearer still, the blood pounded in his ears as his eyes collided with hers. All the emotions previously well-banked flamed to life in the cool night air.

"No." His hand came up and stroked her cheek. His fingers trembled. His lips parted. "I want you."

"Yes."

Something flickered in his eyes. "Yes, you agree? Or yes, you want me, too?"

Their gazes caught and held. Seconds passed. Minutes. A lifetime for all Cameron knew.

"I don't know," she said softly at last.

Never in her life had Gracie Talbot wanted anything or anyone as much as she wanted Cameron McClellan right now. But the very intensity of her feelings made her hold back.

Something about the way she felt about him was special, was unique. It wasn't quite the same as her previous enthusiasms, her earlier forays into interpersonal relationships with the opposite sex.

Was it, she wondered not for the first time, what she'd always been waiting for?

Was *he* what she'd always been waiting for?

She didn't know, wasn't even sure how to find out. But haste wasn't a good idea, she was certain. Whatever was happening to her—to him—was new. It was as fragile, but—dared she hope?—as full of promise as a just-born child.

Gracie didn't know.

But she wasn't taking any chances. She intended to treat it with the reverence it deserved.

She drew a shaky breath, wishing and wanting, yet wary for all that.

Cameron's mouth lifted at one corner. His fingers touched her hair, stroking it, following the curve down to her jawline, then tracing lightly along it to rest for a moment on her chin. "Ah, Grace," he murmured.

She tried to smile. Her hand went out and touched his, wrapping his strong lean fingers in her smaller ones. "Friends, Cameron?" she offered.

One eyebrow lifted. "Friends?"

She gave a helpless shrug. "It's early days yet."

He considered that, then nodded, seeming to agree. "Yes."

There could be more perhaps, Gracie told herself, if things went right, if eventually it was what they both wanted. If her interest didn't flag, if his grew. If eventually there was more than just wanting.

If, perhaps, wanting turned into love.

THE NEXT DAY started Gull Cottage's metamorphosis from a house into a home.

At eight in the morning the furniture arrived, and that, of course, had something to do with it. Couches, chairs, tables, beds and dressers added a lot. And everything seemed to fit, to belong. She and Cameron had good taste, Gracie decided.

She was tempted to tell him so, but she thought it might be a bit forward. They were only just beginning to get on.

But they were getting on. Whatever had been settled by the kiss and the confrontation, it had lasted to live another day.

Gracie wanted to comment on that, too, but she didn't do that, either. Things were too tentative just yet. Safe subjects were best.

In that vein Gracie told him what a great job he was doing fixing the roof.

"Why? Because you want us prepared for another storm?" Cameron had come down in time to take her to work and he was leaning back against the kitchen counter while she packed herself a lunch.

"Of course," Gracie said, slanting him a smile.

She wasn't about to tell him the real reason, which was that she loved seeing him in nothing but a pair of low-slung faded jeans and a leather equipment belt.

All morning long she had been sneaking glimpses of him, memorizing the way the sweat glistened in the hair on his chest as he walked along the roof line and the way his muscles bunched and flexed as he sat or knelt hammering shingles. And later when he came down for a breather and tipped back his head and guzzled milk straight from the carton, she thought she might have to douse herself with the ice jug just to put out the flames.

Something else she couldn't say. Not after she'd said they were going to be "friends."

But the physical attraction she felt towards Cameron McClellan showed no signs of abating, nor did her growing emotional attraction to him.

When he smiled at her, as he was doing now, the sun came out. When he shared a thought, a funny story, a sudden reminiscence as he had done while they'd been arranging the furniture, she felt truly blessed.

She hated having to leave him and go to work, but not more obviously than he hated her leaving. And she understood the reason now. She understood his hangup about actresses and she made up her mind not to call his attention to her job. She had to accept a ride with him this morning. But after that, she'd find one home.

The rehearsal went swimmingly. "You are in the groove," Herschel beamed at the whole cast, clapping his hands. "Stupendous. Just the right note. One more week and it shall be, as you say, cream on the cake."

"Icing," one of the local volunteers, Callista Pendennis, corrected. Mrs. Pendennis and several other townspeople kept things running smoothly, soothed egos, pampered actors and generally made themselves indispensable to the summer production casts and crew. She smiled now and handed the director a cup of tea.

"Just so," Herschel agreed. "Icing. And the lovely Miss Talbot is the icingest of all." He bestowed an even broader smile on her. "I don't blame Algy a bit, my dear. I would be eager, too."

Gracie blushed. "It's just an act."

"A very fine act. You are—" he groped for the right word "—enticing."

"Too right," Des Nolan, who played Algy, assured her.

Gracie just shook her head.

"We are embarrassing Miss Talbot," Herschel said, making a tsking sound. "Enough. That is enough for today anyway. Go home now. Think, study, listen. Feel. Become."

No problem, Gracie thought. She'd never been feeling more in her life. It was odd, that. Unexpected. And she owed it without question to Cameron McClellan. He had awakened something in her that she'd never felt before. A quickening of the spirit, an enthusiasm, a zest, a sense of purpose.

All that from a kiss? she chided herself.

But it was more than that. At least so far it was. Who knew how long it would last?

She stopped Des on his way out of the theater. "I don't suppose you're living out by the beach?"

He shook his head. "Not me. Squalid digs by a bog." Then he laughed. "Just kidding. I'm staying with a friend on the North Fork. Can I give you a lift though?"

"You could take me to Frigate Alley at least."

"Oh, but, dear," interrupted Mrs. Pendennis, still juggling the tea things, "that's right down my lane."

Gracie smiled at her. "We're neighbors then. I live at Gull Cottage."

Mrs. Pendennis's eyes widened. A smile wreathed her grandmotherly face. "Oh, my goodness, you don't say! I had no idea that Poppy was in town."

Gracie blinked. "Poppy?"

Mrs. Pendennis's plump cheeks turned a becoming rose color. "It's short for Lollipop, actually. My nickname for Larry." She giggled, shaking her head. "And I was Cuddles to him. But of course that was years ago."

Gracie nearly swallowed her tongue. Cuddles? And...Lolli...pop? A nickname for *Larry*? Did she mean Laurence McClellan? As far as Gracie was concerned even "Larry" was carrying things too far.

She looked at chubby, energetic Mrs. Pendennis with new eyes. "Er. I'm afraid he's not in town," she said at last.

"No?" Mrs. Pendennis's face fell. "I had heard the cottage was rented earlier in the summer," she said, "but I was sure Poppy would come before the Classic. He always does."

"Classic?"

"The Hampton Classic. It's a horse race, dear. They have it every year, usually in August. Oh, heavens, it won't be the same without Poppy."

"I'm sorry," Gracie said.

Mrs. Pendennis patted her arm. "Not your fault. Are you renting then, my dear?" She looked expectantly at Gracie.

Gracie wasn't quite sure how to answer that. She didn't feel up to explaining what she was doing. That would necessitate talking about her relationship with Cameron, and she didn't know for sure what it was.

"No, actually I'm..." she faltered. "Mr. McClellan's son is here," she said at last.

She didn't say he was renting the house. She didn't know whether Laurence cared if it was known, but she didn't think Cameron would want their estrangement highlighted by the public knowledge that he was paying money to live in his father's house.

"Oh, of course. Tony!" Mrs. Pendennis beamed.

"No. Cameron."

Mrs. Pendennis's eyes practically bugged right out of her round little face. "Cameron? You mean Lily's boy?"

She supposed he must be because Tony's mother was called Amaryllis, and, as far as she knew, "Poppy" had only had the two wives. "Yes."

"Oh, by all that's wonderful!" Mrs. Pendennis seemed about to pirouette down the theater aisle in excitement. "Cameron's home after all these years! Oh, I am so glad!"

Gracie gave her a weak grin. He certainly wasn't "home" in the way Mrs. Pendennis thought. But Gracie wasn't going to correct the impression.

If Cameron wanted to explain it to her, that was his decision. Gracie just asked for a ride. "If it's not too much trouble."

"I'd be delighted," Mrs. Pendennis said. And she drove Gracie right to the door.

Cameron was sitting on the gable, shirtless and bronzed, replacing the shingles. He watched them arrive, but didn't wave.

"Getting the roof redone?" Mrs. Pendennis asked, pulling up to park next to the solarium.

"Doing it, actually," Gracie told her. "That's Cameron."

"On the roof?"

Gracie nodded.

"Goodness me. I'm surprised at Poppy letting him."

"Cameron does what he wants," Gracie said with perfect justification.

"So does Poppy," the older woman confided. "Never saw such a muleheaded man. Gets an idea in his head and you can't budge it."

Family resemblance, Gracie thought.

"I can give you a ride in tomorrow, darling, if you'd like."

"Please." Gracie got out as dexterously as she could, her knee still braced but improving. Mrs. Pendennis continued squinting up at Cameron who was working his way along the gable and then disappeared over the seaward side.

"Would you like to come in and wait for him?" Gracie asked her. "Say hello. Have a cup of tea, perhaps?"

"Not today, dear. When Poppy comes I will. He and the admiral and I always get together."

The admiral, Gracie gathered, was Mrs. Pendennis's husband. "I don't know if Pop—er, Mr. McClellan is coming this year."

"Oh?"

"He's in France, I understand."

Mrs. Pendennis's eyes widened and she made a tsking sound. "France? That Poppy! Such a goer. You never know with him." She shook her head, bright red curls bobbing. "Probably got some young gal with him and they'll be all over the Riviera making whoopee."

Gracie giggled at that. The very thought of starchy, pompous Laurence McClellan "making whoopee" with some young "gal" tickled her fancy. Obviously he had a much broader range than she'd ever imagined.

"Do you need help getting to the house, dear? No? Well, see you tomorrow, then. I'll be here at ten."

"Thank you." Gracie leaned on her crutch and watched "Cuddles" Pendennis drive away. Then she went around the house, found Alice on the deck and walked out to a point where she could see Cameron again.

"Hello up there!"

He was almost down to the eaves now and he turned, surprised, and looked down at her. "You got a ride?"

"Yes. The lady who lives on the corner will take me from now on. Mrs. Pendennis, she's called."

"Poop Deck."

"What?"

He made his way clear down to the edge now and sat down, dangling his legs over. "Mrs. Poop Deck. The lady who gave you the ride. That's what my dad always called her."

Gracie goggled at him. "Poop Deck?"

"She married the admiral instead of him the way I heard it. He didn't take it well. They've been Admiral and Mrs. Poop Deck around our house ever since."

"Ah." Gracie grinned. "That explains it."

"Explains what?"

"Cuddles."

"Cuddles?"

"She said that's what he used to call her, your father, I mean—obviously prior to refusing him. And she called him Lollipop."

It was Cameron's turn to stare. Then he let loose a full-throated laugh. "Lollipop? First time I ever heard that." He shook his head, still grinning.

"Where's Kip?"

"At Bates's. Big baseball game."

"They get along well."

"Bosom buddies." Cameron smiled. "I was afraid the month was going to be a bust for him."

"It's not?"

"Nope. Best time he's ever had," Cameron quoted.

"I'm glad. How's the roof coming?"

"Not bad. We shouldn't float away during the next storm at least. I've taken off the shingles over the attic so I can replace them while I'm up here. They look pretty bad, too. No telling how much water got in there during the last storm."

"Should we look?"

"Don't have a key."

"Want me to call the realtor?"

"If you would."

"Are you coming down soon?"

Cameron glanced at his watch. "Yeah. I've been up here four hours. I'll be sunburned if I don't."

"You should've put on sunscreen."

"Nobody to do it for me." He grinned at her.

Gracie felt her heart skip a beat. She squinted up at him. "Is that a hint?"

"I think it might be."

Gracie swallowed hard. There was nothing she'd like better than spreading a smooth film of lotion across Cameron's strong muscular back. Well, perhaps one or two things she'd prefer, but.... She licked her lips. "Come on down, then."

For a long moment Cameron didn't move, as if he were contemplating the wisdom of that, as if once the words were out of his mouth, he'd begun to regret them.

Gracie, heart in her throat, still stared up at him unblinkingly. Whatever he'd been seeking in her gaze, it seemed at last he found it, for he crawled swiftly over to the ladder and scrambled down.

Suddenly it was Gracie who had second thoughts, who felt the first flutterings of panic. She looked around for moral support and saw only Alice. Alice gave her an encouragingly doggy smile.

She didn't have time for anything else before Cameron took her hand and led her into the house. Alice tagged along behind.

Her leg still made it difficult to climb the stairs, and all at once she felt Cameron swing her into his arms and begin to carry her. Gracie was still melting from the contact of her thin cotton shirt with his sun-warmed skin when he set her down and pressed something into her hand.

She stared up at him, drowning in the warm dark azure of his eyes. Her legs trembled. Her eyes dropped from his to focus on his lips. They were firm and slightly parted, smiling tenderly at her.

"Well?" he said softly after a moment.

"Well, what?"

The smiled broadened fractionally. "Well, what are you waiting for?"

Was he expecting her to start things, then? To touch him? To kiss him? To make love to him? Oh, merciful heavens. Gracie took a deep breath. Trembled again.

"Grace?"

"Mmm?"

"I thought you were going to put sun screen on my back."

The tube fell from nerveless fingers and hit the floor. A tide of consternation—of humiliation—rolled over her.

"Oh, yes. Sure, of course. I—" she babbled, trying to bend, to reach the tube, to pick it up, anything to avoid his eyes and stop herself feeling like such a fool.

Cameron pulled her upright. "Hey," he murmured, "I didn't mean . . . It's all right. It's—"

"No. I—"

His hands held her upper arms, trapping her, keeping her there until she lifted her eyes to look at him.

"Gracie. Trust me," he said softly. "One step at a time."

Then he loosed her and bent over, scooping the tube up himself. Taking her hand, he led her to the bed where he laid the tube down and stretched out flat.

Gracie stood over him staring down, her emotions stampeding in her heart and in her head.

Trust him.

She did. In fact, she thought ruefully, he'd just proven how trustworthy he was. It was herself Gracie was worried about.

But after a long moment's hesitation, she reached for the tube and sat down next to him. She took a deep breath, then squeezed some of the lotion into her palm. She felt it cool and smooth against her skin. She rubbed her hands together to warm the lotion, then lowered her hands slowly and touched his back.

Trust him?

Yeah, sure, Cameron thought, his fingers tightening into fists at his sides as Gracie's hands danced and swirled over his back.

Trust him? How could he even ask it of her when he couldn't even trust himself?

He felt a shiver shoot through him as Gracie's fingers tripped lightly down the length of his spine, then skated smoothly up the sides again. He held his breath.

Don't trust me, he thought. *Don't.* It became a litany singing through his head.

Then, as her hands worked their magic on him, the litany changed, and the words his mind sang were *Don't stop. Don't. Please. Whatever you do, don't stop.*

Gracie didn't. Her fingers kneaded the nape of his neck, smoothing the lotion up to his hairline, then worked their way back down across his shoulders, the backs of his arms, then joined again on either side of his spine and began to slide downward. And downward.

Cameron came alive under her touch. He counted the vertebrae as her fingers slid, knew the exact moment when she had reached that incredibly sensitive spot where the waistband of his jeans brushed the small of his back. He sucked in his breath.

Her hands slowed, stilled.

More, his mind begged her. *Farther.*

They edged another centimeter, then stopped, hovered.

He quivered.

She hesitated.

He felt her fingers tremble, imagined her leaning toward him, her breath warm upon him, her lips descending...

A cold wet tongue slathered up his back.

"Geez!" He jerked bolt upright.

"Alice!" Gracie admonished. "Bad dog!"

Cameron rolled over, flopping onto his back, glaring into the warm loving eager eyes of Alice the mastiff. She grinned. He flung a hand over his eyes. His heart was racing, his loins were aching. "Bad doesn't begin to cover it," he muttered.

Alice lapped at his face.

Cameron swore.

Gracie giggled and continued tugging Alice away from him.

"You think it's funny, do you?" he growled at her.

"It does have a certain amusing side to it." She was laughing openly now.

Cameron scowled at her.

Gracie tried to stifle her giggles unsuccessfully. "Want me to try again?"

She held out the tube as an offering. But before she could do more than that, the door downstairs banged; Kip shouted, "I'm home," and the telephone rang.

Cameron and Gracie looked at each other.

Alice butted Gracie's arm with her nose, asking for a pat on the head.

Kip's feet thundered upstairs. "Hey, Dad, Gracie, where are you?"

The phone rang again.

Cameron sighed and looked ruefully at Gracie. "I don't think so."

Chapter Nine

He had to go back to Boston. That was the gist of the phone call.

Just a couple of days, Roger said. Three at most. To iron out the merger Cameron had set in motion last time.

It wasn't unreasonable. It was just damned hard.

Last time he'd gone to Boston to escape. He'd fled as if all the devils in hell were after him—or at least one blond temptress named Gracie Talbot.

Now she was the reason he wanted to stay.

It wasn't sexual, he told himself. Not entirely at least. Though he certainly couldn't deny that there was a strong sexual attraction between them.

There was, however, more to it than that.

He wasn't sure what changed things. The kiss, of course, had precipitated it. But without Gracie's determination to follow through, to wait patiently until he was ready to explain, without her steadfastness, the kiss would have accomplished nothing. Or at least nothing worth waiting for.

Whatever it was, it wouldn't last, he told himself.

But then, he didn't expect it to. Gracie hadn't offered him "till death do us part." He hadn't asked for it.

They were going to, as she'd suggested, become friends. And if they didn't contain the relationship that way, they were still going to contain it within the context of one month's time.

In that way it would be like the summer when he was ten. A magical time. An interlude. At the end she would go her way and he would go his.

Which was fine, he told himself, as long as you knew it beforehand. It was asking for more that got you into trouble.

But having only a month, he didn't want to waste any time. So he didn't want to go to Boston.

"You could come with me," he said to Gracie as he packed.

She shook her head. "I have rehearsals."

He gritted his teeth, closing his eyes for a long moment, reminding himself again. Then he nodded. "Of course."

Really it was better she hadn't come, he told himself as he headed for the airport. It confined Gracie to one time and one place. It limited her effect on his life.

All the same, he wanted as much as he could reasonably get. And in Boston he couldn't get her out of his mind.

If Roger and Julie had thought he was distracted the first time he'd come, it was nothing compared to this. Roger had to repeat things three and four times. And Julia got so many monosyllabic answers out of him that she thought he was ill.

"Not ill," Roger diagnosed, "just eager to get back. We shouldn't have dragged you away again," he said to Cameron. "You didn't seem to think the vacation was going to work out last time you were here. Things have changed, I take it?"

"Things have changed," Cameron agreed.

So much so that he called Gracie three times a day. "Checking on Kip," he told her.

"Kip's fine," she told him, knowing full well what he was up to. "'Bye."

"Not so fast," Cameron protested.

"Yes?" Gracie said with the sultry note in her voice that made the hairs on the back of his neck stand at attention.

He cleared his throat. "How are you?"

"I'm fine, too. 'Bye."

"Gracie!"

"And so is Alice. And Boris."

"To hell with Boris. What's new?"

"We bought a waffle iron."

"You what?"

"Bought a waffle iron. It's what we had for dinner tonight. Waffles."

"I haven't had waffles in years."

"When you come home, I'll make you some."

"Promise?"

"Yes, I promise. And your secretary phoned."

"What? Why?"

"Don't know. I'm just the hired help. You're supposed to call when you get back."

"You're a damned sight more than the hired help," Cameron said gruffly.

"Oh, yes?" The sultry tone was there again.

"Yes." The word hissed through his teeth.

"When are you coming back?"

Right now, he wanted to say. "Tomorrow, as early as I can manage it."

He heard her sigh. "Good."

He smiled. "Good?"

"Good."

That one word—that affirmation—got him through the rest of the day, through the complicated legal terminology of the merger, through a long but necessary conversation with Roger and Roger's father about the future of the company, and through a virtually sleepless night during which he tormented himself by remembering every stroke of her hands as she had coated his back with that wholly unnecessary sunscreen and through a marvelously frustrating fantasy in which he returned the favor and brought it to a most satisfactory completion.

He practically dashed out of Roger's offices the next afternoon as early as he could get away. He was grateful that it was Sunday and it was only Roger he had to deal with and not a whole staff. The taxi to Logan made good time, and the small commuter plane took off ten minutes late. All the same, it seemed to Cameron as if the world were moving in slow motion.

Once he hopped into the Trooper and shot out of the parking lot, capable of controlling its speed himself, things got a lot better. There was a matinee of the current play at the theater this afternoon, which meant that Gracie wouldn't be there rehearsing. And though it was a slightly gloomy overcast afternoon, he expected to find Gracie and Kip at the beach or by the pool. They were nowhere to be seen.

He prowled the downstairs, then the upstairs, becoming concerned. The house was open, as if they were there. But they weren't. And not only where they missing, but so was Alice. He called out their names softly, then louder.

It was then that he heard the scuffling sounds overhead.

Scowling, Cameron went to the attic door and discovered it wasn't locked anymore. He tugged it open and put his head in, calling up the stairs. "Gracie? Kip?"

"Cameron!" That was Gracie.

"Rrroof." Three guesses who that was.

"Dad, you gotta see this!" And Kip's head appeared at the top of the stairs wearing an old World War I helmet, his eyes shining, his nose smudged with dust, a fox fur complete with beady glass eyes wrapped round his shoulders. "C'm'ere. Look!"

Cameron climbed the stairs quickly, astonished at the sight before him. The attic was jammed full of trunks and boxes, hanging wardrobes and rocking chairs, old chests of drawers and oak framed, beveled glass mirrors. But not just any trunks, boxes, wardrobes and furniture—the pure and undiluted stuff of his childhood. His grandfather's rocking chair, his grandmother's fox! Everything he remembered that he'd thought was missing. And amidst it all were Kip, Alice and Gracie.

He stared, eyes wide, jaw sagging.

Gracie smiled up at him, a broad-brimmed straw hat piled high with fruit perched rakishly on her fair hair. "Welcome home."

"Yeah." Cameron barely managed a croak. His fingers went to the fox's fur, touching it tentatively, remembering—reliving—the feel of the soft but bristly fur beneath his hand. But his hand moved independently of the rest of him. He had eyes, thoughts and emotions only for Gracie.

"Isn't it great, Dad? Can you believe all this stuff?"

Cameron, starting to smile, said, "Yes, I can. I remember my grandmother wearing that." He tugged at the fox's pointed nose. "And that," he added, nodding at Gracie's fruit basket hat. "Holy cow," he murmured. "So this is where it all went."

He sank down on his haunches and surveyed the scene before him, shaking his head slowly, remembering the bare floors down below, remembering when they had been covered with all the things he saw before him now. There was the hat rack that had stood in the entry hall, and there was the rocking horse that had been his mother's and grandfather's before it had been his. Under the eaves was the huge walnut armoire that he used to shut himself in when he and the Poop Deck boys, Bobby and Chris, used to play hide-and-seek on rainy days inside.

"Wow," he muttered. "Oh, wow." He sounded just like Kip and he knew it. He didn't care.

"Didja ever see such great stuff?" Kip demanded.

Cameron just shook his head. "How'd you get up here?"

"Kip found the key," Gracie told him. "This morning. I was changing the sheets and he was helping me. And he got to exploring the snake bed. Did you know that one of those snakes can open its mouth?"

Cameron stared at her.

"Well, it can. It's a secret compartment. Kip discovered it, and in it he found the key."

"That wasn't all, either!" Kip said. "I found a feather, too. A black one from Boris. An' a moonstone. And some whatchamacallits. What'd you call 'em, Gracie?" He looked at her for the answer.

"Condoms," Gracie said.

Cameron choked.

Gracie gave a little shrug. "You said you never lied to him."

"She didn't tell me what they were for though," Kip went on conversationally. "She said you'd do that." He looked at his father, wide blue eyes curious.

"Right," Cameron said, strangling. His eyes were boring into Gracie's, trying to guess how she'd reacted. She seemed perfectly matter-of-fact about it now.

"So, what are they for?" Kip wanted to know.

Cameron opened his mouth and no sound came out. He looked from his inquisitive, bouncing ten-year-old to the smiling woman sitting on the trunk with that absurd basket of fruit on her head, both of them waiting for him to answer.

"I'll tell you later, okay?" he said.

Kip shrugged. "Okay." He grabbed his father's hand. "Come look what else I found," he demanded, and willingly Cameron went.

"Saved," he muttered.

"Postponed," Gracie whispered just loud enough for him to hear. And when he turned to look at her she winked at him.

Cameron grinned ruefully. "I fear you may be right."

"Dad!" Kip implored.

And so Cameron gave his attention over to his son, squatting beside him, carefully lifting out pieces of his past, of his heritage, of the history he'd thought was lost to both of them that once again was found.

Gracie watched the two of them and found herself strangely moved, almost misty-eyed.

It had to do in part, of course, with Cameron's being back. The moment she'd heard his voice calling them, it was as if the sun had come out, as if Santa Claus had come, as if her father's choir of heavenly angels were heard from on high.

But it was more than that as well. It was the look in his eyes when he saw the attic—the boxes and trunks, the mangy fox still hanging around Kip's neck and the crazy pile of fruit on her head. It was his flicker of embarrassment about having to explain the condoms, and then the unspoken acceptance that the responsibility to do so was his.

When Kip had asked, she'd been tempted to tell him they were water balloons. Anything but the truth. But then she remembered Cameron, remembered the first night when he had impressed her with his love for his son, with his statement that he didn't lie to him.

She knew then that a flippant, phony answer wouldn't do. She also knew that the responsibility wasn't hers. If she'd been Kip's mother, yes, she would have done it then. But . . . she wasn't.

The sudden overwhelming desire to *be* his mother that had smitten her at that moment nearly knocked her socks off.

There was something about Cameron McClellan and his son that inspired an incredible variety of intense feelings in her, feelings she'd never known to the depth that she experienced them here. She felt tenderness and passion, need and desire, an urge to laugh and an urge to cry, and, just now, watching them together, their dark heads bent over an old electric train set, she got a lump as big as a moonstone in her throat.

She leaned one elbow on her good knee and rested her chin in her palm. The hat tipped, the banana teetered and fell onto her feet. The sound made Cameron look over at her, and his eyes were shining exactly the way Kip's had been shining since they'd slipped the key into the lock two hours before.

He reached out and scooped up the banana, handing it to her gravely.

"Your banana, madam."

Gracie accepted it, giggling. "D'you suppose I could glue it back on?"

Cameron shook his head. He got to his knees and moved over to face her. "I don't think so. I think that hat has just about had it."

"I think it's wonderful. I wonder who wore it. I wonder *where* she wore it."

"Oh, I can tell you that. It belonged to my grandmother. She wore it to church on Easter, if you can believe."

"The original Easter bonnet, you mean?"

Cameron grinned. "Irving Berlin probably wrote it for her. There were pictures of her in it when she was young and gay." He surveyed the jumbled expanse on the floor beside him. "I bet they're even here somewhere. I could probably find them if I tried." He sighed and raked a hand through his hair. "Cripes, this is unbelievable. I thought all this was lost, too."

"Like the furniture was, you mean?"

He nodded. "But even the furniture is here. The stuff I remember anyway. I wonder what they took."

"I don't know," Gracie said, "and I don't care. I like the stuff we bought."

Cameron looked at her. "Me, too," he said, his voice soft, the way it had been when he'd called her on the phone from Boston, the way he spoke when he made her toes curl.

Gracie swallowed hard. "Y-you ought to see what else we found," she said.

For a moment she didn't know if Cameron was going to allow himself to be distracted or not. But then, when Kip skipped over several boxes, an old World War I gas mask in his hands, Cameron gave in.

"Show me," he said. He looked over the gas mask with Kip, then directed the boy's attention to an old toy box he said he remembered from when he was a child. Kip dove for it as Gracie got up and hobbled over to open the armoire.

"Voilá," she said and flung the door back to show him old ball gowns, suits with padded shoulders, and slinky flapper dresses, all of which were so far out they were in again. She slipped one off the hanger, a sequined peach-colored number that had a matching feather boa. She held the dress up in front of her and looped the boa around her neck, then waggled the end of it under Cameron's nose. "Aren't they gorgeous?"

Cameron was smiling. "You're gorgeous."

Gracie blushed and tickled his nose with the boa, making him sneeze. "I'll bet you say that to all the girls."

He reached for the boa and tugged it, hauling Gracie into his arms. He bent his head and nuzzled her neck, making her squirm. Then he whispered in her ear, "You'd lose."

"Hey, Dad, look. I found some—" Kip, who had been rooting through the toy box with the enthusiasm of a child at Christmas, turned his head at that point. His mouth dropped open and he stared. "Dad?" His voice was hollow, disbelieving, his eyes like saucers.

Cameron lifted his head and took one step back, slowly and deliberately. He turned and cocked an eyebrow. "Yes?"

Kip was grinning all over his face. "Nothin'. Never mind." He turned and ducked back into the toy box again. "Don't mind me. Just go right ahead."

Cameron looked at Gracie, a slight smile playing about the corners of his mouth. "Shall I?" he asked softly.

"Not here, for heaven's sake!" Gracie muttered, mortified. She pulled the feather boa off hastily and wrapped it back around the hanger, then stuffed the garment back into the closet. While she was doing so, something suspiciously like a pair of lips brushed the back of her neck. If her leg had been well she'd have jumped a foot. As it was she managed a creditable four inches.

"I've been wanting to do that since I walked up the stairs." Cameron grinned, wholly unrepentant. "Actually since I saw you asleep in that bed the first day."

Gracie felt her blush deepening. This was a Cameron she'd fantasized about. She gave him a curious look.

"What's got into you?" she mumbled, trying to keep her voice down so Kip wouldn't hear.

"I'm frustrated," Cameron whispered back. "Or can't you tell?"

It would have taken a dead person not to, Gracie thought. But Cameron had been frustrated before.

"I thought we were friends," she said, confused, wanting him to spell things out.

"Oh, yes. Indeed we are," Cameron agreed, and he gave her a Cheshire Cat's grin, his blue eyes hungry and compelling.

Gracie's heart flip-flopped in her chest.

"Dad, Gracie, look. It's magic!"

It certainly was, Gracie thought. But that, as she soon discovered, wasn't what Kip meant.

He had reached the bottom of the toy chest and was just now drawing out a large, flat wooden box. On it in faded and scratched, elaborate but obviously home-drawn red letters, Gracie read, *Dr. Wizard's Wonderful World of Magic*.

"Holy Moses," Cameron breathed, and Gracie didn't have to attempt to distract him anymore. He had eyes only for the box in Kip's hands. He strode across to his son, saying, "Let me see that."

Kip handed it to him. Cameron held the box gingerly, his head bent, his thumbs stroking the top of the box with something approaching reverence. "I can't believe it."

"What is it?" Gracie and Kip both wanted to know.

Cameron smiled at them. "This was my absolutely most favorite present in the whole world. My dad made it and gave it to me on my birthday one year." He knelt down and lay the box gently on top of the nearest trunk. Then carefully, gravely almost, he lifted the lid.

It looked to Gracie like the strangest collection of bits of metal, scarves, cards, long sticks, little pieces of wood and other flotsam and jetsam that she'd ever seen in her life.

"Are they tricks, Dad? Could you do tricks?"

Cameron didn't answer at once. He was running his fingers experimentally over the metal rings, jingling them lightly, then picking up the deck of cards and riffling them in his fingers, at first tentatively, then with more confidence.

"Dad!" Kip persisted.

"What?" Cameron shook his head as if to clear it, as if he were coming back from a very long way away.

"Can you do magic?"

The cards riffled once more slowly, then faster. Cameron looked from the boy down to the cards in his hands and Gracie saw the same curiosity on his face that she saw on his son's. A slow smile lit his face.

"Let's find out, shall we?" Cameron shuffled the cards now, slowly and deliberately, then shuffled them again, his hands big and quick and deft, the fingers square-tipped and strong. Gracie didn't care about the cards, only his hands. But then he dealt out three rows, discarded the rest of the deck, and said to Kip, "Pick one. Don't tell me which."

Kip scanned the cards, then nodded.

"Got one?"

"Yep."

"Which row is it in?"

"The left."

Cameron picked up the cards and repeated the process. "Now which row?"

"The right."

Again Cameron laid them out. "And now?"

"The left again."

Cameron nodded and picked up all the cards, then tossed them face down haphazardly one by one onto the top of the trunk until there were none left in his hands. He scanned the backs of the cards, his hand moving over them slowly, cautiously.

"What're you doing?" Kip asked.

"Feeling for vibrations."

"Dad!"

But just then Cameron's hand swooped, snatched a card and flipped it over. "Your card. The three of clubs."

Kip's eyes bugged. "How'd you do that?"

Cameron grinned and spread his hands. "Magic."

"Dad!"

"Watch. I'll do it again." He took the whole deck, reshuffled and began all over again. He took his time, now, telling Kip to pay attention, to tell him everything he did as he did it, to see if he could pick out the pattern.

Gracie sat, chin resting on her palm, watching the two of them, fascinated, not so much by the "magic" of the card trick as by the magic in the relationship between father and son. It made her smile, made the lump come back to her throat.

"Do you know how he's doin' it, Gracie?" Kip demanded after he'd been shown the card he'd picked a second time and a third.

Gracie shook her head. "Not a clue."

"Will you teach me?" Kip asked his father.

"Of course."

"Now?"

Cameron shrugged. "Why not?"

"Will you teach me all the tricks?"

"Not today."

"But sometime?"

Cameron reached out and ruffled Kip's hair. "Absolutely."

Kip grinned. "Great. C'mon, show me how the card trick works now, 'kay?"

"Okay."

Gracie left them to it. Kip would need someone to try it out on who didn't know the trick. And anyway, it was time for father and son to be together, just the two of them. She stood up slowly. "I think I'll go put together some supper."

"Want some help?" Cameron paused in the middle of his explanation to Kip.

"No, I'll be fine. But I'll want a magic show after," she told them both. "All right?"

Kip beamed and gave her a thumb's-up sign. "A-a-all right."

THE ATTIC WAS DARK but for the spill of moonlight through the dormers. The only sound was the soft rush of the sea. Cameron sat on the floor, his back against the armoire, his knees bent, his forearms resting on his thighs as his fingers idly smoothed the moonstone in his hand.

Once he had found a moonstone. He and his dad had gone up to Rhode Island. It had been at the end of his last summer at Gull Cottage, during the last two weeks, the time he'd most been looking forward to—the time when his dad would be free to come down for the whole two weeks.

Only this time, Laurence hadn't wanted to stay. Instead he'd taken Cameron off on "a jaunt," as he called it, to Rhode Island. Cameron had gone, mystified but willing, always eager to spend time with his dad. He'd had such high hopes for the time they'd spend together—just the two of them. Instead Laurence had been awkward with him, distant. And then he'd explained that he and Cameron's mother were getting a divorce.

Cameron had tuned him out, had deliberately ignored him, as if pretending he hadn't heard would make reality go away. Instead he'd made an enormous production out of shell and rock hunting. The moonstone had been his prize. Every night after he found it, he told himself that if he just kept rubbing the moonstone, none of the things his father said would come true. He took it everywhere with him—to the beach, to meals, to bed.

And then, on the trip home from Rhode Island, somehow he lost it.

Fitting, actually. He'd lost his father then, as well.

He sighed and leaned his head back, closing his eyes, soaking up the past that surrounded him, sorting through it, marveling at the way it colored the present, touching Kip now as well as himself.

Until supper he and Kip had worked through the magic tricks, him explaining, demonstrating, and Kip oohing and ahhing, then trying and, to some extent succeeding in duplicating them. After supper Kip had shown Gracie what he'd learned. Cameron had demonstrated a couple of tricks that he'd remembered but which he'd not had time to teach Kip yet. Then he and the boy had come back up to the attic to explore until bedtime.

It hadn't been easy to get Kip to bed. He remembered about the condoms for one thing. And Cameron had had to pick his way through a minefield of questions about those.

Then, abruptly Kip had had enough of that and started in on the magic tricks again, wanting to go back and see what else they could find. Only the promise that he could come back up first thing in the morning had assuaged his unhappiness. He wanted to see it all. Right now.

Cameron could understand that, though he didn't know if he felt that way himself. He wasn't sure yet exactly how he felt. Stunned. Amazed. Yes, both of them. It was so unexpected, as if the door to the past had just been flung open and he was invited in.

Seeing the attic, filled as it was with relics and remembrances of his past, had been in equal parts daunting and exciting to him. What it all meant, as yet he didn't know.

"You wanted nostalgia," he'd reminded himself as he settled down on the floor and opened one of the trunks. And, of course, he had. But the sheer overwhelming quantity of it was a little hard to take in.

Confronting him in the first trunk was a stack of photograph albums. He'd picked up first one, then another. Past and present ran together. Memories piled one on top of the other, until he couldn't sort through them anymore.

His parents. His grandparents. Great-grandparents he'd never even known. Weddings. Baptisms. School pictures. Silly pictures of himself and his father larking about on the beach, more silly ones he'd never seen before of Tony and Emmy burying each other in the sand. Sailing trips. Fancy balls. Christmases, birthdays and Thanksgivings long past. Opening nights on Broadway. College graduation pictures. His own wedding pictures. Dana and himself, laughing, smiling. Dana, pregnant. Himself, dazed, holding a squalling infant. Kip. The infant Kip. The toddler Kip.

Cameron paged through them, one after another all the way from first to last. Beginning to end. Pausing to stare, to feel, to remember. The joy, the sorrow. The hope, the pain.

The present ceased to exist. He was lost in a swirl of memories. Of ifs and onlys and might have beens. Of promises kept and more that had been long forgotten.

His muscles cramped. His legs felt stiff. Finally he got up and went down to shut off the light. But however late it was, he couldn't go to sleep yet and he couldn't just walk out and talk about it as if it were simply something that he and Gracie could make small talk about.

Gracie, he realized, seemed to understand that. She hadn't demanded his attention after Kip's and his impromptu magic show. She had, in fact, disappeared, leaving him to get Kip off to bed by himself. And afterward, when he had gone back up to the attic, she hadn't joined him there.

He shut off the light and climbed back up the stairs in the dark, sitting down and laying his head back against the armoire, the moonstone in his hand.

He didn't know how long he'd been there, hadn't the faintest notion what time it was when he first heard the creak of the door opening and then, footfalls on the stairs.

Gracie appeared, silhouetted at the top wearing a long robe. He was surprised she hadn't turned the light on. But she hadn't, and she didn't say anything about turning it on now.

She said his name quietly. "Cameron?"

"Here."

It was too dark to see him, but his voice must've been enough to clue her to his whereabouts for she carefully picked her way through the piles and heaps of McClellan memorabilia until she was beside him. Then she sat down.

The moonlight cast her in silver, spun white gold out of her hair. She eased her legs under her, taking care of the knee she no longer had braced. Her toes slipped out of sight beneath the folds of her robe. Then, settled, she reached out and laid a hand on his knee.

For a long moment they just sat like that. Companionable. Silent. Her hand on his knee making it the warmest part of his body. Cameron shifted slightly.

"I loved the magic," she told him, her voice barely louder than the rush of the waves.

He smiled crookedly. "Yeah. Me, too."

"So did Kip."

"Yeah."

"He loved all this." Her head turned and Cameron knew she meant the whole attic, what was in it, what it meant.

"Yeah," he said again.

"Do you?"

He looked at her knowing her eyes were on his face, wondering what they saw, wondering what he was showing. His fingers worried the moonstone. With his other hand he sought Gracie's, wrapping it firmly as it lay against his knee.

"Love it, you mean?" he asked at last.

She nodded.

"I don't know. I need it, I guess," he said softly, realizing only as he spoke that it was true. "The perspective it gives. To come to terms. To remember."

"Are they good memories?"

He sighed and closed his eyes. "Some of them."

Outside far off he heard a motorcycle cut away, the waves beat relentlessly against the shore.

"It's what you came back for."

He sighed. "I don't know for sure what I came back for. I had the best summer of my life here when I was ten. Kip is ten. I thought . . . hell, I don't know what I thought. Maybe it was just a stab at giving him that. I don't seem to have been able to give him much else."

"Not true." Gracie's hand squeezed his gently. "You've given him a great deal. I don't know anybody who ever had a better father, even me. And mine was great."

Cameron gave her a faint smile. "A father's not much."

"It's a very great deal indeed."

It was, but he didn't want to admit it. He ducked his head. "Thank you for saying so."

"It's true," Gracie maintained.

Cameron made a small sound of doubt that Gracie interpreted correctly. She leaned forward and brushed her lips against his cheek. "Very true," she whispered as her lips slid past his ear. He shivered.

Slowly, carefully, Gracie began to get to her feet. Seeing her struggle, knowing it must be hard with her leg still weak, Cameron helped her and in doing so, came to stand beside her.

Wordlessly they stared at each other. Cameron felt a need, a quickening, and didn't know how it had happened to him; it had been so far from his mind all evening. Now it seemed all that he wanted, all that he needed. And the how, he discovered, didn't matter, only that it had.

"Grace?" he whispered.

Wide, dark eyes lifted to meet his in the moonlight. Trusting eyes. Loving eyes.

He swallowed. They were so close he could feel the soft whisper of her breath against his neck, could smell the citrus scent of her shampoo. He drew a breath. She touched his hand. And then she turned, moving toward the door, and the moonlight shimmered in her hair as she went.

She led him down the stairs and along the hallway, pausing by his doorway to look at him. Cameron knew what she was asking. He shook his head.

His narrow cold bed held no appeal for him tonight. Not now. Not alone. Not even with her. He wanted the luxury of space, of comfort, of fantasy. He nodded toward her room and she led him there.

Alice, asleep on the foot of the bed, looked up and made a whuffling sound as they came in. Cameron looked at Gracie. She smiled and shrugged.

"Up and at 'em, Alice, old girl. Time to move out," he said softly.

Alice gave him a baleful stare and put her head back down between her paws.

Cameron looked at Gracie. *She's your dog,* his gaze told her.

Gracie sighed. "C'mon, Ally. There's a girl." She tugged the dog by her collar and managed after a moment to half lug, half shove Alice off the bed. Once she had the dog on the floor though, she could do no more. Cameron knew her leg wouldn't permit wrestling a hundredweight of dog anywhere. And Alice didn't budge, but stood instead staring up accusingly at her mistress.

Gracie looked sternly at Alice and pointed to the door. Alice's gaze didn't even flicker.

"Oh, dear." Gracie murmured. She looked at Cameron and shrugged helplessly.

Cameron, remembering the last time he slept in Gracie's bed and who all had shared it with them, was determined not to let it happen again. He took a firm hold on Alice's collar and hauled her to the door.

Alice dragged her feet, making a low negative sound far back in her throat. Cameron pulled harder.

"Let's go, Alice," he said in the tone he used on Kip when he wasn't brooking any nonsense. "Come on."

Alice looked over her shoulder at Gracie, obviously expecting help from that quarter, but Gracie sat on the bed, smiling, and shaking her head. Alice looked at her, betrayed.

Cameron gave another tug. Alice gave another low protesting moan.

"She'll fuss," Gracie told him. "Even if you get her outside the room, or even outside the house, she'll just sit there and fuss."

"Howl, you mean?"

Gracie sighed. "More or less."

"So what do you suggest?" he asked irritably.

"Let her stay?"

"Let her stay?" Cameron was incredulous. "No way."

Gracie giggled. "Not an exhibitionist, are you?"

He grinned sheepishly, but there was no way he was sharing this. "Guess not."

"We could go down to your bed," Gracie suggested after a moment. "But she might just come along, now you've woken her."

"Great." Cameron's fingers loosened slightly on the collar. Alice turned her head, ever hopeful of a change of heart. She licked his hand. The hairs on the back of Cameron's neck stood up.

Gracie shrugged. "She just likes company. She wants a bed partner."

"So do I," Cameron said dryly.

"What about Kip?"

"What!"

"For Alice, not for you," Gracie said, laughing. "I think that'll work. Here." She eased herself off the bed and took Alice's collar. "Come on, Alice. Let's go see Kip, Alice. Want to see Kip?"

The sound of the boy's name set Alice to immediately wagging her stubby tail.

"C'mon, Ally. Atta girl," Gracie urged. And with Alice's full cooperation, she led the dog from the room. Cameron, amazed, followed after them down the hall. Alice marched right into Kip's room, plopped herself on the foot of his bed, prodded the boy to move him slightly so she wouldn't

fall off. Then she laid her head on her paws and looked at
Cameron and Gracie, yawned and shut her eyes.

Cameron just shook his head.

Then Gracie turned to him, looked up into his eyes and
slid her arms around his waist. "Where were we?"

His heart tripped over and his arms tightened for a second. Then he scooped her up in them and bent to kiss her
lips. "I think if I try, I might just be able to remember."

Chapter Ten

He hadn't forgotten a thing.

He set her gently on the bed, then, button by tiny button, he undid her robe until it fell away, and he slid it off her shoulders to expose the thin cotton gown she wore. He smiled, and Gracie marveled how even the faintest moonlight could still pick up the tender hunger in his eyes.

This was indeed the Cameron she had fantasized about, dreamed about. This was the Cameron she had seen beneath the gruff exterior, the biting tone, the rigid countenance. This was the Cameron she had glimpsed with Kip, with Alice, with his friends in Boston. This was that Cameron—and more.

For she had never seen Cameron look at anyone else with the need in his eyes that she saw there now. She had never seen him touch anyone with the reverence that his fingers demonstrated as they trailed now across the neckline of her gown and brushed lightly across her breasts.

She trembled under his touch. She reveled in it, desired it, unconsciously sought more, inching toward him, resting her hands on the front of his shirt. Its top three buttons were already undone. He'd undone them himself shortly after he'd arrived, rolling up his sleeves and discarding his tie before he had dug into the attic. Now through the thin cotton, she could feel the warmth of his chest, the soft springiness of the dark hair curling there, the steady rapid thudding of his heart. She slid the fourth button free. And the fifth.

Cameron closed his eyes. The soft whisper of Gracie's breath against his chest made him swallow, the warm weight of her hands made him ache. It was like a dream, only when his eyes opened, she was still there smiling at him. And seeing her, he could only smile back.

He didn't think beyond the moment, wouldn't let himself. What would happen after was something best left unprobed.

He'd lived his life planning everything, and look what it had got him. Success, yes. But happiness? No, not really. Not beyond the happiness he had with Kip at least.

Happiness, he decided, was ephemeral. Transitory. Fleetingly tantalizing. Something to grasp briefly but never to hold on to. And so he wouldn't ask for more than the moment's happiness. That would be enough.

He would have the memories, though, no matter what.

Looking through the pictures tonight, he realized that was all he could ever be sure of, all he could ever expect. Memories.

Little enough, to be sure.

But without them, his days would be even lonelier. And Cameron had had enough loneliness to last him a lifetime.

Gracie offered him— Well, he wasn't quite sure what it was that Gracie offered. But whatever it was, he knew he wanted it.

He had tried to fight it and that hadn't worked. It was against his nature, against everything in him. He couldn't fight it anymore, didn't want to. And so he stopped fighting, stopped running. As long as he knew the boundaries, as long as he curbed his expectations, it would be all right. He would accept.

He would take what he was given. And he would give in return.

There was a fine tremor in Cameron's fingers as he plucked at the wide neckline of her gown and drew it open, then slid it down over her arms and over her hips until it pooled in the moonlight at her feet.

Gracie shivered under the intensity of his gaze. And yet she didn't know the self-consciousness that she had feared she might. That was because she knew she had nothing to fear. Not from Cameron.

Her life had been spent up until this moment in a state of perpetual dithering. Was this right? Was that? Should she be here? Or there? Acting? Teaching? In New York? In Akron? In Cincinnati? In East Hampton? Was this man the right one? Or was that one? What about the millions she hadn't met yet? What if he was still out there?

Never before had the answer been clear.

She knew he wasn't out there any longer. He was here. Tonight her life—her purpose—was like crystal, pure and transparent, flawlessly clear. Tonight her doubts and her dithering were gone. Whatever she was supposed to do, whoever she was supposed to become, a part of it, she was convinced, would be realized through this night with Cameron.

She finished unbuttoning his shirt, then drew it apart and laid her hands against the solid wall of his chest. Her fingers curved into hair-roughened skin and she kneaded the firm flesh as if she were a cat. The soft, low sound that came from the back of Cameron's throat sounded remarkably like a lion's purr.

She smiled up at him. "Like that?"

"Mmmm." He arched his back, shrugging off the shirt and letting it fall to the floor. Then his hands went to his belt.

"May I?" Gracie whispered.

Cameron swallowed, but his hands dropped to his sides, permitting her to loosen the buckle.

She paused, wondering how bold she dared be, knowing she'd never been this bold before in her life, expecting any moment that Cameron would take over. But apparently he had taken her request seriously for he made no further

moves. Just waited, though his fists clenched and unclenched at his sides.

Gracie's fingers moved to the fastener of Cameron's
slacks, easing it open, then unzipping them. Her hand
brushed the warm firm flesh of his belly, and at the contact
she felt a faint tremor go through him. He moved then, and
his slacks slid down to join her nightgown on the floor.

Then he joined her in the bed and wrapped her in his
arms. Grace held him, too, her fingers sliding down the
length of his back, learning his muscles, his sinews, his very
bones.

It was, she thought, the warmest, most secure, most
wonderful feeling she'd ever known. Like coming home. It
was what she had always known she was waiting for.

She said so, and felt Cameron smile against her cheek.

"Wait longer," he whispered, nuzzling her. "It gets better."

"Can't."

"Wanna bet?"

"Mmm-hmm." It couldn't, she thought.

But Cameron was right.

It did.

A PART OF CAMERON could not believe he'd done it. A part
of him fully expected him to wake up in his narrow bed,
frustrated and with only the fleeting memory of a dream.

Instead he awoke at half past five with Gracie Talbot snug
in his arms. He had one bare leg thrown over her thigh, one
knee nudged up against her bottom. A soft cloud of golden
hair tickled his nose. He sighed and almost shut his eyes
again, then blinked them open determinedly. He wasn't
about to go back to sleep. This was better than any dream.

With his hand he stroked from her shoulder down to her
arm, then touched his lips to the nape of her neck. He let
them linger a long moment, then sighed again and reluctantly pulled away. He eased his body away from hers, too,
and sat up.

Gracie frowned in her sleep, groping as if to find the warmth that had left when he'd pulled away. Cameron tucked the blanket around her and smiled ruefully when she snuggled into it at peace again and relaxed.

He wanted to lie back down with her, to partake again of the warmth, the caring, the passion that they had shared. Nothing in him wanted to get up and pad down the hall to his own bleak bedroom. Nothing but his sense of responsibility to Kip.

He didn't know exactly what Kip would think if he got up in the morning and found his father in Gracie's bed, but Cameron was sure Kip wouldn't understand what he saw. He was sure that Kip would expect things to last, was sure that Kip would never be able to look at August 31 and know that the world would be different after that.

Kip was a child. He didn't have to know. But Cameron knew. And he wasn't a fool. He wasn't going to raise Kip's hopes—or his own—where there were none.

He swung his legs off the bed and dropped to the floor, picked up his clothes and padded quietly down the hall. He would take his memories and his cold bed and settle for that.

GRACIE WASN'T SURPRISED to awaken in the morning and find Cameron gone. Disappointed, yes. She readily admitted that. But it was in character.

She would have been more surprised to have found him still there beside her when Kip and Alice came bounding in to find out if she wanted waffles as much as they did.

"Both of you want waffles?" Gracie drew the covers up to her chin and looked from one to the other of them—boy and dog with equally eager grins.

"Well, I do," Kip admitted. "But I betcha Alice'd eat some."

"Alice eats everything," Gracie reminded him. "What about . . . your dad?" She had to ask.

"He eats anything, too."

Gracie laughed. "I mean, is he up?"

"Yeah. He went for a swim. I saw him goin' down to the water when I got up."

When had he left her? Gracie wondered. And how did he feel? Was he happy or regretful about their night of loving? Did he wish it had never happened or was he glad it had?

She knew how she felt. She'd never been happier in her life. She wanted to sing and dance and spin like a top. It was only Kip's sturdy presence that kept her in bed and not pirouetting around the room.

"Waffles it is," she said to him, happy to make them for him, but even happier to have a chance to make them for Cameron because she had promised him, especially after the joy he had given her last night. "As soon as I get going. You go make your bed and get dressed and I'll be right down."

"Great! C'mon, Alice." He headed for the door, then stopped. "Hey, Gracie, guess what. Alice slept with me last night, not you."

"Really?"

"Yeah." He got clear to the door. "It must mean she really likes me."

"I'm sure she does."

He turned to look at her. "You didn't mind, did you? You weren't lonely?"

Gracie smiled. "Not in the least."

He grinned, a look of relief passing over his face. "Swell. Could she stay tonight, too?"

"I'm sure that would be fine."

Kip beamed. "Thanks, Gracie. You're the greatest. C'mon, Alice. Let's go make our bed."

GRACIE WAS JUST TAKING the first batch of waffles out of the iron when the kitchen door opened and Cameron came in. He wore only a pair of wet ragged cut-off jeans, his hair was plastered to his skull, and, to Gracie, he'd never looked more beautiful in his life. She cast her fears aside and smiled at him.

Cameron stopped halfway through the door. He looked surprised—no, jolted, actually—to see her there in her *Cats* T-shirt and chambray shorts, forking out waffles onto a plate. It was, Gracie thought, as if he'd forgotten about her.

She felt a momentary stab of panic. But then a warm, slow grin came to light his face. A grin such as one might see on a child on Christmas morning. A grin that warmed her heart, curled her toes and chased all her fears away.

"Waffles?" he asked, his voice almost tentative.

Gracie smiled. "What else?"

Cameron just stood there, nodding to himself. "What else?" he murmured, as if reminding himself. Then he looked at her, the grin back. "I'll grab a shower and be right down."

He started to go past her when Gracie said, "Aren't you forgetting something?"

He stopped, looked at her, baffled.

She turned and leaned toward him, touching her lips to his. "This."

Cameron looked as if steam might come from his ears. He reached for her, sandy hands, sopping jeans and all, but just then Kip and Alice came thundering down the stairs.

"Great! Are all those for me? Hi, Dad," Kip said all in one breath as he slid into a chair at the table and beamed up at Gracie.

"Those are for you," Gracie agreed and put the plate in front of him. She gave Cameron a rueful smile and held up the mixing bowl. "And these will be for you if you hurry."

"Tease," he muttered and Gracie felt herself blushing. But then he grinned, stole a glance at Kip and seeing that he was wholly occupied with his waffles, stole a hard, quick kiss as he headed for the steps.

"Who's a tease?" Gracie said after him.

But Cameron didn't answer. He was taking the stairs two at a time.

By the time he got back down Gracie had finished making the waffles and was sitting at the table eating with Kip.

She had put Cameron's waffles in the oven to keep them warm, and when he reappeared, she jumped up to get them.

"I can do it," he said, but Gracie shook her head.

"Sit down," she told him. And when he did, she heaped them onto his plate and passed him the syrup and the butter, then sat back to watch him eat.

Kip chattered on about the baseball game he was going to play with Danny today, and about how first he wanted to spend time exploring the attic and practicing his magic. But neither Cameron nor Gracie seemed to hear or even to be aware of him at all. Their eyes were only for each other, their thoughts only for each other, their smiles for absolutely no one else.

It was far, far better than Gracie had ever hoped.

She completely forgot she had to get to rehearsal until there came the rattle on the kitchen door and Mrs. Pendennis bounced in.

"Are you ready, Gracie love?" she began, then spotting the newcomer at the breakfast table she burbled, "Cameron! Cameron, my dear!" She practically flung her arms around him.

Cameron stiffened under her embrace. His smile for Gracie vanished, and it took him a few moments to find another, forced this time, to paste in its place.

"Good to see you, Mrs. Poop Deck," he said to the older woman, but his face was shuttered. There was none of the joy that had been there just moments before.

Mrs. Pendennis cuffed him lightly on the shoulder. "Oh, you! Larry should never have started that. The admiral would like to kill him. What do you hear from the old reprobate?"

"Not a word."

"No?" Mrs. Pendennis looked amazed, then shrugged. "Well, I suppose he's far too busy to keep us abreast of his busy life."

"Undoubtedly." Cameron's voice was dry. But Gracie detected a brittleness in it, too. A hurt, she thought, and wondered why. But now, of all times, she could not ask.

"I have to run," she said to Cameron.

He nodded but he didn't look at her.

"I wish I could stay."

"Uh-huh." He had tucked his thumbs into the belt loops of his jeans. She thought he wasn't going to look at her, but finally he did. His expression, however, didn't reveal a thing. It was closed, remote almost. She touched his arm, but he didn't respond, and her fingers fell away.

"I'll just get my bag," she told Mrs. Pendennis hurriedly, "and be right with you."

"Can I come?" Kip asked.

"I don't think—" Gracie began.

"No." The word was hard, but Cameron must have realized how it sounded for he softened it almost at once. "I thought we were doing the attic this morning, Kip."

The boy's face cheered immediately. "Yeah. That's right. You should see how well my dad does magic," he told Mrs. Pendennis.

Mrs. Pendennis gave Cameron a look of wide-eyed amazement. "Magic?"

"Some old tricks," he muttered. "Used to do 'em when I was a kid."

"Larry did magic tricks, too. I remember one that—"

But Gracie could see that whatever Mrs. Pendennis was going to recall, Cameron didn't want to any part of it, so she said quickly, "I guess I don't need my bag after all. Perhaps we should just move along."

Mrs. Pendennis sighed. "Yes, I suppose perhaps we should." She turned to Cameron. "Lovely to see you again, dear. So glad you've come back to us."

Gracie looked at Cameron to see how he was taking that, but, as with everything else, it was impossible to tell.

She gave him an encouraging smile as she went to the door. "I'll be back by five."

He nodded wordlessly. But she noticed that he stood with his hand on the doorjamb, watching until the car was out of sight.

"YOU CALLED?" Cameron said to his secretary later that afternoon. He'd buried himself in the attic doing magic with Kip until well past noon, keeping busy, trying not to think about Gracie at rehearsal. He was even fairly successful at it. Mostly because Kip kept saying he was sure she wouldn't be late. She never was, Kip assured him. Other people went out after, but Gracie always brought him right home. He'd see, Cameron decided. In the meantime he remembered Jeannie's phone call and decided to return it.

"Friday," she agreed. "A lady said you were in Boston." The way she said *lady* told Cameron she wanted details the way a terrier wanted bones.

Another time he might have obliged her. His relationships, such as they were, had never been classified information. Perhaps, he thought now, because they'd never before been worth classifying.

But there was no way on earth he was going to satisfy Jeannie's curiosity about Gracie Talbot. He might only have a month with her, but however much he had, he wasn't sharing it.

He said, "Uh-huh," then waited for her to get on with it.

Jeannie, seeing, after thirty seconds of long-distance silence, that she was not going to be further enlightened, told him instead, "The real estate people want to know if you're interested in buying the house."

"What real estate people? What house?"

"The house you're in. Bird Cottage or whatever it's called."

"Gull," Cameron corrected. "Gull Cottage. *Buy* it? He's selling, you mean?" The full impact of her words hit suddenly, and he felt as if someone had socked him in the gut.

"Very confidential, the realtor said," Jeannie went on. "Not on the market yet. They're only testing the waters.

And since we had the month's lease, they thought they'd try us first.''

Cameron breathed a profanity, astonished.

"So what do you think? Are you even vaguely interested?''

Cameron didn't speak. He couldn't. The very thought of buying Gull Cottage poleaxed him.

He'd allowed himself a month here. A vacation from reality. A retreat, as it were. Like Cinderella at the ball he was winging on a flight of fancy. But that was all it was. He knew damned well—always had—that he was supposed to be back to work on September 1.

He'd never given a thought to a prince with a slipper. Or, in his case, a realtor with a cottage to sell. Correction: a *father* with a cottage to sell.

What in hell was going on with the old geezer? What was he up to now?

He stared around the sparsely furnished living room, liking what he saw, in part, of course, because he'd furnished it himself. Did he like it enough to consider moving here?

And if he did . . . ?

He hadn't thought about living at Gull Cottage in years. Not since he and Dana were first married. Not since his head had been filled with sugar plums and other starry-eyed notions that Dana had proceeded to prove to him had no grounding in reality at all. He chewed the inside of his cheek. He raked a hand through his hair. He rubbed the tense muscles at the back of his neck.

Buy Gull Cottage?

Give up San Francisco? Move Kip? Change schools?

Be less than two hundred miles from his old man. Heaven help him.

All those things preyed on him, but nothing more so than: did he dare commit himself to living in the house where he'd just made love to Gracie?

Gracie.

He'd promised himself a month's worth of memories. A hidden stash to tide him over when the going got rough, when the loneliness closed in. A treasure chest of the mind. His very own personal portable attic in which to store the beautiful moments of his life and which he could root through to sustain him in hard times.

In San Francisco, that would have been enough. By the time he was back there, this month with Gracie would have been long enough ago and far enough away.

But though time would pass if he moved to Gull Cottage, the place would remain. And Cameron would have to live with it—with her—or, rather, with memories of her for the rest of his days.

"I don't know, Jeannie," he said, his voice hollow. "I'd have to think about it."

"Well, go ahead and think. They're sure they can sell it. They just wanted to make the offer. I'm sure it's just a courtesy. Don't feel you have to."

"No. But . . ." He found that he couldn't say no, either, not right away. "I'll think. And Jeannie, see what else you can find out. Like why he's selling."

"Will do. I'll call you when I know anything else."

"Thanks."

"And, Cameron." Jeannie paused, then apparently decided to get in her two cents' worth anyway. "Your lady has a lovely voice."

HIS LADY. The words had a tempting ring to them. They lingered in Cameron's mind long after Jeannie had hung up. He liked the sound of them and wished they were true. That was no way to be thinking, he told himself and climbed up onto the roof and set about reshingling the area above the attic in a determined effort to ignore them. But they wouldn't go away.

It wasn't only the night he'd spent in her bed that made him weave fantasies as he sat and hammered away. Though he'd be the first to admit that last night had had an impact he'd never forget, there was more to it than that. There was everything that had gone before the night; and, if he was scrupulously honest, there was this morning, too. There were the waffles.

He felt a fool admitting it, even to himself, but he was being seduced by a plateful of waffles. Just the sight of them sitting on the table with a pat of melting butter, a dollop of maple syrup, had raised a lump in his throat. It was crazy. *He* was crazy. But it had really knocked him for a loop.

Gracie had promised, of course. But it had been a silly promise, one he hadn't really expected her to keep. Heaven knew he could count into the hundreds before he reached the number of promises made to him that had never been kept before.

But Gracie had kept hers, as small and insignificant as it was. And what's more, she'd sat and smiled at him and talked to him while he ate. As if he'd mattered.

Did he?

The thought almost knocked him off the roof. It scared the hell out of him. For one thing, it questioned the boundaries that he'd already determined. It implied a relationship.

And a relationship was something Cameron wasn't interested in.

Was he?

He whacked the hammer down hard, missing the roofing tack and nailing his thumb. The expletive could've been heard in Montauk if the wind had been blowing that way. He sucked on his thumb, cursing it, cursing himself, cursing Gracie.

"That's reality, McClellan," he reminded himself. "It's what happens when you fantasize your life away."

He replaced the tack and with great determination pounded it in.

"Dad!"

He turned and looked down toward the pool. Kip was backing across the deck, squinting up at him.

"Phone call!" Kip yelled when Cameron waved at him.

"Urgent?"

Kip shrugged. "Some lady. Got to talk to Mr. McClellan right now."

Not a lot of people knew where he was. But if they did, it was probably important. "Tell her to hang on," he shouted to Kip. "I'll be right there."

He scrambled down there and took the phone from Kip who was standing in the kitchen door. "McClellan here."

"Ah, yes, Mr. McClellan," said a female voice he didn't recognize. "There's a bit of a problem."

Cameron scowled, still worrying his thumb with his index finger. "Problem. What problem? Who is this?"

"This is Mia, from Forresters' Fine Furniture. You were in last week. And I'm afraid there's been a mistake."

"Forresters'...?" Cameron groped. "Oh, right." The place he and Gracie had done their pantomime furniture purchase. "What's the problem?"

"I'm afraid we'll have to come by and pick everything up."

"What? Why?"

"The, uh...name on the charge...I'm afraid it's...oh, dear..."

"It's what?" Cameron growled.

"The man...this Mr. Laurence McClellan who was supposed to pay..."

"What about him?"

"He used to do business with us, but recently I'm afraid we've had to...well, what I mean to say is, his credit isn't good."

The expletive Cameron breathed this time reached no one's ears but his own, but the personal shockwaves vibrating through him were a hundred times as great. Laurence McClellan, credit risk?

Holy cow.

But at least the great equation that he'd been toying with since he'd rented the place finally made sense.

First the house was for rent; then the furniture vanished; then the house was for sale; then Laurence McClellan's credit was no good. It all added up to one thing—the old man was flat broke.

"So, if you could tell us a time you'll be home, we can send a truck out and ... pick up ... the furniture."

He could tell the woman wasn't used to doing this. She sounded as if she might have an anxiety attack any moment.

"I'll pay."

"What?"

"As long as someone pays, there isn't a problem, is there?"

"Well, no, but—"

"Then charge it to me." He wasn't going to go back to camping out. Not now. And he wasn't leaving here the way things were, either. He was going to get to the bottom of this business with his father.

And he was damned if he was leaving Gracie. Not before he had to. No way.

He rattled off his own name and charge card number. "Check it," he told her. "See if it's good."

"Yes, sir." Moments later she was back, anxiety gone. "Oh, it's fine, sir. I'll just redo the paperwork. Thank you, sir. It's most kind of you."

Was it? Cameron didn't think so. *Idiotic* was the word that sprang to his lips.

What the hell was he going to do with five rooms of furniture when he only had the house for less than three more weeks? Was he serious about buying it?

Of course he wasn't. But then why had he done such a stupid thing?

"Cameron, ol' buddy, you are losing it," he said to himself.

"Who was that?" Kip asked, when he hung up.

"A saleslady." It was, after all, at least partly the truth.

"What was she selling?"

"Furniture."

"We already got all the furniture we need, don't we?" Kip said, opening the refrigerator and taking out a carton of milk.

Cameron shrugged wryly. "We do now at least."

Kip poured himself a glass of milk. "Want one?"

"Sure."

Carefully the boy poured another one and handed it to his father, then looked at him with satisfaction when Cameron downed it in one gulp.

"You know what we do need, though," Kip said conversationally.

"What's that?"

"A mother."

Cameron choked. He wiped his mouth on the back of his hand, staring at Kip over the top of it. Kip stared back, the epitome of guilelessness.

"Why?" Cameron managed at last.

"Well, we could have waffles more often."

"You don't need a mother to have waffles, Kip."

The boy shrugged. "I think it would help."

Cameron raked a hand through his hair. "I can make waffles," he said in a strangled voice.

"Yeah," Kip said reasonably. "But a mother'd be nice anyway."

Cameron looked at the boy closely, seeing in the determinedly nonchalant stance and detached air a loneliness that he didn't remember seeing—or hadn't he wanted to see?—in Kip before.

How long had it been there? How could he have missed it?

And now, even having seen it, what could he do?

He knew what Kip wanted—*who* Kip wanted. Somewhere deep inside, in some tiny hidden part of him, he wanted it himself. But he was terrified of it, too.

He reached for the boy and pulled him close. "Life doesn't always give you everything you want, Kip."

For a few moments it seemed as if Kip were going to resist him. He held himself stiff against his father's embrace. But then small hard arms went around Cameron's waist and the boy burrowed his face into Cameron's middle.

"I know," he mumbled into Cameron's shirt. "I love you, Dad."

Cameron just stood there, eyes closed, throat aching, stroking the boy's soft hair. God, what a pair they were.

Chapter Eleven

"What's the matter with your father?" Gracie asked, staring at the man on the roof.

When she'd come into the house, she hadn't been able to find him. She'd called and called and got no answer.

Finally she found Kip in the attic.

"He's on the roof," Kip had said, so she went to look.

She saw him then, just over the top on the seaward side, not roofing at all, simply sitting there like some sort of statuary, staring out to sea.

Gracie had called to him, but he didn't respond, just kept staring. She'd tried again and got no response. Finally she went back inside and found Kip now in the kitchen.

"He's just sitting there," Gracie said. "What's wrong with him?"

Kip shrugged. "Dunno."

"Has he been up there long?"

Another shrug. "Couple of hours. Maybe three."

"Working or sitting?"

"Sitting mostly. He hammers every now and then." Kip seemed unconcerned as he made himself a peanut butter and jelly sandwich. "Want one?" he asked Gracie.

"No, thanks." She wasn't hungry; she was worried. The man she'd left this morning had been perhaps a bit non-plussed by Mrs. Poop Deck, but he certainly wasn't cata-tonic. She wasn't sure what the man on the roof was.

She left Kip chomping down his sandwich and went back outside, going down the steps toward the beach so she could get enough of an angle to see where Cameron sat.

He hadn't moved. He was still sitting immobile, his back against one of the chimneys as he stared out into the distance. What he saw, Gracie didn't know.

"Cam?" she called. "Cameron!"

The sight of him there worried her. Something was wrong, she could tell. All had been wonderful last night and this morning. But all was not right now.

She flexed her knee carefully. It was still a little sore, but if she was careful, she could manage. Her wrist was better, too.

She stuck her head in the kitchen one more. "I'm going up on the roof."

"Can I come, too?"

"No. I want someone down here in case I . . . well, just in case."

Kip looked horrified. "You're not gonna fall, are you?"

"Of course not." Gracie gave him a bright smile, went back outside and began to climb.

It was not a short climb. It was, in truth, a decidedly long one. It didn't matter, she told herself. One rung was just like any other. There were just more of them, that was all. And anyway, she didn't have to look down.

She simply focused on each rung as she reached it, and when she finally arrived at the eaves and could see Cameron still sitting against the chimney, she breathed a huge sigh of relief.

"Cameron." She didn't know what she'd do if he didn't answer now.

But the sound of his name jerked him back from wherever he'd been, and his head whipped around to stare at the wide-eyed, white face that peered at him from just above the eaves.

"Gracie? What the hell?" He started scrambled toward her. She inched her way over the top of the ladder and sank gratefully onto the shingled roof, shutting her eyes and breathing deeply. The wind buffeted her slightly and she swallowed hard.

"Here. Grab on."

She opened her eyes just enough to see that Cameron had reached out a hand to her. She took it thankfully and let him pull her up to the chimney where he'd been sitting. Once there she sat again and hooked an arm around it as an anchor.

Cameron looked at her closely. "What'd you come up here for?"

He seemed perfectly normal now. Not catatonic in the least. And Gracie felt foolish until she remembered that he hadn't answered her at all, that he'd just sat and stared.

"I called and called and you didn't answer."

"I didn't hear you."

"Didn't hear me? Cameron, they can hear me in the last row."

He grimaced and she realized that reminders of her profession weren't welcome even yet. She shrugged quickly. "Oh, well, maybe you didn't. Maybe the wind was blowing the wrong way." She looked at him closely. "Is something wrong?"

Another grimace. Cameron shook his head looking slightly sheepish, but still worried. "I was thinking," he said slowly.

Gracie waited. She knew she'd get nowhere if she forced his confidences. She concentrated on staring out at the horizon, picking out a freighter moving toward New York City, trying to speculate about what it might be carrying, but unable to think of anything else other than the man sitting beside her.

"I own the furniture," he said at last.

Gracie looked at him, confused by that unexpected comment.

"The furniture we picked out," he clarified.

"The furniture you charged to your father?"

"And which his credit isn't good enough to purchase."

"You're kidding."

Cameron shook his head. "I'm not. Apparently the old man's broke, or giving a reasonable impression of it at least. And that," he added heavily, "goes a long way toward explaining what my secretary called about."

Gracie had forgotten his secretary had even called. "What did she call about?"

"To know if I wanted to buy the house."

"This house? Gull Cottage?"

Cameron nodded and patted the newly shingled roof. "Gull Cottage."

Gracie's heart lodged in her throat. She had spent all day at rehearsal going through the motions while rehearsing another scenario in her mind—one in which she and Cameron and Kip bought Gull Cottage and lived in it happily ever after. She was amazed, also petrified. "What did you say?"

He stared out at the horizon again without replying. Finally he sighed. "I said I'd think about it." One hand was clenched into a fist against his thigh. The other gripped the chimney so tightly she could see the white strain outlining his knuckles.

And what do you think? she wanted to ask him.

She bit back the question because she didn't want to sound desperate, frantic. She hoped that Cameron would answer it in his own good time.

He didn't. He just sat there and finally said, "I don't know what's going on with him."

Gracie, not following, asked, "Who?"

"My old man."

So much for other scenarios. Gracie shoved that one out of her mind and set herself to concentrating on Cameron's father. She remembered thinking early on that Laurence McClellan had had money troubles. Obviously she hadn't guessed the half of it.

"You could ask him," she suggested.

Cameron gave a short bark of laughter. "There's a joke."

"Well, he is your father," she said. "I'd ask my father."

"You probably have a damned sight better relationship with your father than I do with mine."

He'd said something to that effect before. She hoped now he would amplify it. "You don't . . . get on?"

"Putting it mildly." Cameron drew his knees up and wrapped his arms around them, resting his chin on his knees. A seagull landed on the farthest dormer and stared at him quizzically as if considering him for perching possibilities. Cameron stared back. Finally he blinked, and the bird, disappointed, flew away.

Cameron sighed and spoke at last. "I am his one big mistake."

Gracie was shocked. "How can you say that? You're wonderfully successful. You're healthy and handsome and you have a marvelous son."

"None of which matters to my old man," Cameron said gruffly. "It's a matter of values, you see. He values creativity, talent, drama." His mouth twisted. "Cripes, when he married Amaryllis he even named his kids after awards. With Tony and Emmy coming along, I'm lucky he didn't call me Oscar, I guess. And probably the only reason he didn't is because he named me after himself. The ultimate egotist!"

"He named you after himself?" Gracie hadn't known that.

Cameron snorted. "Laurence Cameron McClellan. The Cameron was a sop to my mother. It was her maiden name. It's what everybody calls me, except him."

"He calls you Mac?" Gracie ventured, remembering that Tony did.

Another snort. "Don't I wish? I'm thirty-six years old and all I'll ever be is 'little Larry' to him!"

Gracie couldn't stifle the giggle. "Little Larry?"

Cameron scowled, his fingers worrying the ragged edge of his cut-offs. "It's ridiculous."

Gracie, looking at him, thought that it was, rather. "So what are you going to do, then? If you can't ask him?"

Cameron shrugged. "I don't know. What can I do? He's never trusted me with a single confidence in his life. We aren't exactly close."

"Do you want to be?"

Cameron didn't answer that. He plucked at a stray thread dangling from his cut-off jeans. He chewed the corner of his mouth. He pressed his lips together in a firm, uncompromising line.

Gracie, watching him, sensed that in his mind a whole relationship was being replayed, weighed and evaluated.

Finally he sighed. "It's a bit late for that." He stretched out his long bare legs and contemplated his toes. "Besides, I've never noticed that what one wants makes a hell of a lot of difference."

"Oh, it does," Gracie said adamantly.

He jerked as if she'd hit him. Then he turned his head and looked at her hard.

"You can't give up on what you want," she told him earnestly. "You have to believe in yourself, forge on, struggle."

One brow lifted sardonically. "And you think that guarantees you'll get it?"

Gracie flushed. "Perhaps it doesn't guarantee it, but it's almost certain you won't if you don't."

Cameron gave a negligent shrug and didn't say any more.

Gracie stared at him, wondering if she'd said too much, too little, the wrong thing, or what?

Certainly he didn't seem to be convinced. But what else could she say?

"I'll think about it," Cameron said noncommittally. And she supposed she would have to be satisfied with that, for it seemed that confidences were over as he shoved himself to his feet.

"Come on. Let's go down." He started carefully down the steep slope of the roof without looking back.

Gracie, watching him go like a cat down the steeply shingled roof, froze right where she was.

For the first time since she'd climbed up, she considered the prospect of going back down again. Her mind reeled. She stopped considering it at once.

Quickly lifting her eyes to the horizon, she stared out to sea until the vertigo lessened and the white panic receded a bit.

Cameron was on the ladder before he glanced back at her. "Come on."

Gracie swallowed, tried to speak, couldn't manage a word.

Cameron frowned. "Gracie?"

She just looked at him, shaking her head, her jaw clenched tight.

"Gracie, what's wrong?"

Another shake of her head. Looking at him had been a mistake. Miles below him, she'd seen the ground. She felt the blood draining from her face, her neck, her arms, her legs. It all seemed to be pooling in the middle of her stomach, which was about to stage a revolt. Her head started to spin and her ears to ring again. She shut her eyes.

The next thing she knew Cameron was beside her again. "Are you sick?"

"N-no."

"Then what's wrong?"

"Th-the ground."

"What about the ground?"

"It's d-down there."

Cameron looked perplexed. "So?"

"I'm not," she almost wailed.

"Oh, God. You're not afraid of heights?"

"I didn't think so."

"But?"

"I was wrong."

"Oh, God," Cameron said again. It sounded like a prayer this time.

"My feelings, precisely," Gracie concurred with fervency and shoved her back more firmly against the chimney. As long as she didn't look down or contemplate climbing down, she was fine. The moment she did, her entire misspent life seemed to flash before her eyes.

Cameron glared at her. "Why the hell did you climb up here then?"

"I didn't know, did I?" Gracie retorted. "D'you think I would've if I had."

He sighed and raked a hand through his hair. "No, of course not." He looked slightly abashed. "Well, wait a second. I'll think of something."

Gracie forbore telling him that she would wait forever unless he did think of something. She was incapable of coherent thought herself. It amazed her how she could have sat here perfectly calmly until the moment came to descend. But she had, and now it was up to Cameron to save her from herself.

"I'll be right back," he said after a moment. "Don't move."

"No fear." Gracie gave him a shaky smile.

He shook his head, then started down the roof again. Gracie, watching, swallowed hard and audibly.

"Shut your eyes," Cameron commanded.

"With pleasure," Gracie muttered, and did.

She didn't know how long she sat there. Minutes. Hours. Weeks. It seemed like forever. Certainly it was long enough for her to have chastised herself a thousand times over for having done anything so foolish.

But the trouble was, when it came right down to it, even though she was terrified out of her mind, still she couldn't be sorry.

She had been worried about Cameron. He mattered to her. Mattered more than anyone she'd ever met in her life. And so she'd had to come. She was glad she had; he'd talked to her, had trusted her. And now, she thought, she was trusting him with her life.

It seemed a fair return somehow. She only wished he would hurry the hell up.

And then, just when she had given up hope, he was there unaccountably beside her. Without the aid of the ladder. Without, it seemed, having climbed at all.

"Come on."

"What?"

"Hang on to me and come on."

"Wh-where?"

"Here." He gestured toward the far side of the chimney. "Through the dormer. Only ten feet. Straight across. You don't even have to look down. Come on, Grace. You can do it."

Gracie looked at him doubtfully. He looked steadily back. His deep blue eyes encouraged, cajoled, promised.

"The window's open. You just hold on to me and we walk across the roofline to the dormer. Then you hang on to the dormer and come around the front of it and into the window. Piece of cake."

"Piece of cake," Gracie repeated shakily and stayed where she was.

"Or," said Cameron when she still didn't move, "I could call the fire department and they could bring the net and you could jump."

That galvanized her. *Jump?* Who did he think he was kidding? She pulled herself to her feet, grabbed his arm so tightly she knew he'd be bruised for weeks.

"Easy, there," Cameron's voice was calm and steady, the way it was when he talked to Kip at night. "If you want to close your eyes, it's all right. I can get you there."

"No." She didn't want to close her eyes. She only wanted to look at Cameron, to watch his face, to trust his eyes, to put her faith in the steady encouragement of his smile.

One step at a time, he walked her along the rooftop, then edged around her and got below her by the window and drew her down into his waiting arms. "In you go," he said

and, blessedly, in she went, face first, and kissed the attic
floor.

Seconds later Cameron was beside her. "Are you all
right?"

Gracie, still reeling, gave him a world-beating smile.
"Fine," she breathed. "Now."

He knelt on the floor next to her, his face still lined with
concern. "You're sure?" He touched her tentatively, running his hands over her arms, legs, ribcage.

"Well, I might have a black eye in the morning," she admitted. "But it's better than spending the night on the roof.

"And," she added impishly, "I still have all the same reactions when you touch me."

She gave a small hysterical giggle because just the feel of
his hands made her so recent terror recede instantly.

"Oh, Cameron," she murmured shakily, and that was
enough.

Cameron drew her into his arms and touched his lips to
hers.

HE INTENDED IT to be a comforting kiss, a reviving kiss. One
that would compensate her for the terror she'd felt and show
his concern.

He didn't know what it did for her, but it was a good thing
he was already on his knees or he'd have been knocked right
off his feet.

His lips caressed hers hungrily, seeking and finding, giving and receiving everything that they had shared the night
before. Cameron drank it in, desperate for it, his knees still
weak at the sight of her terror, his mind still reeling at the
sense of his life gone out of control.

She was sweetness and warmth and yielding as she clung
to him. And he couldn't stop kissing her.

The whole crazy day spun in his mind: the proposed sale
of the house; the business with the furniture, with his father, the waffles; the ecstasy of the night he'd just spent with
Gracie; her ascent to the roof; the things he told her that

he'd never told anyone else; her debilitating fear of heights, which had scared him witless, too, until he'd remembered the dormers.

He felt as if the world were reeling out of control, as if he could do nothing to stop it or to help himself, save hang on.

And so he would. He was going to hang on to Gracie Talbot as long as he could. She was his anchor.

And that meant he was going to keep right on kissing Gracie Talbot until something or someone made him stop.

Suddenly he heard footsteps behind them and Kip said, "How come you came in this way?"

Heart hammering, ears ringing, Cameron reluctantly pulled away to see Kip coming up the steps to the attic trailed by Alice.

"We—we were—" But he couldn't speak. He had no more breath left.

"I panicked," Gracie said. "I didn't know heights bothered me, but they do. I couldn't have come down that ladder to save my life. So your dad brought me in this way."

"That was smart." Kip bestowed an admiring glance on his father.

Gracie smiled at Cameron. "It certainly was."

Cameron was dismayed to find that the compliment made him blush. But he blushed even more a moment later when Gracie deliberately put her arms around his neck and kissed him again.

"My hero," she said, and while Cameron was still recovering from that, she said, "How about a picnic?"

A picnic? Right after she'd been petrified out of her mind? He couldn't fathom it.

But once the suggestion had been made, Kip latched on to it, and even Cameron found himself being swept along with him in his enthusiasm.

"But why?" he asked.

"To celebrate."

He looked at her, perplexed.

"It's a big day," she explained. "You've had an opportunity given to you. You have to make a decision. And I survived the roof!" She grinned. "A day like this deserves to be celebrated. Besides, I can remember another reason, too," she added and gave him a smile that made his toes curl.

Cameron couldn't help smiling either when he remembered that. "But we don't have any picnic stuff," he protested. "Or any portable food."

Gracie waved the phone. "Fear not. No one has starved picnicking in East Hampton in at least a hundred years."

The next thing he knew she was on the phone to Madame Makarova's deli, making arrangements to pick everything up.

"Everything?" Cameron asked when she requested a ride into town.

"Everything," Gracie promised.

She was right about that, too.

Two hours later they were spreading a red-and-white checkered tablecloth on the sand in the one small, wholly deserted cove that Gracie insisted must exist somewhere on Long Island and which they searched for until they found it.

Once the tablecloth was spread, while Kip tossed the Frisbee for Alice and Cameron watched in bemused amazement, she set out plates, silverware, stemmed wineglasses, napkins, and began lining up an impressive array of small and not-so-small cartons whose myriad colors and intricate designs reminded him of nothing so much as Ukrainian Easter Eggs.

"I'm not surprised," Gracie said when he told her. "Madame Makarova is a former Ukrainian princess."

"I thought she was the former food editor of *Izvestia*," Cameron said, having read the clippings in the foyer while Gracie picked up her order.

"Probably," Gracie said and laid out the last of the cartons. "But that would only qualify her to provide four hundred ways to fix beets economically. I suspect it's her royal background we're seeing here.''

She gave Cameron such a look of ingenuousness that he couldn't help smiling at her. Half the time he never knew if she was serious or not. He only knew that, serious or not, she made the world a happier place.

The world was definitely a happier place that evening.

They sat cross-legged on the table cloth, chomping down deviled eggs and slices of smoked turkey, nibbling *pirozhki*, sipping borscht—which even Kip was persuaded to try—and quaffing *kvass*, which Madame Makarova touted as a Russian equivalent to beer, except for Kip who got a bottle of sparkling grape juice instead.

Nothing was said about the house or the furniture or Laurence McClellan. It was there in the background, of course. But it ceased to be the trial and the trauma that Cameron had anticipated it would become, the way everything connected with his father had always become.

He finished off the *kvass* and lay back in the sand, pillowing his head on his folded arms, watching Gracie unpack still another surprise from her unending picnic basket of goodies.

It was a pie, and she cut three large pieces, put them on clean plates, and handed him the biggest one.

"Raspberry?" he guessed gazing down at the ruby red fruit oozing from beneath the flaky crust.

"Mmm-hmm."

He grinned. "My favorite."

She returned the grin. "Mine, too."

It was funny how something as insignificant as a shared liking of raspberry pie could seem like an omen, particularly to a man to whom omens had always been if not unbelievable, then invariably bad.

This one wasn't. It seemed a portent of the future—a good future.

How long a future, Cameron didn't let himself consider. The world might as well end September 1 as far as he was concerned.

He ate his piece of pie, then stole a bite of hers while Gracie was calling Kip. But she looked back just in time to see him snitching it, and shook her head, making a tsking sound.

She didn't offer to cut him another piece, however. Instead she sat down beside him again, cut off a piece of hers with her fork and wordlessly held it out to him.

Cameron looked at her, at it, then back at her again. Her eyes were warm, tempting. He swallowed. Slowly he leaned forward and took it into his mouth, savoring it.

Why, he asked himself as the tart fruit and flaky crust slid down his throat, did that one piece taste better than all the rest?

He knew all about magic tricks, knew everything there was to know about sleight of hand and illusion. But he didn't understand the magic that Gracie Talbot was bringing into his life.

The sun was low in the sky now, and the stiff breeze of the afternoon had trailed off. The sea was calmer, ripply, but no longer choppy. The world seemed a gentle place, comfortable, accepting. And Cameron taking bites that Gracie fed him and watching as Kip and Alice darted in and out of the waves that broke upon the shore, felt comfortable, too. He accepted.

He smiled at Gracie and reached for her hand once she put down the pie plate. Then he tugged her closely and wrapped an arm around her shoulders. They lay back together into the slight slope of the dune. Gracie leaned her head against him, her hair brushing the curve of his neck and grazing his jawline. Cameron smiled, turned his head and kissed her temple.

Briefly she turned her head and kissed him back. But then she turned again to watch Kip and Alice. And, shoving aside the frustration, Cameron did, too.

It was late, almost midnight, before they packed everything back in the car and headed for home. The roads were nearly deserted, the town fairly quiet as they drove through. Kip was already asleep in the back seat, his head pillowed on Alice's side, his arms around her.

Cameron remembered riding home late at night in the back seat of his father's Oldsmobile, remembered the soft sounds of his parents talking up front, his father's soft laughter, his mother's gentle response. And he had snuggled down into Blackie's soft fur, content with the knowledge that all was right with the world.

He hadn't remembered feeling that way since. He'd had isolated moments of joy—when Dana had said yes, when Kip was born—but nothing resembling contentment.

Until now.

Tonight, despite the decisions that lay ahead, despite the questions and answers that plagued his life, he felt good. It was crazy, perhaps. Perhaps he was living in a dream world. But it had been a long time since Cameron had allowed himself any dreams.

Right now he had Gracie's hand wrapped in his, resting on his thigh as he drove. He had the lilting melodies of Debussy on the radio and the soft whuffle of Alice, laying her chin on Kip's head and closing her eyes. Not much. But more than enough for a man who'd forsaken dreams long ago.

Cameron didn't ask what would happen when he woke up.

Chapter Twelve

"Told you so," Tony told Gracie when she called him to invite him to the play.

"Huh?"

"You're happy, aren't you?"

"Oh, yes." Never more so. But not for the reason he thought.

"Well, then...good thing I talked you into it, isn't it?" Tony congratulated himself.

Gracie smiled—she'd been smiling for a week—and agreed with him. What difference did it make? "The very best thing that ever happened to me," she said.

She could almost hear Tony preening over the phone lines.

"Great! I'll be down tomorrow. What time's the curtain?"

"Eight."

"I'll come early. Take you to dinner first."

"After," Gracie said. "I can't eat first. You know that." And besides, she needed all the time she could get beforehand to convince Cameron to come.

"After, then," Tony conceded. "How's Mac?"

"Uh, fine." Marvelous. Stupendous. The most wonderful man in the world.

"Tell him I'm looking forward to seeing him. Maybe I'll bring Em. We can have a family reunion."

"Sounds like fun," Gracie said, but when she told Cameron that, he groaned.

"Tony? Coming here? What for?" His obvious displeasure puzzled Gracie and put a damper on her rampant enthusiasm.

"I . . . invited him," she confessed.

Cameron stared at her as if she'd lost her mind.

She gave a defensive shrug. "Well, it was his idea that I come here at all, you know. For the play."

"Oh. Right." A long strained silence ensued.

Cameron never talked about the play. He just seemed to pretend it wasn't there. He knew more or less what time her rehearsals were, and even if they were together until almost the time she left, he always contrived to leave first—to go up to the attic or out onto the beach or into town. He was never there when Mrs. Poop Deck picked her up. He was also never there when she returned, although he seemed to appear within minutes after she walked back in the door. It was uncanny, as if he'd been waiting or something.

Maybe he had been. Gracie didn't ask.

Everything else was wonderful between them. Magical, in fact. They went for long walks on the beach now that her leg was getting better. They swam in the pool. They cooked and ate and talked and laughed. And every night they shared the barge down the Nile, loving each other with such tenderness and fervor that Gracie felt as if, in Cameron McClellan, she'd found the other half of her soul.

She had no intention, then, of rocking the boat. It was hard for Cameron to face her acting, and she knew it. So she wasn't going to force him. It would happen, she thought, in its own good time.

Besides, it wasn't as if she were planning to take the world by storm and rake in Tonys, Emmys and Oscars by the score. She was merely doing her best in a regional theater. No Ethel Barrymore, she.

"So when's he coming?" Cameron asked her, apparently resigned by the look on his face.

"Tomorrow. Opening night." Gracie tried to sound casual, but she couldn't quite pull it off. She was excited; she couldn't help it. The play had developed marvelously. Something as oft-done as *The Importance of Being Earnest* should've seemed old hat, hackneyed, not worth the time and effort.

But with Herschel's brilliant direction and hard work on the part of the cast, not to mention marvelous period sets, it was going to be grand.

Gracie herself was going to be grand, and she knew it. All the happiness she'd found with Cameron seemed to come out in her work. She threw herself into Cecily and made her come alive.

She owed that to Cameron, especially. She just wished he'd appreciate it.

He wouldn't, of course. She didn't even bother to say anything. Not about that. She did say, "I do hope you'll come."

They were sitting on the edge of the pool, dangling their feet in, and for a long moment they continued to sit there, Gracie awaiting a response and Cameron—well, she wasn't quite sure what Cameron was doing. At last he simply shoved himself into the water and began a vigorous crawl in the other direction without so much as a word. In no time he reached the other end, did a racing turn and headed back.

Gracie expected him to surface and give her an answer. He did another racing turn and headed the other way.

A dozen more laps and she began to get the idea. She watched him churning his way up and down the pool as if all the devils in hell were after him, and she began to realize something of the magnitude of what she'd asked.

At first she was irritated. Then, on further reflection, she felt oddly pleased. Elated, almost. For she was certain he would have said, "Sure," if he hadn't cared. But she suspected—hoped—that he did care, and possibly in the same way that he'd cared for Dana, if he thought of Gracie and the theater as somehow connected with Dana's place in his life. She didn't know what the circumstances had been of their split. She did know that once he'd loved Dana—at least at first he had.

They'd both agreed that she wasn't Dana. But when she saw a reaction like this one, she couldn't help asking herself: did Cameron, perhaps, love her?

He'd certainly never said so. But sometimes she caught a look in his eye, an expression of tenderness or fierceness that made her wonder. Watching him swimming now, his long powerful body surging through the water, Gracie prayed to God that he might.

He swam fifty-four laps before he reached either the end of his endurance or a decision. Hauling himself out of the pool, chest heaving, dark hair streaming water into his face, he looked her straight in the eye.

"All right. I'll come," he said.

THE DAY OF THE PLAY, Cameron was amazed to note, began like any other. He had spent the night with Gracie, waking by habit to creep back to his own bed just past dawn.

He was still unwilling to let Kip get his hopes up, though his own, if the truth were known, had crept up considerably.

It was foolish, and he knew it. It would probably all come crashing down around his ears today when the play wholly and irrevocably took over Gracie's life. But in the meantime, he took things at face value, protecting Kip, but not entirely protecting himself.

He slept another hour in his own bed, then got up and went for an early-morning run on the beach as had become his habit. He got back expecting to find Kip eating cereal and Gracie already gone. Instead he walked into the kitchen to find the two of them making blueberry pancakes while Kip taught Gracie the starting line-up of the Mets.

He looked from one to the other, surprised at the everydayness of the situation.

"Hurry up and get a shower, Dad," Kip said. "There'll be more ready by the time you get out."

"Okay." Cameron crossed the room, smiling, feeling suddenly as if a great weight had been lifted from his chest. He passed closely behind Gracie on his way to the stairs, close enough to be unable to resist the temptation to nibble the back of her neck.

She spun around and gave him a hug. "Good morning, handsome."

Kip snickered.

Cameron flushed, but couldn't quell the surge of desire he felt at the mere contact of her body with his. "Morning, Gracie," he mumbled into her hair. Then he retreated up the stairs as quickly as he could.

After breakfast Gracie sat in the kitchen writing a letter to her parents while he and Kip practiced magic tricks. Then Kip wandered off to play with Alice, and Cameron searched for Gracie, expecting to find her holed up in her room, getting into her character. He was surprised to find her in the solarium with Boris.

"What are you doing?"

He couldn't imagine why she'd be wasting her time with this miserable bird, not with a show this evening. Whenever Dana'd had a performance she went incommunicado for the entire day, not wanting to be disturbed so she could "get in touch with her character's soul."

"I'm not Dana," he remembered Gracie telling him.

Well, no, of course not. But an actress was an actress.

Boris hopped onto his perch, scattering the seed that Gracie had just put out for him. He cocked his head and glared at Cameron. "You are my sunshine," he warbled in a Texas baritone.

"I was trying to clean his cage," Gracie explained. "I thought perhaps with Tony coming it might be a good idea. He might be spying for your father."

"He doesn't even known Dad's renting the place," Cameron reminded her.

"Maybe not. But then he's going to wonder anyway why you got Boris and he didn't."

Cameron grimaced. "Just lucky, I guess." He gave Boris a baleful look.

Boris preened, first ruffling his feathers, then smoothing them. Then he hopped onto his food dish and kicked seed at Cameron.

"Boris!" Gracie admonished him. "Stop that."

"Never!" the bird said. "Never, never, never!"

He stuck his beak in the air exactly, Cameron thought, the way his father stuck his nose skyward when offended.

"Birds of a feather..." Cameron muttered.

Boris hopped back onto his perch and gave a credible imitation of a slightly inebriated McClellan swagger. "Ya wanna make somethin' of it?"

Cameron clenched his fists.

"Honestly." Gracie glared at him. "Until I came here I didn't imagine it was possible to referee a fight between a man and a bird."

Cameron scowled and muttered something about mynah fricassee. "How much longer are you going to be?"

"Five minutes," Gracie promised. "Less if he cooperates."

Boris poked his beak through the bars of the cage. "If you've got the money, I've got the time."

Gracie shook her head. "What on earth have you been listening to, you wretched bird?"

"Sounds like Grand Ole Opry to me," Cameron said. "Dad'll love that."

Dad would hate it, in fact. Laurence was a pure snob. Nothing but classical music or Broadway tunes was ever allowed in his house. Cameron grinned.

"The television was on all night," Gracie admitted. "I think Kip forgot to shut it off after he watched *The Wizard of Oz* last night. Oh, dear."

"Don't worry about it," Cameron told her. "The old man's not going to be here anytime soon. And he'll never know who taught it to Boris, anyway. Probably think it was one of his earlier tenants."

"I hope so," Gracie said, unconvinced.

"Your cheatin' heart," Boris sang.

"Oh, heavens."

"Forget him," Cameron insisted.

"But—"

Cameron took the bird seed pack from her hand and set it on the floor. He secured the cage firmly, then took Gracie by the shoulders and turned her to face him. She still looked worried, preoccupied.

He bent his head, touching his lips to hers, moving them gently, then more firmly, more persuasively across hers. He drew her into his arms and held her close, savoring the feel of her, smiling at her quickening response, at the way her arms lifted and went around his neck, at the way her body moulded itself to his.

Teasing became tasting. Promise became passion. Cameron's mouth grew hungrier, his body tauter, and he could feel Gracie responding the same way. The heat between them grew from a hint of a flickering flame to the threat of a full-scale conflagration.

There was a sudden shrill whistle behind them. "Only you can prevent forest fires," Boris said.

THE FIRST TIME Gracie met Emmy McClellan she'd thought the other girl was flamboyant. Nothing she saw this time caused her to change her impression.

When Tony and his sister breezed up to Gull Cottage at four o'clock, Gracie was on the beach tossing a football with Kip. Cameron had gone back on the roof, though Gracie couldn't see that he was doing much. He'd been acting strangely all day, watching her as if she might be coming down with something. She tried to ask him what the problem was, but he brushed her off.

She wasn't surprised when he headed for the roof. It was, she was beginning to think, his refuge. Certainly *she* wasn't

apt to bother him up there again. And when she saw Tony
and Emmy alight from the taxi, she began to understand
another reason why Cameron was where he was.

Tony was wearing fashionably pleated dark trousers and
a billowing white silk shirt. It was perhaps a bit more glitzy
than the sloganed T-shirts and jeans Gracie usually saw him
in, but the only thing that really set him apart was the purple
paisley ascot tucked into the neck of the shirt.

Emmy, however, was a sight to behold. She wore a sil-
very sequined dress that looked as if she'd got it by mug-
ging Betty Boop. Looped around her neck were seven—
Gracie counted them—*seven* strands of beads, all different,
the most striking a long strand of what appeared to be de-
cayed rhinoceros teeth. She wore four-inch black patent
leather heels with patterned stockings of bright blue, and on
her head she wore a tiny pill box hat with one brilliant pea-
cock feather sticking straight up.

Kip, seeing them, stopped dead and stared. "What's
that?"

Gracie blinked. "You don't know who that is?"

Kip shook his head. "If I did, I think I'd have remembered," he said frankly.

Gracie smiled. "No doubt. That, my dear, is your Auntie
Em."

Kip stared. "All the way from Kansas?"

Gracie laughed and threw him the football. "All the way
from the Village, I should think."

"What village?"

"Don't ask her that. I imagine she thinks she lives in the
hub of the western cultural world." Gracie didn't have a
chance to say more for at that moment Emmy launched
herself from the deck.

"Gracie, love!" she exclaimed, tottering down the slope
and flinging her arms around Gracie. "My dear, how are
you?" She held Gracie out at arm's length. "When Tony
told me he'd convinced you to hie to the far reaches of Long

Island, I couldn't believe it. But I must say, rusticating seems to agree with you.''

"Yes. It does." Gracie hauled Kip forward. "Emmy, this is Kip.

Emmy's eyes grew round and astonished. "Kip? Little Kip? Kippy, baby!" She minced across the sand and scooped him into her arms, squeezing the stuffing out of him.

Kip, like Raggedy Andy, went limp, suffering himself to be hugged but managing, Gracie noted, to keep the football between himself and his aunt. The moment she relinquished her grip, he jumped back and aligned himself firmly with Gracie.

"Pleased to meet you," he said in an even, dignified voice so reminiscent of his father that Gracie couldn't help smiling. Her eyes went automatically to the roof. Cameron had his back turned, but he wasn't hammering and he couldn't have missed the twins' arrival. He just wasn't acknowledging it.

He *was* hiding out, she thought with a tiny smile. She was relieved at least that it wasn't her he was hiding from.

Emmy laughed, a tinkling, melodic sound. The perfect stage laugh. "Tony, look! It's Kippy! Look how big he is. Imagine that.''

Tony dumped the luggage on the deck, bounded down the steps and swept Gracie into his arms. "How you doin', beautiful?" He gave her a great smacking kiss that had Gracie looking roofward again. But Cameron, thank heavens, was still facing the other way.

"I'm nervous," she said. "It's not long now."

"You'll do fine. Told you you would," Tony said blithely. "Been hearing great things about you. Word of mouth. Grapevine and all."

"Oh?"

He nodded, eyes sparkling. "Great things," he repeated and winked. Then he turned to Kip. "Hi ya, Kipper."

"Tony! I think you just called him some kind of fish," Emmy protested.

Tony shrugged and ruffled his nephew's hair. "Better'n what some people have called me. Where's your old man, kiddo?"

Kip pointed. "Up there."

Emmy and Tony both swiveled to stare.

"What'n hell's he doing up there?" Tony wanted to know.

"Fixing the roof," Kip said. "It leaks."

Tony stared at his nephew. "Leaks?" He shook his head astonished. "Then why doesn't he hire somebody to fix it? Dad should be notified."

"Cameron's taking care of it," Gracie said firmly.

Tony sighed. "Trust Cameron. Nobody can do it better. I know him. Stubborn cuss. Well, there's not a cloud in the sky. He can stop fixing it for a few minutes at least. Yo! Mac!" he yelled. "C'mon down and be sociable!"

For a moment Gracie thought Cameron was going to do his statuary act and pretend not to hear. But then he slowly turned, lifted a hand in acknowledgment, and began to make his way down the roof.

Gracie had seen Cameron scale that roof often enough to know how swiftly he could do it if he wanted to. He was clearly in no hurry now. When at last he did hit ground, he walked slowly across the deck toward the them, wiping his hands on his jeans as he came.

He looked to Gracie as if he were building invisible fortifications around himself, erecting walls even as he walked. His face gave nothing away; he was even smiling slightly. But there was something in the way he held himself—a defensiveness, if you would—that made her wonder.

"Tony, Emmy." He nodded to them both.

Tony might've let him get away with it. Emmy didn't. She threw her arms around him. "Oh, Mac, lovey, it's so good to see you. I can't believe you're here, that you and Daddy have made up. It's just the most wonderful thing! It'll be just like old times, won't it?''

Cameron didn't answer that. Gracie thought he looked exactly like Kip had when suffering under his aunt's attack. But for all her flamboyance, Emmy wasn't insincere, and Cameron seemed to know it for, after a long moment during which Gracie saw him struggling to get his bearings, he hugged her, too.

"Isn't this just too exciting?" she babbled on, hooking her arm through Gracie's. "I couldn't believe it when Tony told me what you were up to. What a coup, working for Dimante. You lucky lady!" Then she turned to Cameron. "Isn't she lucky? I'd sell my soul for a Dimante part."

"What soul?" Tony teased before Cameron could speak.

Emmy socked her twin in the arm. "You beast."

Cameron stepped between them. "Come on, you two, stop squabbling. You sound just like you did when you were kids. Let's get your gear into the house." He was already moving quickly, gathering up the luggage, heading that way.

"Fine with me," Emmy said, sticking out her tongue at Tony.

Tony smirked back it her but then concurred. "I've been with her since ten this morning. I could use a stiff drink."

He followed Cameron into the house and stopped dead. "What in hell did you do with the furniture?"

"Nothing," Cameron said, ushering them into the living room. "It was gone when I got here."

"Gone?" repeated Tony.

"Gone?" shrieked Emmy. "What about the wicker? The filigreed mirror in the entry way? My canopy bed?"

"Gone," Cameron said implacably.

"Everything?" Emmy demanded.

"The slot machine's still here," Kip said cheerfully. "And Gracie's got the barge."

"Barge?"

"You remember," Tony said. "Dad's relic from the Cleopatra play. The one that closed after one night. Well, I'm glad that didn't get stolen at least."

"Nothing was stolen."

Both Tony and Emmy stared at Cameron.

"Dad sold it all."

"What!"

Gracie was sure they could get jobs in a Greek chorus. She knew this was hard for Cameron. She gave him an encouraging smile. He received it gratefully if the brief flicker of his eyes in her direction was any indication.

"He sold everything," Cameron reiterated. He didn't say, Gracie noted, anything about Laurence offering to sell the house. Perhaps he knew there was only so much Tony and Emmy could take in at once. He seemed to be right.

"But why?" The Greek chorus again.

Cameron shrugged. "It's his."

"Yes, but—"

"You'll have to ask him," he told them firmly.

Emmy stared at him, aghast. Tony sank down on the newly purchased sofa and stared around the sparsely furnished room that now contained only the sofa Cameron and Gracie had picked out, three armchairs, two lamps and an end table they'd dragged down from the attic.

Gracie thought the room had a certain eclectic charm. Tony, from the expression on his face, did not.

"I could really use that drink," he said to Cameron now, and Emmy, sinking down next to him, found her voice again and said, "Make mine a double."

CAMERON DIDN'T TOUCH a drop, though everything in him wanted to stay home and drink himself under the table. There was no way on earth he wanted to sit there and watch while Gracie enthralled the audience at the John Drew Theater.

He went because he promised her he would go. And Cameron, like Horton the Elephant, kept his word. He gritted his teeth, put on a suit, got Kip spiffed up and accompanied his glitzy brother and ditzy sister into town.

Mrs. Poop Deck had come for Gracie at just past six. She'd grabbed her duffel bag and waved everyone a quick good-bye. Everyone except Cameron.

She'd given him a kiss.

That had raised Tony's and Emmy's eyebrows. But no more, he had to admit, than it had raised his own. On a night like tonight he had expected she'd forget his very existence.

Thanks to Emmy they got to the theater fashionably late. If there was an entrance to be made, Emmy McClellan could be counted on to make it. There was never any doubt whose daughter she was. Even Tony, ordinarily less showy, seemed to be thriving on it tonight.

"If you can't squelch it, outdo it, that's my motto," he'd told Cameron when they left the house. "Whenever Emmy goes anywhere it's An Event."

It was certainly An Event tonight. They arrived just before the house lights were beginning to dim, Emmy and Tony in the lead, turning everyone's heads as they breezed down the aisle, smiling and nodding to new acquaintances and old friends.

Kip and Cameron trailed along behind, Cameron still wishing he weren't here and Kip still insisting he thought it was rotten that they couldn't bring Alice.

Cameron would've traded places with her if he could. But the die was cast. Now all he had to do was endure. He lowered himself into his seat and leaned back, and felt the familiar sensation of doom settle over him.

As he'd feared, the play was good. No, it wasn't merely good; it was outstanding.

The man playing Algy was a sly charmer, Jack was wonderfully two-faced, Lady Bracknell was as delightfully acerbic as she could be, and Gracie's Cecily had just the right amount of coquettishness to balance her innocent lines.

They were all good, but Gracie was the best. She was a natural, and Cameron knew it. She was by turns beguiling and bemused, charmed and charming. And they were close enough to the front that when she batted her eyelashes at Jack, he could feel the tightness in his own chest remembering how she'd batted those same eyelashes at him—with much the same effect.

"Tol'ja she was good," Kip whispered in his ear. "Isn't she good?"

"Mmm."

"Wish I could do that," Kip continued.

Cameron gave him a hard stare. "What?"

"Act."

Cameron growled.

"I do," Kip insisted. "I really liked it when I came to rehearsals with her."

Something else Cameron didn't want to hear. He sank deeper into his seat, closed his eyes, and waited for the end to come.

WHEN THE END CAME, Gracie was ecstatic. She'd never done better and she knew it. For two hours, give or take a bit, she'd *been* Cecily Cardew. The thrill, the sense of accomplishment, was terrific. But now in the backstage crush, her eyes were scanning the crowds of milling people, looking for Cameron, needing him to make the celebration complete.

She'd glimpsed him beyond the footlights, third row center, right where she'd wanted him. Just past the staring eyes of the people in the first couple of rows. Close, but not so close she'd forget herself, do something foolish. He was there for her inspiration, not distraction, and he'd done it marvelously.

Every time she'd seen him, he'd been staring at her, his expression grave, even during the funny bits. She hadn't minded. She knew he didn't think drama was funny for whatever reasons—something having to do with Dana, she supposed. But whatever he had felt for Dana, he had come for her. And for that she loved him.

She looked for him now, brushing past well-wishers with smiles and expressions of gratitude, Thank-you-so-much's and You're-very-kind-to-say-so's, all the while her eyes darting from one person to another, seeking him.

She found Herschel—or rather he found her, and enveloped her in a bone-crushing hug. "Stupendous, my dear! Simply marvelous. You've done everything I asked—and more. I couldn't be more pleased."

Gracie beamed. "Thank *you*," she told him. "I couldn't have done it without you."

Herschel continued squeezing her shoulders. "We make a great team."

Did he really think so? Gracie wondered. Or was he just building her ego so she'd do as well tomorrow night? Did she even care? No, not really. She wanted to find Cameron. Where was he?

And then, at last, Emmy swooped down upon her, drawing her out of Herschel's grasp. "You were stunning, darling. Delightful. I couldn't have done it better myself!"

The ultimate compliment, Gracie thought wryly.

"Truly," Tony seconded. "How 'bout another 'I told you so.'" He turned to the other man who had materialized at her side as well. "Didn't you think so, old man?"

And there, at last, he was.

Gracie felt relief shoot through her. She'd had the awful fear that once the lights came up, Cameron had vanished into thin air. But he hadn't. And now he stood right beside her looking as solemn as a judge.

His expression was unreadable, his beautiful blue eyes dark, and betraying some sort of vague nameless concern. He might've been at a wake, waiting to pay his respects to the bereaved.

"Cameron?"

"You were marvelous," he said quietly. And though Gracie knew the words sounded as if he'd dredged them up from his toes, she also knew he meant every word.

She gave him a stunning smile, but before she could speak, "Super!" Kip boomed and flung his arms around her. "Super, super, super! I didn't know you were so funny."

Gracie returned his hug, tousled his hair and gave him a fleeting smile in return. "A laugh a minute around here."

"You bet! It was great!"

"Thank you, Kip." Then her eyes went back to Cameron. "Thank you for coming," she said, guessing what it had cost him.

She wanted to throw her arms around him. She'd hugged everyone else, for heaven's sake. But Cameron just nodded briefly, as if she were some remote stranger passing in the street.

Unable to stand it any longer, Gracie touched his arm.

He hadn't touched her yet at all, this man who made such beautiful love to her night after night as they floated down a dreamy Nile. It was as if, from his side at least, an invisible shield surrounded her. But when her fingers touched the sleeve of his coat, something happened.

His gaze jerked at once to her hand, as if its touch surprised him. Then his own fingers came up and tentatively, touched hers. He would have drawn away, but she grasped his hand in hers. The surprise in his eyes was almost palpable. He looked at her, dazed.

"Let's get out of here," she said.

He stared. "What?"

Emmy and Tony were bubbling away, chatting up Algy and Lady Bracknell. Mrs. Poop Deck was ushering people toward the doors for an opening-night reception. Herschel was like a sheep dog, herding his cast and hangers-on toward the party.

"I said," Gracie repeated, "let's get out of here."

"But—"

"Come along, come along." Herschel boomed at them. "Everyone to my place for the celebration."

But Gracie gave him a regretful smile and shook her head. "Thanks, but we've got to be running along."

"Oh, my dear, no. You can't. You must—"

But the play was over. There were more important things in her life now—more important people. She gave Herschel a quick peck on the cheek. "I'll see you tomorrow. Right on time. Six-thirty, all right?"

And Herschel, as nonplussed as Cameron, managed a bemused smile and nodded his head.

"See you then." And Gracie, still holding onto Cameron's hand, tugged him toward the door, herding Kip in front of her as she went.

"What about your makeup?" Cameron asked.

"I'll take it off at home."

"What about Auntie Emmy and Uncle Tony?" Kip asked, craning his neck, looking for them.

"They'll be fine. They'll be out all night, I bet. And I'm sure when they want to come home, they'll manage." She turned to Cameron and gave him a hopeful smile. "And we can manage without them, can't we?"

Cameron was standing stock-still on the sidewalk, a rock in the way of the river of humanity passing out the doors. "Are you serious?"

"What do you think?"

A moment later she saw the first smile out of him she'd seen all night. It was a stunning smile, one that would have knocked the socks off every woman from here to the Mississippi River.

"Let's go home," he said.

THEY STOPPED and bought homemade ice cream bars at a local place called Popsicles Plus, then sped through the dark streets like hooky players with the truant officer after them.

"Are you sure?" Cameron asked Gracie once more as he pulled into the driveway of Gull Cottage. He could turn around now, could take her back and be philosophical about it even yet. But once they were inside . . .

"Sure about what?" Kip asked sleepily from the backseat.

Gracie touched his cheek. "I'm sure." And before he could say a word, she hopped out of the car and led the way into the house.

Still dazed and disbelieving, as if he'd been drinking after all, Cameron followed her.

The evening hadn't gone as he'd expected in the least. The *whole day* hadn't gone as he'd expected, for that matter.

He'd anticipated a preoccupied Gracie, one who brushed him off, who immersed herself in Cecily, who couldn't be bothered with him or Kip or Tony and Emmy. He hadn't found that.

He'd expected her to bask in her triumph after the play. It was after all a triumph well deserved. But she'd been more intent on getting out of there than he had. He couldn't figure it out. He didn't try, just let himself be tugged along by the undertow.

"It's magic," he muttered to himself as he started a fire in the fireplace while Gracie removed her makeup and showered. He tried to sound sarcastic, but it didn't quite come out that way. His voice had more of a sense of wonder to it. Awe.

He removed his coat and tie, rolled up his sleeves and put Kip to bed. Then he came back down and sat on the couch in front of the fire.

He heard Gracie first in Kip's room, then in his own, and wondered if she might just be so exhausted she'd wanted to come home and go to bed. Maybe that was why she'd wanted to come back. Maybe she wasn't keyed up before, but exhausted after.

But moments later, she came down the steps.

She was wearing a long, pale blue dressing gown, her fair hair still slightly damp from the shower, but beginning to fluff becomingly around her head.

She looked like an angel; he thought and wondered, not for the first time, if he wasn't dreaming this, if he mightn't open his eyes and find himself back in the John Drew Theater, waiting for the start of the second act.

But the bright nimbus of hair picked up the glow of the firelight and accentuated the roundness of her cheeks and the darkness of her eyes as she descended the steps. Her eyes fastened on his, and she crossed the room to go straight into his arms.

If he'd questioned the reality of the moment, the warm weight of her body and the gentle persuasiveness of her lips on his taught him quickly that this was no dream.

It was too beautiful, too marvelous. Even the very best of dreams were never like this.

"Ah, Grace." He smiled into her eyes, shifting around to lie on the couch, arranging her on top of him, welcoming her home.

His hands glided softly down her back, brushing her shoulder blades, her ribs, the slope of her buttocks, needing the contact, needing to let his sense of touch reinforce what was happening to him—to them.

Gracie pulled back just slightly, far enough to look down into his eyes while she threaded her fingers through his hair. Her body moved restlessly against his, evoking an equally restless response.

Cameron's hands moved to divest her of the gown, then he stripped off his own clothes. The firelight painted them both in rosy warm hues, fanning the flames of desire that were growing each second between them.

He'd loved her before, but never like this. Never with a thought of tomorrow.

But he thought of tomorrow now. Of tomorrow and tomorrow and tomorrow.

"I love you," Gracie whispered.

And as he laid her gently back against the cushions, and the two of them joined together in that love, Cameron believed for the first time that there could be life after August 31st.

Chapter Thirteen

Cameron's tolerance for Tony usually lasted a few days, for Emmy a few hours. He was amazed, therefore, that he managed to put up with both of them for the next six days and scarcely felt a thing.

Well, not exactly nothing, but hardly the negative heaven-help-me-get-them-out-of-here desperation that he customarily felt. He owed it all to Gracie.

She brought out a tolerance in him he never knew he had. She put Emmy's histrionics and Tony's glibness in perspective. She jollied them along, teased them out of the worst of their eccentricities, and made them almost enjoyable to be around.

They said the same about him.

"I don't know what you've done to Mac, but whatever it is, you ought to bottle it," he heard Emmy tell Gracie one morning over her daily bowl of wheat germ, oat bran and dried apples. "You could make a fortune."

Gracie just smiled vaguely as if she had no idea what Emmy meant.

Maybe she didn't. But Cameron did. He knew the miracle she'd wrought even if she didn't know it herself. He actually found himself liking his younger brother and sister.

"But I'd like them better if they'd leave," he told Gracie candidly. "I want you alone."

"We wouldn't be alone even then," she reminded him. "We'd still have Kip and Alice. And Boris," she added with a fleeting glance toward the solarium.

"Saints preserve us, yes. Don't let's forget Boris." Cameron grinned.

It was, Gracie told him, a measure of his growing equanimity that he could even joke about that blackguard of a bird.

Cameron could joke about virtually anything these days. Gracie had made all the difference in the world. The love she had professed had given him hope and joy and courage.

He decided to buy the house.

Gracie's face had lit up when he told her his decision that Thursday afternoon as they sat in the den, stealing a few moments from the whirl that Emmy and Tony and Kip perpetually surrounded them with.

"I'm so glad," she said to him, snuggling against him, making him feel warm, comfortable, content. "This house is meant for you. You love it."

He did. He also loved Gracie.

Gracie. A woman like no other he'd ever met. A woman who had the ability to make him believe in dreams again, who had the humor to make him laugh again, who had the power to make him love again.

He took a deep breath. The phone rang. He ignored it. Instead he looked deep into her eyes. "Will you share it with me, Grace?"

She blinked. "Share...?"

He smiled, touched her cheek, rubbed a tendril of that golden hair between his finger and his thumb. "Marry me, I mean."

Gracie simply stared.

Cameron waited, tense, hopeful, and suddenly terrified. Then at last she launched herself at him. "Oh, Cameron, yes!"

She threw her arms around him, hugging him tightly and knowing that the joy of her love was returned in his embrace.

There was a discreet "ahem" from the doorway. Kip stood there, a half-silly, half-bewildered smile on his face.

"Dad?" His tone was hesitant.

"We're getting married," Cameron told him.

The hesitancy vanished. The smile became one of pure unadulterated joy. "Oh, wow." Kip looked from one to the other of them, his eyes shining now, his enthusiasm simply brimming in them. "Married? Really? For sure? When?"

Cameron looked at Gracie expectantly. She shrugged.

"As soon as possible," he told Kip. "All right?" he asked Gracie.

"As soon as possible," she agreed.

"Super!" Kip cheered. He flew to them, hugging them both. Then suddenly he dropped his arms. "I almost forgot. Grandpa's on the phone."

"What?"

Kip shrugged. "Grandpa. That's what he said, anyway."

Cameron frowned at Gracie who gave him a shrug in return.

Grandpa?

Dana's father was dead, but it seemed to Cameron almost more likely that he'd be calling from beyond the grave than that his own would be on the other end of the telephone line.

Curious, still disbelieving, he went into the sun room and picked up the telephone. "Cameron McClellan here."

There was a fleeting pause, a crackle of long-distance wires, then, "Little Larry? Glory be, Larry, it is you!"

"Dad." Cameron felt as if someone had just slung a two-hundred-and-ten-pound albatross around his neck.

"Didn't believe it for a moment when she wrote and told me you were there," Laurence went on after a transatlantic lapse. "Preposterous, I thought. He'd never, I thought. But I wanted to check."

"Who, Dad? Who said?"

"Callista. Mrs. Poop Deck, of course! In her letter."

Of course. He should've known she couldn't keep the news to herself. She probably thought Laurence knew, probably wrote and congratulated him on getting Cameron back into the fold.

"You don't—I mean, you're not—I'd intended—" Laurence seemed to be stumbling for a moment, no doubt trying to square Cameron's presence with his own rental of the house. "What *are* you doing there?" he asked at last.

"Renting."

"Renting?" Laurence was clearly stunned. Then he said hastily, "Oh, yes, well, I did let a realtor have it for the summer. Knew I was going to be in France myself. Couldn't stand to see it going to waste."

"Uh-huh." So he still wasn't going to tell his son he needed the money. So what else was new?

"The realtor rented it to you?" Laurence probed.

"I got it from a west coast firm, Trailblazers, who took it for the month," Cameron said. If Laurence wanted to continue the pretense, he'd play along. He wasn't going to admit he'd known from the first whom he was renting from. "I'm subletting."

"Ah." The sound of relief easily crossed the five thousand miles. Then, "Why?"

"No special reason. A lark really. Kip and I needed a break. He doesn't remember the east coast. I thought, why not?" He made it sound as blasé and disinterested as possible.

"Oh, yes. Right. Good idea," Laurence said a shade too heartily. "I thought it might be . . . thought perhaps you had . . ."

But he didn't say what he thought it might be or what he thought Cameron had; he just went silent. That in itself was a rare and beautiful event.

In fact his father was silent so long Cameron thought the conversation might end right there. Suddenly he found that he couldn't let Laurence off so easily.

"What happened to the furniture, by the way?"

The connection developed a stutter. "F-f-f-f-churniture?"

"Place was bare when I got here."

"Er, yes." A pause. "Oh, well, I lent some to friends. Took some into the city for the winter and never thought to bring it back. You know how it is."

"Didn't need the money, then?"

"Money?" Laurence sounded as if it were a dirty word. "Of course not. How's Kip?" The change of subject didn't off-balance Cameron but the choice of it did. He wasn't used to paternal or grand-paternal concern.

"Fine," he said shortly.

"Must be getting big."

"Yes."

"How old is he now?"

"Ten."

"Imagine that."

Cameron was silent.

"Love to see him," Laurence said heartily. "You should bring him to France."

Cameron didn't reply to that, either. Laurence hadn't seen Kip since the boy was two. If he never saw him that would suit Cameron. He sure as hell wasn't dragging the boy to France.

His father seemed to get the message. There was a sudden clearing of throat and a muttered, "harrumph," on the other end of the line. "Let me speak to Boris."

"What?"

"You do have Boris? He is there?" The sudden note of panic in Laurence's voice told Cameron that at least one of his father's priorities hadn't changed. Suddenly he'd had enough. He handed the phone to Gracie. "He wants to talk to Boris," he said and walked straight out of the room.

The conversation between Laurence and Boris was one of the strangest Gracie had ever overheard, consisting as it did of questions about the bird's health, eating habits and emotional well-being on the part of Laurence, and quotes from Desdemona, Portia, Juliet and Viola by Boris who had been listening to Emmy display her dramatic range for the past few nights.

Laurence was clearly pleased with Boris's repertoire. At least he was until Boris ended the conversation by saying in his best Tennessee drawl, "Great balls o' fire!"

Gracie decided that the conversation had gone on long enough at that point and, without giving Laurence a chance to do more than splutter, she quietly hung up.

"I walk the line," Boris told her.

"You certainly do," she said and went to find Cameron, more than a little concerned about where he'd got to. The roof, she feared. Thank heavens she was wrong.

She found him in the pool, as a matter of fact, churning up and down the length of it with the force of a tidal bore.

Kip looked at her from where he was sitting on the chaise longue. "Was that really my grandpa?"

"Yes."

"D'you know him?"

"By reputation," Gracie said.

"I don't think my dad likes him much."

Gracie didn't know what to say to that. She just gave Kip a hug, relieved when his friend Danny appeared at that moment and Kip, Alice in tow, went off with him to play on the beach. He stopped, though, at the top of the stairs.

"Gracie?"

"Mmm-hmm."

"I'm glad you're gonna be my mom."

Gracie's heart felt as if it would burst for love of him. "Me, too, Kip. Oh, me, too."

She stood watching until he and Danny had reached the beach, then she sat down on the chaise and watched Cameron swim.

When he finally hauled himself out of the water and stood dripping on the deck, wiping his face with a towel and looking down at her over the top of it. His eyes looked dark, almost haunted, and she wondered what was going on inside his head. What had happened to him while he was talking to his father?

But then he smiled at her, and it was such an excruciatingly tender smile that her heart turned over in her chest.

He dropped the towel and held out his hands to her. She took them, letting him pull her to her feet so that they stood toe to toe, eye to eye, heart to heart.

"Oh, Lord, Grace, I love you," he muttered and hauled her into his arms.

CAMERON DIDN'T THINK Tony and Emmy were ever going to leave.

"Why should we?" Emmy said, waving a scarf in his face, "when you've finally learned to be a decent host? Besides, I've just met the most divine man. He's a producer."

But Tony had more compassion. "Come on, Mata Hari, let's be kind and leave the love birds to it."

He was clearly pleased at his brother's announcement that he was going to marry Gracie. He took all the credit for it.

"Why not?" he said Saturday morning as the train hissed to a stop in the station and he and Emmy prepared to board it. "After all, if it hadn't been for me, you wouldn't be here," he reminded Gracie. "You owe me," he said to his brother.

"Yes." Cameron agreed to that.

"Are you getting married in the city or shall we be coming back?"

"You'll have to come back," Cameron told him. "I'll give you a call."

"You're still not fond of New York?"

Cameron shook his head. "Not very."

"Well, you'll have to come in when Gracie's on Broadway, won't you?" Tony gave his brother a comradely punch on the arm and followed Emmy up the steps, hanging out the door as the train pulled away. "Don't do anything I wouldn't do." He winked and waved as the train picked up speed. "That gives you a lot of latitude, bro."

"Do you need a lot of latitude?" Gracie asked him, smiling.

Cameron shoved away the thoughts that Tony's comment about Broadway had evoked and smiled at her in return, looping his arm across her shoulders as he walked her back to the car. "I have all the latitude I want."

AT LEAST he thought he did.

Then Sunday evening while he and Kip were demonstrating the floating table trick for Gracie, he heard a car pull up outside and a door slam.

"Herschel?" he guessed because Gracie's director had been threatening to come by some evening and steal her away for a fancy dinner.

"Mrs. Poop Deck," Gracie bet, for since she'd discovered that Cameron was here, she was never far away.

But minutes passed and there was no knock.

"C'mon, Dad," Kip urged.

"We can't start and then have to stop in the middle," Cameron said. "It isn't that sort of trick. Not like making a quarter disappear."

Kip sighed. "But—"

"I'll see who it is." Cameron shoved back his chair and strode out to the entry hall. Opening the door he could only stare.

There on the porch stood a huge pile of luggage, burgundy with leather trim, all matched. Beyond it was a taxi, trunk gaping. Two men were bent over the trunk extracting more of the same. The first to emerge was quite clearly the taxi driver, struggling under the load of what amounted to a steamer trunk, which he dragged toward the porch.

Cameron opened his mouth to say that he was sure they'd come to the wrong place, when the other man straightened.

It was Laurence.

Cameron felt as if he'd just taken a barge pole in the gut. He stood stock-still, staring, and didn't say a word.

For a long moment, longer than Cameron would have thought possible, Laurence didn't speak, either. And then he plastered on his jaunty grin, mustered his best bluster and strode forward, hand outstretched.

"Came for the Classic," he said heartily. "Always do. Would've stayed with Mrs. Poop Deck, of course, because I let the place this year. But since you're here . . . family and all that." His hand clasped Cameron's nerveless fingers.

Work, damn you, Cameron commanded them, and was vastly, though invisibly, relieved when they did.

"Looking well, Larry, looking well. Just put those there, my good man." He pointed with the toe of his custom-made Italian shoe, and the taxi driver, huffing and puffing, did as he was bid.

"That's all, sir," the driver said.

"Fine, fine." Laurence brushed past Cameron into the house. "Dying to sit down," he mumbled. "Long ride. Ghastly long trip. Hours and hours..." His voice faded off into the distance.

Cameron stared after him, then, hearing a vague, "Ahem," turned back to see the cab driver still standing there, looking at him expectantly.

Cameron rolled his eyes and dug down for the fare. "How much?"

The driver told him.

Cameron stared.

The man gave an apologetic shrug. "I drove him all the way from JFK, sir."

Cameron swallowed a curse. "Hang on a minute." He spun on his heel and stalked into the house.

"The driver needs to be paid," he said to his father when he found him admiring the new living room furniture.

Laurence waved him away. "I've only a pocketful of *francs*, dear boy. Do take care of it, will you?"

Sighing, outfoxed again, Cameron did.

The driver gave him a grateful smile when he handed over the money. "Oh, thank you, sir." He started back to the cab, then paused and confided, "I couldn't believe it when he told me where we were going."

"Neither," Cameron said heavily, "can I." Then he strode back into the house.

Laurence had, exactly as he'd feared, made himself at home. He had already commandeered the best armchair in the living room and was holding court. Gracie and Kip, having come out at the sound of voices, were now standing in astonished attendance on him.

"Fine-looking sprout," Laurence told Cameron, clamping a beefy hand on Kip's shoulder and squeezing hard. "Spitting image of myself at that age. Damned fine," he said again, giving another squeeze. Kip winced.

Cameron scowled, his mind whirling a hundred miles a minute. Having been outfoxed on the taxi and having had the old man slip past him to ensconce himself in the house, he was trying to figure out how to pry him out again. It wasn't going to be easy.

And what the hell had he come for anyway? Not the Classic, that was certain. At least not entirely. Laurence McClellan was nothing if not devious. And he never did one thing if he could do three as well. So there had to be more to it than that. Cameron's eyes narrowed speculatively, trying to fathom the inner workings of his father's devious mind.

But Laurence was in his "what you see is what you get" frame of mind, all jolly and hail-fellow-well-met. Cameron ground his teeth.

Just now Laurence demanded bluffly to know precisely who Gracie was and what she was doing there.

"She's my fiancée," Cameron said sharply before she could say a word.

Laurence started, clearly taken aback. "Fiancée? You're getting married?"

"Yes," Cameron said through his teeth.

"Married." Laurence said the word like a large smug cat trying to decide if he liked the taste of a particular meal. His expression went from consternation to skepticism to pleasure as he decided he did. "Well, well, well. How happy I am to meet you, then, m'dear. What did you say your name was?"

If there were any way to avoid telling him, Cameron would have. There wasn't. "Her name is Grace Talbot."

"Ah, Grace. Yes, indeed. Grace, Grace, Grace." Laurence rubbed his hands together, beaming.

Cameron wondered if perhaps saying things three times was some sort of incantation his father was working. He'd heard from Tony that last year the old man had consulted an astrologer to figure out his stock market investments; he supposed he could have got even loonier in the meantime.

Laurence cocked his head and regarded Gracie speculatively. "Haven't I seen you somewhere before?"

Whether he had or not, Cameron wasn't going to let him find out. "I doubt that."

But Laurence wasn't put off. "And what do you do when you're at home, dear?"

"She's an actress," Kip said proudly when Cameron would happily have said nothing at all.

"An actress." Laurence's eyes got very wide indeed. "Well, well, well."

Cameron waited. Either he would remember her and blather on for hours about about what he'd seen her in or, possibly worse, he wouldn't remember but would take that for occasion to compare her to Dana.

He was surprised then, when Laurence merely said, "I could do with a drink."

He watched warily as his father got up and headed for the dining room's built-in liquor cabinet. Laurence stopped for a moment and considered the new furniture. He opened his mouth as if he might venture a comment, then seemed to realize where such a topic might lead and promptly shut it again and began rooting about in the liquor cabinet, making disgruntled exclamations almost at once.

"I can't believe it! Bloody hooligans!" His voice was muffled by the confines of the cabinet into which he'd stuck his head. "They've filched it all. Every last drop! I sold 'em the dining room set, not the Remy and the Courvoisier, for goodness' sake!"

His head popped back out again, outrage apparent on his ruddy face. "The world is full of thieves and robbers! Can't trust a soul these days."

"I, uh, think I could get you something from the kitchen," Gracie offered.

Cameron shot her a dirty look, but she persisted. "I'd be happy to look."

Laurence blessed her with a smile. "Thank you, m'dear. Too kind of you."

"I'll help her," Cameron said and dogged her footsteps out of the room. "What in hell are you doing? Why make him feel at home?"

"He *is* home." Gracie was opening the kitchen cabinet and stretching up to get the bottle of Courvoisier that Tony had bought earlier in the week.

"Not for long," Cameron muttered.

"Is everything settled with the agent?"

"Last I heard. Jeannie's handling the paperwork." He raked his fingers through his hair. "Damn him. What's he doing here? He's just come to harass me."

Gracie laughed as she poured some Courvoisier into a snifter. "I hardly think so."

"Well, why then?"

"To see you, perhaps?"

Cameron snorted.

"Want one?"

"No."

"It might improve your mood."

"Seeing the back of him would improve my mood."

"Well, maybe he won't stay," Gracie consoled.

"Yeah? Take a look on the porch."

"What's on the porch?"

"All his worldly belongings, at a guess."

"Oh, dear." Gracie raised herself on her toes and kissed Cameron's cheek. "Courage, my love. My father says it's always there when you need it."

Cameron drew a deep breath and prayed Gracie's father was right.

He'd need to be, Cameron realized shortly, for while he and Gracie were in the kitchen, Laurence had manipulated Kip into hauling in all his luggage and dragging it upstairs. Laurence himself was communing with Boris.

"And how is Daddy's handsome fellow today?" Cameron heard him ask as they approached the solarium.

There was no reply.

"Boris?" Laurence's voice was cajoling. "Don't be like that, Boris. Boris!" His voice rose a little.

Cameron and Gracie peered around the edge of the door. Laurence's nose was practically against the cage. Boris was as far on the other side as it was possible to get. His beak was in the air and he was facing the opposite wall. Laurence edged around. Boris did an about-face on the perch and marched to the other end.

"Boris." Laurence was imploring now.

Cameron almost smiled.

Gracie stepped on his foot. "Here's your drink, Mr. McClellan."

Laurence jumped back from the cage and straightened up, clearing his throat. "Thank you, m'dear. Thank you, thank you."

Cameron looked at him narrowly.

Laurence sniffed the cognac appreciatively, then knocked it straight back. Gracie's eyes grew to the size of plates.

"Er, could I get you another, sir?"

Laurence gave her a beneficent smile and handed her the snifter. "Don't mind if you do."

Gracie headed toward the kitchen. Cameron stayed where he was.

Laurence scowled. "What're you waiting for? Why don't you go with her?"

Shrugging, Cameron left.

As he did so he heard Laurence wheedling, "Boris, old fellow, listen...this isn't like you at all. I was only gone three months. Surely you can speak to Papa. Boris, don't be like this, please..."

Boris was eventually cajoled into a recitation of some incredibly corny soap opera dialogue, a fairly accurate imitation of Julia Child doing something culinary to a goose, and a laundry list of his once and future ills. Then he fixed Laurence with one beady eye and sidled up to him along the perch.

"See!" Laurence beamed like a proud father. "I knew you could do it."

Boris gave a little hop. "Why don't you make like a banana and split?"

For the first time in history, Cameron thought, he and Boris agreed.

As luck had it, of course, Laurence dug in for the duration. Kip had deposited his luggage, at Laurence's command, in the master bedroom. Later, when he discovered that that was where Gracie was sleeping, he was the soul of accommodation, evicting Cameron and commandeering his room instead.

"I'll make do," he announced, surveying Cameron's monklike domain with distaste. "You can move in with Grace."

Cameron stared at him. "What if she doesn't want..."

"To sleep with you?" Laurence smiled like the Cheshire Cat. "Well then I, of course, would be willing to accommodate..." By sleeping with Gracie himself, no doubt.

Cameron ground his teeth, grabbed his things and stalked out of the room.

Gracie met him at the doorway to hers. "Such enthusiasm," she chided.

"It isn't you; it's Kip." They'd managed a certain amount of discretion so far.

"It's all right, Dad," Kip said from his own doorway. "I understand."

Cameron stared at his son, nonplussed.

Kip gave him a pat on the arm. "Just remember what you told me about condoms."

GRACIE TOLD CAMERON he was needlessly upset. She told him to stop worrying, that everything would be fine. She told him that he and his father were adults now and they could come to terms. Cameron didn't say anything, but his eyes told her he thought she was crazy.

Forty-eight hours later Gracie was inclined to agree with him. Laurence McClellan was indeed a force to be reckoned with—perhaps more in real life than on stage.

He didn't simply talk; he proclaimed. He didn't only feel; he emoted. Though what he felt, Gracie thought, was largely concealed by a lifetime of saying whatever he thought people didn't want to hear.

She watched the way he and Cameron interacted—or rather, didn't interact—and wondered at it.

"Two porcupines locked in mortal combat," was the way she described it to her mother when her parents called Monday night.

"Oh, my dear." Gracie's mother, who only said nice things about everyone and who always looked on the bright side, would have met her match in speaking about Laurence and Cameron. "Surely you can smooth things over."

Gracie tried. But the more she tried, the more smugly irritable Laurence got and the spikier Cameron became. She would've happily washed her hands of both of them.

Yet sometimes when the hostilities abated, she caught Laurence looking at Cameron speculatively, irritably, sometimes almost even sadly. But if he noticed she was watching, he quickly looked away or made some new cutting remark that Cameron either ignored or—if he absolutely couldn't ignore it—took exception to.

Laurence came to her play one evening, which Cameron objected to heartily. "She won't want you there."

Laurence's white brows lifted. "Oh. Can't she act?"

"Of course she can act!"

"Well, then..."

Cameron glowered at his father, a muscle in his jaw working.

"Or is it you who doesn't want me there, my boy?" Laurence asked silkily.

Gracie watched in astonishment as Cameron's face went white. Then, "Go to hell," he snarled and stalked out of the room.

THE ONLY ONE who gave any indication of being pleased with the current course of events was Kip.

Kip, much to Cameron's dismay, liked his grandfather. He sat in rapt silence while Laurence held forth on everything from the state of the world to the state of his lunch. And the admiration appeared mutual.

Cameron said it was to get back at him. "He knows I don't want him anywhere near Kip. That's why he's doing it."

But Gracie didn't think so. Not entirely, anyway. There was no doubt that sometimes Laurence took almost perverse pleasure in needling his older son. But if his interest in Kip had begun out of a desire to annoy Cameron, it soon became an end in itself.

Laurence was clearly delighted by the boy. Whereas he didn't seem to want to move an inch to accommodate Cameron and would only go a foot or two if Gracie asked, he walked for miles on the beach with Kip.

He also spent hours up in the attic going through old photos and boxes of assorted junk with Kip, and even did his own particular version of the swan dive into the pool for Kip.

"Don't laugh," Gracie heard him admonishing the boy. "I know I look like an old walrus. But I feel the need of a swim."

He went through the water like a wounded walrus, Gracie thought. He hadn't the steady, relentless stroke that his son brought to swimming. It was more of a forward flounder.

But watching him do it after he'd had a particular stiff confrontation with Cameron over his suggestion to his son that Kip be encouraged to take acting lessons, Gracie suspected it served the same purpose for him that it did for his son: a release of aggression.

"Interfering old coot," Cameron muttered, stomping through the kitchen.

Gracie didn't say anything.

Cameron glowered at her. "You're on his side," he accused.

"I'm not on anyone's side. Except maybe Kip's in this case. Did you—either of you—ask what he wanted?"

Cameron's glower got, if possible, fiercer. "Nobody asked me what I wanted when I was his age."

"About acting?"

"About anything!" He slammed his hand against the cabinet, banging the door shut. Then he stalked out of the room.

Gracie saw little of him the rest of the day. He scarcely got back from a long solitary walk on the beach before she had to leave for the theater. And when he came in he hardly said a word.

Laurence took up the slack, of course, egged on by Kip. He talked at length about Gracie's performance, which he had gone to see, whether out of spite or simply because he was interested she didn't know.

Cameron ignored the discussion completely. He looked as if he were on another plane of reality altogether, so remote did he seem. Whenever Laurence directed a question to him, he had to repeat it. And even then he barely got a mono-syllable for an answer.

That night after the play he was already in bed when Gracie got home. She showered quickly, but came to bed expecting him to be asleep. He wasn't. He lay stiffly on his back, his arms folded under his head, a muscle in his cheek twitching. She snuggled up to him and rested a hand on his chest. He took her hand in his.

"Tired?" she asked.

"Mmm. You?"

"Not very. Keyed up, really."

"Did it go well?" He rarely asked her. He'd gone to the play the first night, but hadn't gone since. He seemed to want to pretend it didn't exist not only to his father but to her as well. Gracie let him. It wasn't that important.

"It went fine. Wonderful, in fact. We're in a groove."

"Good." But the response was rote.

"What'd you do?"

"Went for a walk on the beach."

"Another one?"

"Mmm."

"With Kip?"

Cameron shook his head. "Alice. Kip was with my dad." His mouth twisted. "They were in the attic, exploring."

"Why didn't you?"

He shifted irritably. "Why didn't I what?"

"Explore with them."

"I didn't want to."

Gracie was silent, her head turned so she could trace his profile in the light of the moon. It was hard and unyielding. Gently she touched his cheek. "I thought you said you didn't have a creative bone in your body."

Cameron's head turned and he looked at her, frowning. "I don't."

"You do, you know," Gracie said softly. "I think perhaps you're the best damned actor of them all."

He stared at her. "What do you mean?"

"All this indifference. This 'I don't care' attitude."

"I don't—"

She touched his lips. "You do. You care, Cameron. You try to pretend you don't. You try to pretend you don't even like him. I think you've pretended that for years now. Maybe you've even halfway convinced yourself. But it isn't true, my love." Her lips brushed the line of his jaw. "It isn't true at all."

"*He* doesn't," Cameron said almost angrily.

Gracie brushed her hand across his chest. "I think he does."

Cameron shook his head. "He couldn't. If he did, then why—" His anguish was almost palpable.

But Gracie couldn't give him answers. For those he would have to go to the man himself. "Ask him," she urged. "Talk to him."

"Sure. You've seen the way he is with me."

"You need to."

Their eyes met and locked.

Then, "I need *you*," he muttered and turned her in his arms, loving her with a desperation that told her more than words could ever tell.

GRACIE WAS RIGHT, of course. He did care—had always cared. But after years of rebuffs, disinterested yawns, impatient glances, awkward moments, it was hard to believe his father did.

It was especially hard when Jeannie called the next morning to say that they couldn't come to terms on the sale of the house.

"What d'you mean, 'can't come to terms'?" Cameron demanded. "I made an offer. He accepted it."

"Not exactly."

"What's that mean?"

"Apparently the woman who accepted it didn't have the authority to do so."

The pencil Cameron was holding snapped in half. "Says who?"

"Well, she did. She said the owner has just recently come back into the country and claims he knows nothing of the proposed sale."

Cameron's eyes narrowed. He stared across the room and out the French doors to where his father was standing on the deck talking to Kip. Didn't know? Ha. He knew all right. He'd probably just heard who was buying it.

And Gracie thought the old man cared? Damn him. "That son of a buck," he breathed.

"Sorry?"

"Nothing, Jeannie," he said heavily. "Nothing."

"What do you want me to do?"

"Forget it. It doesn't matter at all."

It didn't, he told himself as he slammed out the door and stalked out to the beach.

He didn't need this house. He could live without it. After all, he already had a house in San Francisco. He could live without his father, too. He had for years. It would've been nice if Gracie'd been right, if they could've talked, reached some sort of accord. But the old man's feelings were clear.

Well, so what? It wasn't as if he needed a father. He had Kip and, to some extent, he had Tony and Emmy.

But, most especially, he had Gracie.

That was all that really mattered now.

He slowed his pace, meandering along the shore, getting his balance, glad he'd found out now. Because after tonight's performance—the last performance—they could move on.

They could pack their bags and say farewell to this whole miserable mess. They could remember Gull Cottage with fondness—except for the last few days—but when they walked away it wouldn't matter. Together they would get on with their lives.

Two weeks ago, Cameron knew, if anyone had told him he was going to be looking forward to this moment, he wouldn't have believed it.

Back then he hadn't believed in love. Hadn't wanted to try. Back then he was neck-deep in a fantasy world that would have come to an end August 31st.

Now, in spite of all the havoc the old man could wreak, there was no end. Now life was just beginning.

LAURENCE'S ARTICLE appeared in the following morning's issue of the *Times*. It was supposed to be a vacationer's look at regional theaters. It was a rave review for Gracie.

"No matter how many times a good play is done, there are always things that make it better," he wrote. "The best part of Herschel Dimante's revival of Oscar Wilde's *The Importance of Being Earnest* is Grace Talbot. Her ingenuousness is engaging, her voice enchanting, her ability astonishing. In a limited role she brings freshness and verve. Definitely a woman to watch. I am not being overly optimistic when I say that Miss Talbot is herself that precious commodity—a star just waiting to be born."

It was a tribute as much to Laurence's reputation as to Gracie's talent that almost as soon as the paper hit the stands, the phone began to ring.

There were calls from two Broadway directors before ten. Each of them was expecting cast changes, each thought Gracie might do admirably, when could she return their calls? The director of an off-Broadway show in the works called at eleven to express an interest in her as his second female lead. By noon a Chicago repertory company had called. Herschel himself rang up at one to invite her along to be part of his cast in L.A. where he was going next.

Gracie wasn't there for any of them.

The "star just waiting to be born" had gone with Laurence to a post play-run brunch at Mrs. Poop Deck's. Cameron had been invited, too. He'd declined. It wasn't his thing, he'd said. He'd come a long way, but hobnobbing with theater people was still beyond him. Also, the less time he had to spend with his two-faced old man, the happier he felt.

That was why he was home with time on his hands. That was why he bothered to read the entertainment section in the first place. That was why he even saw his father's article and felt his heart stop in his chest.

And of course, that was why he was the one who answered the phone when the offers and expressions of interest began to come in.

Physically he felt sick. Emotionally he felt demolished. Dutifully he wrote them down.

He had to. He couldn't lie and pretend they hadn't happened. He couldn't fight them and make them go away. Once before he'd faced the same demons. Then he hadn't understood their strength.

Now he paced through the house, hearing the sound of Gracie's cheerful voice saying, "I figured why not? It might be my one big break. You have to forge on. Struggle. Believe in yourself. You'll never get what you want if you don't."

He heard Tony say after the play, "Aren't you glad you came?"

He heard the final sentence of Laurence's review, " . . . a star just waiting to be born."

And if that was true—and he knew it was—then Cameron also knew he had no right to hold her. He *couldn't* hold her.

He also knew—God help him—that the pain was about to begin all over again.

Chapter Fourteen

A Poop Deck brunch always became an all-day affair. This one began at nine with drinks on the veranda, and by three Gracie still hadn't contrived a good excuse for getting away.

Part of the problem, naturally, was Laurence. If all the world was a stage, Laurence was ever ready to play his part. And today he was basking in the glow of the review that had appeared in this morning's *Times*.

He was getting more mileage out of having written it than Gracie was out of being written about. But she didn't care. Acting, she'd discovered, filled a need, but not a soul. She liked the challenge of a new part, of putting herself into someone else's shoes for a time. But she wasn't interested in spotlights and accolades forevermore, not that she hadn't appreciated the compliment, of course.

She'd told him so shortly after they'd arrived and she'd first been shown a copy by the admiral. "It was nice of you," she'd said.

Laurence had pooh-poohed it. "It's only what you deserve, m'dear. Only what you deserve."

Gracie had smiled, grateful for the recognition. But his comments had made her the center of attention, and so she'd been swept into the party, whisked from this group to that, all of them treating her to a mixture of congratulations and cattiness. She'd had to stay far longer than she preferred.

At first she wished Cameron had come along. She could've used a bit of moral support. But the backstage gossip and theatrical affectations swirling around her gave her second thoughts. As much as she would have liked him there, she knew he would've hated it.

It was better that he and Kip had stayed home.

Still, as she stood on the Poop Decks' veranda nursing her fifth Virgin Mary, she wished Laurence would finish whatever interminable anecdote he was telling the admiral so they could at last get underway.

It was almost four when, still talking nineteen to the dozen, he finally permitted himself to be steered down the driveway and tucked into a cab. Gracie would have walked. It was all of ten minutes to Gull Cottage from the Poop Decks'. But Laurence wouldn't hear of it.

"You must needs go out in a blaze of triumph, m'dear," he told her grandly.

Gracie thought rather it was Laurence who needed—a ride to spare his gouty toe.

Still, she was past quibbling. And she bounded out of the cab and into the house, eagerly searching for Cameron, when they arrived three minutes later.

She searched the downstairs, the upstairs, the deck, the pool, the beach. She even checked the roof. Everything was neat and tidy, as if he'd spent the morning housecleaning. But now she didn't see him anywhere.

"That's odd," she muttered. But probably he'd got tired of waiting for her and had gone into town. Or maybe he and Kip had driven out to Montauk. It was a breezy sunlit day, the sort that demanded being outdoors. She was about to go herself just to kill some time when she noticed the proliferation of notes next to the telephone.

The names on them made her gape. What they wanted made her stammer. But the coup de grace was the one on the bottom.

Her hand shook as she stared at the note. "Congratulations on your big break," it read. "I wouldn't dream of standing in your way. It's been fun. Cameron."

Gracie read it three times over before the words penetrated. First she wanted to laugh, then she wanted to cry. Then she wanted to punch Cameron McClellan in the nose.

Fun? *Fun?* He thought what they'd shared was *fun?*

That jerk. That dirty rotten lowlife. That complete and total idiot.

How dare he take all those messages, decide what they meant to her and end their relationship with nothing more than a note?

"Damn it all, Cameron McClellan!" Gracie flew up the stairs to confirm her fears.

Just as she'd expected, his closet and dresser were empty. So were Kip's. Even the shirt Cameron had left in her room—the shirt she'd grown used to sleeping in—was gone.

She didn't need a trip outside to tell her that the Isuzu was not in the garage.

She wandered back out into the hallway, stunned, bereft. Did he really think he was being generous, or was he perhaps just looking for an excuse?

Maybe he wanted to dump her. Maybe his interest in her had waned.

She supposed she could understand if it had. Heaven knew in the past her own had waned often enough. In her whole life, in her myriad jobs, in her other relationships, she'd never felt the sense of rightness, of commitment, that she'd felt with him.

But perhaps Cameron really didn't feel it as well.

"Serves you right," she mumbled aloud, trying to convince herself.

But she wasn't convinced. She was hurt. She was angry. And what was worst—she was alone.

Heavy footsteps on the stairs contradicted that conclusion almost at once. "Can't find Kip," Laurence said

plaintively when he saw Gracie standing at the top of the
steps. "Have you seen him?"

"He's . . . gone."

Laurence frowned. "What do you mean, gone? Where'd
he go? We were going to play chess. The little scoundrel's
getting too blasted good, he can almost beat me."

"They left," Gracie said.

"Obscurity doesn't become you, Grace. Stop talking in
riddles and make sense."

"Here!" She thrust Cameron's note at him. "Read it
yourself."

Laurence did. Gracie was astonished to see him go white
as a ghost. His hand went to the banister, his eyes closed,
and he seemed actually to sway where he stood.

"My Lord, what have I done?"

Gracie stared. "*You*? What on earth are you talking
about?" Trust Laurence to go godlike over this as well as
everything else.

"I did it. It's all my fault."

"What?"

"My review."

"It was a wonderful review. It appears to have got me a
ton of offers. That doesn't mean I'm going to take them,
does it?"

There was a long silence during which Gracie almost
watched Laurence age before her eyes. Then in a voice so
quiet she had to strain to hear it, he whispered, "Dana did."

"Dana did what?" Gracie said, not sure she completely
understood.

"Dana took the job offers she got after a review I did."

"I'm not Dana!" Gracie practically shouted at him.

"I know that," Laurence said heavily. "I thought Cameron knew it, too. But I thought sometimes he felt a few
doubts, a few twinges, as it were." He looked hopefully at
Gracie who didn't look hopefully back. He sighed. "So I
thought this way I could prove it to him."

"What!"

"My opinion carries a lot of weight," Laurence said matter-of-factly. "People in the business heed what I say. If I praise you, you get offers."

"Indeed you do," Gracie said. She had a fistful, and an ache in her heart.

"Well, Dana took those offers and dumped Cameron and Kip flat. Acting mattered more to her than the two of them ever did. I'd always suspected it. There was a restlessness about her, a hunger, a desire." He shook his head. The expression on his face told her he was seeing Dana in his mind's eye. "She would have made him miserable. I could see that. So I gave her what she wanted most in life: a good review."

"You *gave* it to her? And ruined their marriage?" Gracie was aghast.

"She deserved the review, just as you did," Laurence said defensively. "I would never compromise my integrity."

"Just your son's marriage."

"It was going to happen anyway, sooner or later. It was inevitable. She married Cameron to get noticed by me."

Gracie looked at him narrowly. "You're sure?"

Laurence nodded.

Gracie wished she knew whether to believe him or not. His manipulativeness appalled her. But the motive behind it was equally amazing.

And what had he meant about proving to Cameron that he was different?

"Just what I said," he told her when she asked. "I sensed his reluctance. It was obvious. He still isn't comfortable around the theater, around actors, actresses. I could see he loved you, but I didn't think he was entirely comfortable around you, either." Laurence's pale blue eyes fixed on her. "Am I wrong?"

Reluctantly Gracie shook her head. "No."

"It was his one big fear—that you would leave him the way Dana did."

"How do you know?" Gracie challenged.

"I know because he is my son!" There was an authority in Laurence, a depth of certainty that went far beyond the pomposity and arrogance that Gracie had heard from him before. She stared at him, shocked.

Laurence shook his head ruefully. "So I thought I could help him over it. I thought I could do the same for you—give you the review you deserved and let you choose." The blue eyes fastened on her with respect and warmth. "*I* knew what you'd choose."

Gracie felt a shudder run through her. "He didn't," she said softly.

"No." Laurence shook his head. "That was my mistake." He gave a bitter laugh. "Why should I expect things to be different now? They've been this way all his life. Or most of it. Ever since his mother and I divorced, I haven't been able to do a thing right as far as he's concerned."

"Have you tried?" If he had, it was news to her.

"For years. Made a complete botch of it," Laurence said with uncharacteristic humility. "I loved his mother—more than I've ever loved anyone in my life. But we couldn't live together. And after we split up, things were never the same between him and me. I didn't know what to say to him. He's hard to know."

Like you, Gracie thought.

"The summer it happened," Laurence said, "I took him on a trip to Rhode Island with me. To the shore. Thought perhaps we might find there a bit of the magic we had here—the two of us. I tried to talk to him. To tell him about the divorce. I wanted him to know I still loved him, wanted him to know he'd be welcome with me. But I don't think he heard." Laurence rubbed a hand through his meticulously combed hair.

"I told him and he didn't say a word. He just walked on the beach for miles, hunting for shells and moonstones." Then he smiled ruefully. "Found a truckload of shells and one moonstone. It was the one good thing about the trip."

And then he left it in the car when I took him back to Lilian. Shows how much he cared.

"Anyway, a year later I married Amaryllis, and I never spent much time with him again. He went off to school shortly thereafter. I thought our relationship might improve after his mother died. If anything it got worse. He reminded me of Lilian so much it almost killed me. I don't know what I reminded him of. All I know is, every time I saw him he was cold and distant and disapproving. He didn't want anything to do with me."

Laurence stared out over the ocean unseeing, then shook his head and confessed, "I kept the moonstone. Sometimes I thought it was all I had of him."

The moonstone in the drawer of the barge, Gracie thought and found herself blinking back tears.

Laurence gave her a twisted smile. "I haven't always managed my life in the best fashion. This past year has been a rather stunning example of that. My financial situation has bordered on ruin a good part of the time. I thought I was going to have to sell this house."

Gracie just looked at him.

His smile became less twisted. "I knew I couldn't when I found Larry—I mean, Cameron—out here."

Gracie's eyes got wider.

"It's his inheritance, after all. It was his mother's. And I nearly gambled it away."

"You mean you reneged on selling it because you're going to give it to him?" Gracie demanded.

Laurence nodded.

"Oh, my very word." She wondered what Cameron would think of that. "So your...finances have...straightened themselves out?"

"Regrettably no. Not entirely at least. Though I did make a bundle on the Classic. And I've had some good return on my investments lately." There was just a hint of the arrogant Laurence in that last statement. "But it wouldn't matter even if I hadn't. I'm moving out here permanently. I've

decided to preserve Lar—Cameron's—inheritance by sel
ing my penthouse instead.''

That sat Gracie right down on the step.

"That's very...commendable of you," she managed.

"It is," Laurence agreed. "One thing that didn't g
wrong. The question is, what am I going to do about wha
did go wrong? What about my review?"

"I suppose you could print a retraction," Gracie sai
wryly.

Laurence brightened. "Do you think it would work?"

"No."

His face fell.

"Laurence, tell me something honestly?"

He looked right at her. "Of course, m'dear."

"Did you really think I would give it all up for Cam
eron?"

"Yes, I really did. You're a fine actress, Grace Talbo
You could be a star if you willed it. But quite honestl
m'dear, the hunger isn't there."

"And what about Cameron?" she pressed. "Do yo
think he really loved me?"

"He *loves* you," Laurence told her emphatically. "H
gave you what he thought would be your heart's desire eve
though it wasn't his own."

"He didn't even ask me."

"He was afraid to. What man wants rejection to his face
Especially a man who's had it before. Trust me, m'dear.
know."

Did he?

"I STILL DON'T SEE why we had to leave so fast," Kip wa
saying as they crossed the Bay Bridge into San Francisco. I
wasn't the first time he'd said it, either. The words had be
come to the westbound journey what "How much farthe
is it?" had been to the eastbound one.

And Cameron, patience personified, had lied again an
again.

Of course, he who never lied to his son, didn't admit consciously that he was lying this time. He said merely, "It's a long drive back, and school starts practically right after Labor Day."

And then Kip would wail the second part of the refrain, "But what about Gracie?" and Cameron would shrug and say, "She has things to do right now in New York."

After that the conversation took one of several turns. Either Kip asked, "What things?" and Cameron was forced to detail all the various offers she had, making himself sound cheerful and upbeat and "why not?" as he did so. Or Kip asked, "Well, when is she coming?" and Cameron would have to lift his shoulders negligently again and say, "In good time."

He could never bring himself to say she wasn't.

The other question Kip asked was "What about Grandpa?"

And Cameron could think of very little to say to that. Grandpa was Grandpa, that was certain. He hadn't changed a bit. Laurence McClellan seemed just as determined to make Cameron's life as big a hell now as he had for years. First the house, then the review. If he weren't out to get his son, why had he written it? He knew what would happen when he did.

Cameron wanted to say, "Forget Grandpa," but he knew he shouldn't. Maybe someday Kip would be able to see the old man again. But Cameron knew without a doubt that he wouldn't. Not ever.

Kip bounced on the seat all the way through the downtown traffic, pointing out landmarks, and Cameron thought the worst was past, that now they would focus on the present and the future.

But as they began to climb Nob Hill to the street where they lived, Kip spoke up. "It's too bad we had to leave so fast," he said, "but I'm sure glad we went. You were right about that." He looked at his father with shining eyes. "It was a great summer, wasn't it, Dad?"

Cameron couldn't answer that at all.

Sophia knew when they'd be arriving. Cameron ha
called her from Reno that morning.

"I'll have dinner waiting," she'd promised.

And as they climbed the steps now, Cameron could sme
spaghetti sauce and garlic bread. Kip was pounding ahead
eager to throw himself in her arms, to regale her with tal
of the summer, to tell her about the woman who was goir
to be his "new mom."

Sooner or later, Cameron knew, he would have to co
rect Kip's impression, would have to offer some lame e.
cuse about how they'd decided against it, how they didn
really think they'd suit each other after all.

But at the moment he didn't have the heart—or the guts—
to do so.

He lagged behind, dredging up a smile, hoping that Sⴏ
phia had lost some of her perceptiveness over the summe
She was going to know in a moment that something w:
wrong if he didn't look the part of the happy almos
bridegroom.

Kip flung open the door. "We're home! Sophie, we'
home!"

But it wasn't Sophia who stood in the doorway to tʰ
kitchen, brandishing a spoon, as Cameron came in.

It was Grace.

Kip stopped dead, then let out a whoop and flew into h
arms. "You're here! You tricked us! I thought you we
comin' later. That's what Dad said." He turned to beam
Cameron.

"Is that what Dad said?" And though the words were fⴏ
Kip, Cameron knew Gracie's question was directed straig
at him.

Stunned, he shifted from one foot to the other, as ba
fled as Kip. He wanted to hope and didn't dare. One ⴏ
those offers was from a San Francisco company. Maybe sⷰ
was just in town.

He shrugged awkwardly. "I . . . wasn't sure."

"I'm not surprised," Gracie said acidly, "inasmuch as you didn't even wait around to ask me."

"I thought—"

"I have a very good idea what you thought." She turned to Kip. "Listen, sweetie, Sophie's out in back dying to hear about your summer. Maybe you could go talk to her."

"Sure." Kip gave her one more bone-crushing hug. "I'm so glad you're here." Then he dashed through the kitchen and out the back door.

And Cameron and Gracie were alone.

Facing off like gunfighters, Grace thought and wondered again if she was doing the right thing. The welcome from Kip might've been everything she could've hoped for. But the look on Cameron's face was less than encouraging.

He didn't speak, just stood there looking at her as if he didn't quite believe his eyes. But whether he hoped he did or didn't, she couldn't tell.

"What are you doing here?" he asked finally.

She faced him squarely. "Guess."

He dropped the suitcase. "Come on, Gracie. This is no time for games."

"I thought you were all for 'fun,'" she jibed. "Isn't that what you said? 'It's been fun.'"

Pain flickered in his eyes. "You know damned well it was more than that."

"I *hoped* it was more than that. I didn't know anything except that you'd gone and left me standing there!"

"You saw the phone messages!"

"Of course I did. So what?"

"What do you mean, so what? Cripes, you can take your pick now. Anything you want, for heaven's sake!"

"I want you."

Three words and the world seemed to stop.

Gracie stood braced in the doorway as if expecting a re-run of the San Francisco earthquake. Cameron looked as if it had already hit. His face was pale but there was a hectic flush along his cheekbones and his eyes glittered as he stared at her.

"Grace?" The word strangled him.

Grace only looked at him. She didn't move, she didn't blink, she didn't breathe. She had said it all.

What happened now was up to him.

Cameron stood a mere ten feet from her, but it might have been a tightrope across the Grand Canyon between them and not a solid floor and an oriental rug.

He knew in that instant the terror that Gracie had felt when she'd been on that roof. The panic set in, took root, grew.

But he knew as well that if he couldn't make that move, they had no future.

Gracie Talbot had said her piece. She had flown across the country to face him. She hadn't said what she intended to do with the offers, what she would do with any future offers. She was asking if he had enough faith to trust her to do the right thing for both of them.

She was asking him to face his biggest fear.

"Silence," Herschel had once told the cast, "is harder to say than words." Gracie understood now what he meant. And waiting, trusting, praying and yet knowing it was out of one's hands was hardest of all.

She had found the one person in her life who mattered, and she had done everything she could do to show her love, to prove her commitment. Now it was Cameron's turn.

She didn't speak; she didn't breathe. Her heart—her whole life—hung suspended.

And then—praise God—he moved.

Came to her and wrapped her in his arms, buried his face against her neck, hanging on as if she were the only thing between him and disaster. She felt the shudders run through him.

"Oh, Lord, Grace, I love you. I . . . trust you."

And Gracie thought she might faint from the sheer joy of it all. She clung to him, breathing again, taking great gasping gulps of air, filling her lungs with happiness, her heart with gratitude.

"Thank you, Lord," she breathed, and in the next breath, "Thank you, Laurence."

Cameron jerked as if he'd been shot. "What's he got to do with this?"

Gracie smiled. An impish smile. "He gave me the courage to come. And he bought my ticket!"

Cameron gaped. "*Bought your ticket?* I don't believe it."

She touched his cheek gently. "Believe."

"But—"

But she didn't let him protest. She told him instead what his father had said, the reason he'd written the review.

Cameron looked at her suspiciously. He shook his head. "I thought . . . He wrote . . ." His voice trailed off. Then he swallowed and began again. "Dana did that—got a review like that, got offers like those. Her big break." His mouth twisted. "She took them, and she never looked back."

"Yes." Gracie paused, then looped her arms around his neck, lacing her fingers together behind him and looking up into his eyes. "But I won't. Laurence is right, I don't have the hunger."

"But you're a fantastic actress."

"Thank you."

"'A star about to be born,'" he quoted.

Gracie nodded. "But each star has its own place in the sky." She smiled, lifted up on her toes and kissed the tip of his nose. "Mine's with you."

He just shook his head again. His arms tightened around her as if, should he let go, she would be swept away. And then he seemed to realize it, for he dropped his hands and stood looking at her, a wry smile on his face. When she didn't vanish before his eyes, the smile widened. He breathed more easily. He touched his lips to hers.

"Gull Cottage is going to be yours," she told him.

"What?"

"You're the reason Laurence took it off the market."

"I knew that." There was an edge to his voice.

"No," Gracie said quickly. "Not to spite you. To save your inheritance. He came back from France, found you there and knew he didn't want to let it get away. He says it belongs to you."

That took some getting used to, as well. So did hearing what else she told him about his father, about his feelings, about his worries, his concerns.

Cameron wanted to believe it, but he didn't know if he dared—until she told him about the moonstone. She fished in the pocket of her jeans, pulled it out and pressed it into his hand.

"It's the one Kip found in the barge. It's also the one you and your Dad found together in Rhode Island years ago. The prize of the trip, he said."

Cameron shook his head, stunned. "I lost it. I never knew...I..."

"He's kept it all these years." Gracie smiled gently at him. "He said sometimes he thought it was all he had of you."

Cameron shut his eyes and leaned his forehead against Gracie's. His fingers closed around the moonstone. He felt an aching tightness in his throat. His eyes stung.

"You two have a lot in common," she told him softly.

He gave her a wry smile. "An awful thought."

"Not so awful. I'm quite fond of both of you."

"Fond?"

"Fond of him. I love you."

He opened his eyes and met hers, then. "I love you, too. I'm sorry for leaving you," he said. "I should have trusted you. I...couldn't."

"You can now?"

"Oh, yes. I can." He framed her face with his hands, looked down at her with love. There was a pause. A heartbeat. And then a promise. "I will."

It came closer to a marriage vow than anything Gracie had ever heard. She knew it meant more, too, for this promise wasn't spoken for the sake of ceremony.

It was the beginning of a lifelong covenant between them—a promise that came from the heart.

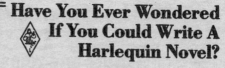

Have You Ever Wondered If You Could Write A Harlequin Novel?

Here's great news—Harlequin is offering a series of cassette tapes to help you do just that. Written by Harlequin editors, these tapes give practical advice on how to make your characters—and your story— come alive. There's a tape for each contemporary romance series Harlequin publishes.

Mail order only

All sales final

TO: ***Harlequin Reader Service***
      Audiocassette Tape Offer
      P.O. Box 1396
      Buffalo, NY   14269-1396

I enclose a check/money order payable to HARLEQUIN READER SERVICE® for $9.70 ($8.95 plus 75¢ postage and handling) for EACH tape ordered for the total sum of $_____*
Please send:

☐ Romance and Presents   ☐ Intrigue
☐ American Romance   ☐ Temptation
☐ Superromance   ☐ All five tapes ($38.80 total)

Signature_____

Name:_____
                                    (please print clearly)
Address:_____

State:_____ Zip:_____

*Iowa and New York residents add appropriate sales tax.

AUDIO-H

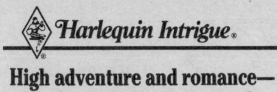

◆ *Harlequin Intrigue* ®

High adventure and romance— with three sisters on a search . . .

Linsey Deane uses clues left by their father to search the Colorado Rockies for a legendary wagonload of Confederate gold, in #120 *Treasure Hunt* by Leona Karr (August 1989).

Kate Deane picks up the trail in a mad chase to the Deep South and glitzy Las Vegas, with menace and romance at her heels, in #122 *Hide and Seek* by Cassie Miles (September 1989).

Abigail Deane matches wits with a murderer and hunts for the people behind the threat to the Deane family fortune, in #124 *Charades* by Jasmine Crasswell (October 1989).

Don't miss Harlequin Intrigue's three-book series The Deane Trilogy. Available where Harlequin books are sold.

DEA-G